KEVIN HOPKINS

Reserved For Murder

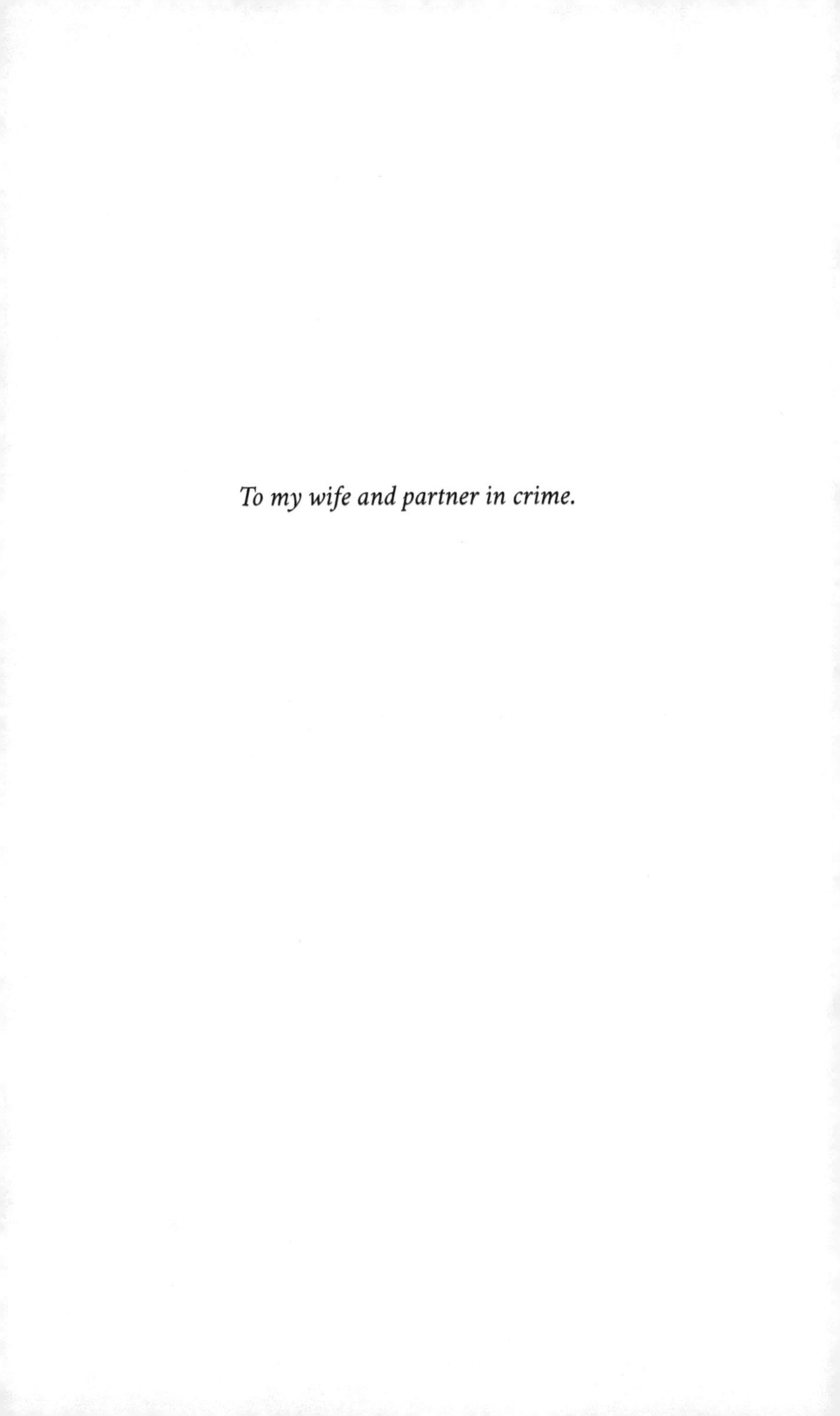

To my wife and partner in crime.

CHAPTER ONE

Sarah Greycrow closed the door to the restaurant, locked it and started on her way home. She was grateful to finally be done her shift. It had felt like a very long night—almost like working a double. It didn't help that the restaurant had been packed for most of the night and the air conditioning wasn't working. The AC unit had been acting up for the last month and finally gave its last blast of cool air three nights ago. The owner said he had contacted a repair guy, but no one had come by yet. 'Maybe tomorrow,' the owner had told her unconvincingly. Sarah knew that fixing up the restaurant wasn't his top priority—he liked his drugs more than anything else. But, maybe he'd surprise her. Maybe he'd get it fixed. Chances were good he'd just wait until the cool fall air arrived and people stopped complaining. Doing nothing was always the easiest route to take.

As she walked, Sarah wiped the sweat from her forehead. Her hair was tied back in a double braid that ran to her waist, which didn't help soak up any of the sweat. The night air was hot and thick. Even though it was one in the morning, the humidity made it feel like it was 36°C. In other words, a typical summer night. Too hot to sleep if you didn't have air conditioning at home, which Sarah didn't.

At the end of the block, she paused, weighing her options. She decided to take the path down by the river to get home. It was a longer walk, but she was counting on there being a bit of cool air coming off the water. Turning to her right, she cut through the school's football field at the end of the street and started heading west down Page Boulevard. The houses along the boulevard were on really big lots with a lot of space in between. Definitely some money in this part of town—not like at home. Not like on the reserve. Things there were tough. Not enough jobs, no money for fixing up the infrastructure, small houses needing too many repairs with too many people living in them. Sarah had been so happy when she got her job at the restaurant. She had been looking for something on the reserve, but no one was hiring. One of her friends had landed a job at the gas station, but she was making five dollars an hour less than Sarah. Sure it would be nice to be able to work closer to home, but Sarah had goals and making money was part of the plan. She wanted to get a better place—somewhere off the reserve, so she and her family could finally have good, clean water at home instead of having to use the bottled water the government supplied. There was a limited supply for each house and once it was gone, that was it until the next month. It never lasted an entire month, especially in the summer heat. The thought of being able to turn on a tap and take a drink, whenever she felt like it, kept Sarah going on nights like this one.

She took another turn and was finally on the path that ran along the shore of the river. It was a bit cooler, but not much. She walked to the river's edge and took out a bandanna from her back pocket, dipping it in the water, wringing it out and tying it around her neck over her beaded necklace.

The cool water helped lower her core temperature, making her more comfortable almost instantly. As she continued her walk, she began to hear the chorus frogs singing to each other in the reeds. She stopped for a minute to listen to their songs, enjoying the slight breeze that rustled the leaves in the tree tops. It felt like rain was on its way—maybe it would finally break the humidity. She continued along the path until she came to the large culvert that ran under the road above, the river continuing its path beside it. It was dark in the culvert. There were no lights at all, and the moonless night wasn't helping. Sarah pulled out her phone and turned on the flashlight, shining it into the culvert to make sure no animals were using it as a home for the night. Two years ago, her younger brother had ridden his bike through the culvert, without checking first, and had been sprayed by an overprotective mother skunk. It took weeks before he had washed out all of the smell. For the first week, their mom wouldn't even let him sleep in the house. He had to set up a pup tent in the backyard. Sarah remembered how he had scrubbed his bike with tomato juice, but there was no saving his shoes and shorts. He ended up having to throw those away.

As Sarah started walking through the culvert, she moved her phone back and forth, checking that all was clear. She saw a lot of graffiti on the walls and the odd can of spray paint on the ground. It looked like some of the *artwork* was relatively new—at least, she hadn't noticed it the last time she took this way home. Some of it was actually pretty good—paintings of people and animals. Lots of people's names and indistinguishable marks. Then there was the racist stuff. There was a lot of hostility in this area, with the reserve being so close. Growing up on the reserve, you were pretty much taught to distrust anyone who wasn't like you, and it seemed like people living around the reserve were taught the same lesson. Not everyone, of course. She'd had a few white friends over the years, but it wasn't easy. There was so much animosity in the community. When she first took the job off the reserve, she had been worried about how hard it might be. She hadn't known how the restaurant patrons would treat her, but for the most part they were really nice. Every now and then, she would get a customer who would make comments behind her back, or not leave a tip because of who she was, but those people were few and far between. She found the worst people were actually her friends back on the reserve. Once she got the job, they started calling her Sarah Whitecrow, saying she was turning her back on her own kind and was becoming 'one of them.' It hurt. She had even gotten into a couple of fights with one of the girls, but for the most part, she tried not to dwell on it. She had goals. She had a plan.

Coming out the other side of the culvert, she met up with the river again. The wind was beginning to blow harder, blocking out the songs of the frogs. The air smelled different, too. She looked up and saw dark clouds moving across the sky. Great. It was definitely going to rain before she made it home. Picking up the pace, she turned to head into the woods. It was really dark under the trees, but she didn't mind. She felt safer in the woods than on a city street at night. Nature was where she felt at home. Ever since she was a kid, she would spend a couple of weeks at a time on the land—trapping, hunting and foraging. Her grandmother had been a good teacher of the 'old ways,' as she called them.

She turned off the flashlight on her phone and waited a couple of minutes for her eyes to adjust to the darkness that surrounded her. It may have been quicker walking with the light, but she didn't like using technology among the trees if she didn't have to. It almost felt disrespectful. Her eyes began to pick out shapes in the various shades of grey, and soon she continued on her way.

She could hear the wind picking up even more—the leaves in the canopy were rustling harder, but she couldn't feel the breeze where she was. The air was still, thick and hot. She was starting to wish she had brought a bottle of water with her. Walking along, she came to the small brook that crossed the path. As she knelt down to remove her bandanna, she noticed some tracks in the soft dirt beside the water. Looked like a raccoon had been here recently to have a drink or to look for his dinner. Sarah soaked her bandanna again, not bothering to wring it out this time, before wrapping it back around her neck. She felt something hit the top of her head. A drop of rain had made it through the trees. Time to get home. She walked a bit to her right, to a point in the brook where it was narrow enough to jump across. She had tried jumping over at different spots over the years, but she was never as successful as here. As she landed, she heard something scurrying off in the bushes beside her. It didn't sound too big, probably another raccoon. She looked around to see if she could see any tracks. It was almost instinct for her to track anytime she could. This time she had no luck. Whatever it was had made a clean getaway.

More raindrops were making their way through the tight tree canopy to the plants along the ground. It felt like a good, hard rain. The humidity still hung in the air, but at least the water helped to cool off Sarah's skin. She took a moment to enjoy the feeling, tilting her head back to let the rain run across her face. It was starting to really come down hard now. A crack of thunder boomed nearby, startling her and reminding her to keep moving.

The path Sarah was following was definitely not a straight cut through the woods. It had started out as an animal trail, connecting the river with the field on the other side of the woods. Over the years, it became a good way to get from the reserve to town. A lot of people used it to sneak booze back home—the reserve had been dry for the last decade, and not everyone was happy about it. Some people thought they should have the right to drink—those were usually the ones who shouldn't be drinking to begin with.

As she got close to the clearing at the end of the woods, a flash of lightning briefly lit up the forest around her. Out of the corner of her eye, something odd in one of the trees to her left caught her attention. She let her eyes readjust to the darkness and cautiously headed in the general direction of what she thought she had seen. She stepped carefully over fallen logs and moved aside low-hanging branches.

As she got closer, she noticed a smell—a smell she was familiar with from her time trapping on the land. The smell of death. It wasn't very strong, but it was definitely noticeable. With the heat and humidity of the past couple of days, it could be a day old, two at most. She grabbed her phone out of her pocket and turned on the flashlight. She needed to be able to see properly. Shining the light into one of the trees, she saw something that seemed familiar, yet surprising. Her brain couldn't seem to make sense of what she was seeing. She moved around slightly to get a better look. Slowly looking up, she saw the body of a young man hanging from a large limb up in the tree, a rope tied around his neck.

Sarah almost tripped over a root as she jumped back, more surprised than scared at the sight of the body. Taking a breath, she composed herself and stepped forward to get a better look. She was certain that the young man was dead—his skin was a blueish grey colour and he wasn't moving. And then there was the smell. A dead giveaway. She shone her light up to the young man's face, trying to see if she recognized him, but his long, black hair was hanging down, blocking his features. She looked around on the ground and found a branch that had fallen off of a neighbouring tree, just long enough to reach up to his head. Holding the phone in one hand to shine the light, she tried to gently move the hair out of his face with the stick, making sure not to disturb the body. It wasn't easy balancing the seven-foot long branch with one hand. After several failed attempts, she finally got the end of the stick into position, gingerly moving his long, wet hair out of the way. His mouth was slightly open as though he had gasped for one last breath before he crossed over to the spirit world, eyes bulging as they had watched the darkness take over. Even in its current state, Sarah knew she had seen that face before. Jonny Two Bears. He was a year younger than Sarah, in the same grade as her brother. She hadn't known him well, but she knew who he was. He was a hoop dancer with the Bear Clan. He was good. And too young to have crossed over.

Collecting herself, Sarah knew she needed to get help. She checked her phone but there was no service here—either because of the trees or the storm. She needed to get out of the woods so she could phone the band police. She tossed the branch aside and started back along the trail towards home, keeping the flashlight on and trained to the ground, so she could make up time. As she walked, her thoughts kept going to Jonny. He was one of those people who always seemed to be in good spirits. A real joker. A lover of life. He had gone hunting with her brother a few times and he always seemed to love being on the land. He wasn't interested in moving to the city or anything. He liked the freedom that the old ways gave him. He just didn't seem like the type to take his own life. But maybe something had been going on with him that she didn't know about. She would ask her brother. Unfortunately, suicides were not uncommon in the community. Times were hard and most kids couldn't see far enough into the future to realize that things could improve. A kid's world is the here and now, not five years from next Tuesday.

Sarah emerged from the edge of the woods and checked her phone again. She had service. There was no 911 for the band police. 911 would put you in touch with the city police. Local boy, local police, she thought. She was worried the city cops would just brush it off as another dead kid from the reserve and not give him the respect he deserved. She went into her phone contacts and found the number for the band office, pressing the button to dial. As it rang, she continued walking towards her house, getting soaked by the cool summer rain. Finally, the call was answered by an automated message. She knew no one would be answering the phones at this time of the morning. She listened to the message and when prompted, pushed three to be put through to the police station. A couple more rings and finally a voice answered her call.

'Hi, this is Sarah, Sarah Greycrow. I found a body in the woods.'

CHAPTER TWO

Constable Grant was woken up by the phone ringing on the bedside table. At least, he assumed he was woken up. He never really slept well in the room the band office provided him—definitely not the first night he was there. The room was small. The bed was strangely lumpy. And it was almost too quiet. By his last night he was usually sleeping better, but that was more from sheer exhaustion than from being comfortable. He fumbled around in the dark, switched on the lamp beside the bed and answered the phone.

'Hello?'

'*Constable Grant? It's Barry. Sorry for waking you.*'

'No problem. What time is it anyway?'

'*About one forty-five. We just got a call. Do you know Sarah Greycrow?*'

'Um, yeah. She comes to the drop-in. Is she okay?'

'*Yeah, she's fine. But, she found a body.*'

'What?' Grant was wide awake now. 'Where?'

'*In the woods, this side of the old culvert. Are you able to meet up with her so she can show you where it is? I gotta stay here and man the phones, and Pete's not available—he's still out turkey hunting. Won't be back until after lunch sometime.*'

'Sure. No problem. Where can I meet her?'

'I asked her to head towards your place. Figured it would be easiest.'

'Pretty presumptuous of you, no?' Grant commented, getting out of bed.

'I figured you'd do it. Just the type of guy you are. Thanks, eh? I owe you one.'

'I'll hold you to that. You can buy me a bannock at the powwow later.'

'Deal. Let me know how it goes.'

'Will do.' Grant hung up the phone and went into the bathroom to splash some water on his face. Looking in the mirror, he noticed that his hair was plastered to his forehead. He must have been sweating a lot—the room didn't have very good air conditioning. As he was finishing up, there was a knock on his door. 'One second,' he called out, grabbing a shirt from his drawer. He opened the door, still pulling the shirt over his head.

Sarah stood on the porch, soaked through. 'Morning. Lovely night, eh?'

'Sarah, come in and get out of the rain for a minute,' Grant said, stepping out of the way to let Sarah in. He looked out the door and saw the heavy rain bouncing off the asphalt. 'Not looking forward to going out in that,' he thought as a flash of lightning lit up the parking lot. 'Did you want some tea or anything?'

'No, I'm good. Thanks,' Sarah said, water dripping off of her onto the carpeted entranceway. 'Sorry 'bout your floor,' she added, looking down.

'No worries. It's not really mine. I'm just borrowing it,' Grant said, walking to the bathroom to grab a towel. 'So, what's going on? You found a body?'

'Thanks,' Sarah said, taking the towel and trying to squeeze the water from her braids. 'Yeah. I was cutting through the woods on my way home from work. Jonny Two Bears hung himself.'

Constable Grant tried to think if the name was familiar. He wasn't sure if he knew who Jonny was. There were some kids, like Sarah, who were regulars at the drop-in centre, and there were some who showed up from time to time. Some kids had never been, but he was trying to change that. 'Don't think I know Jonny. Your age?'

'No, same age as Sammy. Sixteen.' Her brother, Sammy, would sometimes go to the centre with Sarah, but not all the time. Usually he preferred to just hang out with friends, riding their bikes.

'You sure it's him?' Grant asked.

'Yeah, we don't all look alike to each other,' Sarah said, smiling. The first couple of times he'd run the drop-in centre at the reserve, Grant had confused several of the girls with each other. Same dark eyes, same smiles, same long braided hair, all around the same build. One day four of them showed up to the centre all dressed exactly the same, just to mess with him. It had worked—he had no idea who was who.

'Cute. Okay, can you tell me where he is? Easy enough to find?'

'Maybe. Probably easier if I just show you.'

'Won't your mom be worrying? It's getting pretty late. What time was she expecting you home?'

'She won't notice,' Sarah replied. 'She sleeps with earplugs in, so she never wakes up when I come home late. Besides, sometimes on hot nights I just sleep in the backyard—it's cooler than in the house.'

'You really want to go back out in that?' Grant asked, just as another crack of thunder rumbled, as if on cue.

'I'm wet already. Doesn't matter now,' Sarah replied, opening the door. 'Come on, City Boy, time to hit the road.'

'Really? City Boy?' Grant grabbed a raincoat and his flashlight from the hall closet before locking the door and joining Sarah in the rain. 'Should we drive partway?'

'What, afraid you'll melt? You're not that sweet,' Sarah said, twirling around, arms outstretched, looking up at the heavens. 'It's not far. Come on! Some fresh air will do you good.' She started walking back towards the woods, Constable Grant just behind her.

'How far a walk is it?' Grant asked as he caught up to Sarah.

'Um, not far really. Ten minutes, maybe. Well, to the edge of the woods. Then a bit further in. Don't know—never timed it.'

'Do you always cut through the woods to get home after work? Isn't it quicker to follow the road?'

'Yeah, but it's not as nice a walk. Don't see any animals on the roads. Well, cats and people, and the odd roadkill, but that's not very nice.'

'At least you aren't likely to get eaten by a cat or roadkill,' Grant said. 'Any bears or cougars here?'

'Are you serious?' Sarah asked with a laugh. 'Lots of bears. But just blacks. Chances are you'll never see one.'

'Well that's encouraging, I guess.'

'Doesn't mean they don't see you, though!' Sarah gave him a sly little smile and a wink. They arrived at the edge of the woods. 'Let's go. Might want to turn on your light. Watch for eye-shine in the trees.'

'You're really not helping matters,' Grant said, turning on

his flashlight. Sarah had already started into the woods and he struggled to catch up. 'Wait for me!'

They followed the path for several hundred yards, weaving around, ducking under low hanging limbs. The smell in the air changed.

'Getting close,' Sarah said, turning off the path towards the tree where she'd left Jonny. Constable Grant reached out for her shoulder to pull her back.

'Wait here,' he said. 'I'll go check him out.'

'I've already seen him, remember. I found him,' Sarah said, shrugging his hand off to continue on.

'Sarah, please. Just wait here 'til I have a look around, okay?'

'Fine.'

Constable Grant slowly approached the tree, shining his light up to the branch, the rope and then moving down to the body. Jonny was still in the same position he'd been earlier, when Sarah first came upon him. His hair had fallen back around his face. An off-white rope was tied into a loop and placed around his neck. Grant noticed that it wasn't quite a traditional tying of a noose, but evidently it was close enough to do the job. The rope stretched about two feet above his head where it was tied off to a large limb stretching out from the trunk of the tree. A gust of wind suddenly blew through the forest, making Jonny's body sway ever so slightly and catching Constable Grant off guard. He played his light down the boy's body, checking out his clothes. T-shirt. Old, ripped jeans held up by a worn black leather belt which had a large bear buckle. Black converse runners.

'Poor kid,' Constable Grant said out loud.

'Whatcha gonna do now?' Sarah's voice came from just behind Constable Grant, making him jump.

'Geez, Sarah! I thought I told you to stay over there!'

'Like I said, I already saw him, so no big deal if I see him again,' Sarah said. 'Death's no big thing. Happens to us all, apparently.'

'Well, next time I ask you to do something, just do it, okay? At least, don't sneak up on me.'

'Sorry,' Sarah said, smiling. She liked Constable Grant. He'd been a big help at the centre and he was fun to be around. For a City Boy. 'So, like I said. What now?'

'Good question,' Grant answered, unsure. 'Do you know if the band has a coroner?'

'Dude, we don't even have a family doctor we can go see. Ya think we have a coroner?' Sarah replied, shaking her head.

'Right, makes sense. So, any idea who gets called when someone dies?'

'City doctor has to come out,' Sarah said. 'Someone from the hospital, I think. Can we take him down?'

'No, we should leave him until a doctor gets here.'

'Why? He's dead. What's a doctor going to do, try to revive him? Bit late for that, dontcha think?' She had a point.

'Just procedure is all,' Grant said. 'A medical doctor has to pronounce him dead before we can move him.'

'That's pretty dumb, ya know,' Sarah said. 'Sometimes I really don't understand you white folk.'

'Rules are rules,' Grant said, realizing it really did sound dumb. 'Crap.'

'What's wrong?'

'I forgot to bring a roll of tape.'

Sarah looked around. 'What're you planning to tape together out here?'

'No, not like scotch tape. Crime tape. I gotta tape off the

area to keep people out.' Grant pulled out his phone to try and call Barry at the office. No service. 'Great. Can you do me a favour?' he said to Sarah.

'Of course,' Sarah said, happily.

'Can you go back to the police station and get a roll of tape from Barry? I gotta stay here with the body and make sure no one disturbs it.'

'Who's going to come out here? In the middle of the night? During a storm? To disturb a body?'

'Chances are, no one.'

'Let me guess, rules are rules?'

'You got it,' Grant said. 'Do you mind?'

'No problem. You gonna be okay out here by yourself? In the dark?'

'I'll be fine,' Grant said, assuming a confidence he didn't really have. 'Just hurry back, okay? And get him to call for a coroner. I assume he knows who to get in touch with.'

'Will do, City Boy,' Sarah said, starting back towards the path. 'Try not to get eaten!'

Constable Grant watched as Sarah disappeared into the darkness. The wind still rustled through the leaves, which was a good thing, as far as he was concerned. In the dark, a familiar sound was better than no sound at all. 'Right, probably got twenty minutes, half an hour. Now what?' he said to himself. He aimlessly wandered around the immediate area, looking at the ground as he went. 'Don't know how anyone can track an animal through here, all I can see are leaves.' He wandered back over towards the body as another crack of thunder made him jump. 'Sarah was right. Who would be out here on a night like this?' he thought. He looked up at Jonny. 'Such a young kid. What was so bad in your life that you figured this was the best option? Maybe if I'd been able to talk to you at the centre, we could have helped you out.' He knew it was pointless to think like that. There may not have been anything anyone could have done. But still. One of the reasons he was here was to try and help out the community. There had to have been something he could have done.

He pulled out his phone again. Still no signal. He checked the time. 'Where is she?' he wondered. He realized that it had finally stopped raining and the wind had died down. Unfortunately, the humidity was starting to creep up again. Typical Ontario weather. A nice hard rain can drop the temperature several degrees, but as soon as it stops, the humidity returns and it's worse than ever. He unbuttoned his coat, which now felt like a personal rubber sauna, and took it off. Laying it on the ground next to a tree, he suddenly heard a snapping sound off to his left. He froze, shining his light in the general direction he thought the sound came from. Nothing but leaves. Impossible to see anything through the dense brush. His mind started to race, and his breathing wasn't far behind. Maybe it was a bear. Or worse, a cougar. He had heard of cougars dropping out of trees onto people's backs and grabbing onto their necks with their powerful jaws. He shone his flashlight up into the branches above him. 'There's nothing there,' he said out loud, trying, unsuccessfully, to calm himself down. Another rustling sound—this time from behind him. He spun around, almost falling as he did. Suddenly, something hit the ground right beside him, making him scream and jump out of the way, almost right into a tree. He moved his light to reveal a roll of yellow caution tape as Sarah came out of the darkness in hysterics.

'Nice high-pitched scream there, City Boy. Or should I say,

City Girl,' she said, still laughing.

'Very funny. You could have given me a heart attack!' Grant was not amused.

'Couldn't resist. Sorry,' Sarah said, wiping a tear from her eye. 'It was pretty funny, though.'

'Glad you think so,' Grant said, his heart starting to slow back to a more normal pace. 'So, did Barry call the coroner?'

'Oh, shoot,' Sarah said, slapping her palm to her forehead dramatically.

'You forgot to tell him? Great.'

'Nah, just kidding. He called. Should be out in the next hour or so,' Sarah said. 'So, what do we do now?'

'*We* don't do anything,' Grant replied. 'I'm going to put up the tape around the area and you're going to go home.'

'I can help. No way I'm going to sleep in this heat,' Sarah said. 'Plus, who's going to keep you safe?'

'Funny,' Grant said, shaking his head. 'I'll be fine. The sun should be up soon anyway. Go home. Are you going to the powwow? You dancing this year?'

'Wouldn't miss it. Mom made me a new jingle dress. Lots of extra beads and cones.'

'Cool. Why don't you go on home and get some rest. I'll see you at the opening ceremonies,' Grant said, starting to string out the tape.

'Fine,' Sarah said. 'Stay safe out here. The predators get real hungry right before sun-up.'

'Very funny,' Grant retorted, pretty sure she was joking. 'Thanks for your help tonight. And, Sarah, if you need to talk to a counsellor about this, I can arrange it.'

'I'm good. Like I said, we all die, right? Have a good night, City Boy,' Sarah called out over her shoulder as she wandered back to the path.

'Night,' Grant called back, wrapping the tape around another tree. He paused to listen to her footsteps, half expecting her to circle back around to try and scare him again. When he was sure that she was really gone, he pulled out his phone again to check the time. Three thirty. It was going to be a long wait for sunrise.

CHAPTER THREE

For the next half an hour, Constable Grant jumped at every little sound he heard. Sarah's comment about the predators had put him on edge. He had never spent too much time in the woods. Definitely never alone. He had gone camping a few times when he was in school, but sitting around a fire with twenty other people was very different than standing alone in a dark, unfamiliar forest. Even though he knew that the sounds he was hearing were nothing to be concerned with, his mind was playing tricks on him. Every little rustle in the ground cover was a bear, sniffing him out for a late night snack. Anytime the wind blew the leaves in the canopy of the trees, it was a cougar, ready to pounce on him, clamping its jaws around the back of his neck, holding him still as his life slowly slipped away. 'This is crazy,' he thought. 'I gotta find a way to occupy my mind.' He decided to walk around the area, looking for tracks on the ground. Sarah and some of the other kids who came to the drop-in centre would often talk about tracking different animals. They tried to figure out where they came from, or where they were going, so they could set up traps or find a good vantage point for hunting. He wasn't really sure what he needed to look for. He trained his light on the ground and started slowly walking, moving the light from side to side. Occasionally he would see a mark in the ground that looked like it could be a track, but, upon closer inspection, there was nothing definitive. He knew there were animals around. He had heard something run along the path earlier, but by the time he turned his light towards the sound to see what it was, it was gone. He convinced himself it was just a raccoon, even though he really had no idea. 'Maybe if I start bigger.' He placed his right foot in front of himself, pressing down hard, and moving it back, looking to see what type of mark it left. He was surprised at how little a mark it actually left to be seen. After the rain, he thought the ground would have been soft and muddy, but it wasn't the case. It was still hard and dry. Not enough water had made it through the leaves above to penetrate the packed dirt. He moved his light to a different angle, bending down slightly. The outline of the tread of his boot slowly became visible, revealing itself as an indent in the leaves below. 'Cool,' he said out loud. He squatted down on his haunches and slowly moved his light across the path he had walked earlier to put up the police tape. His old footsteps came into view, showing a brief history of his actions. 'This is awesome!' he said, marvelling at what he was seeing. He got up and moved over towards the path he and Sarah had used earlier, again getting low to the ground and shining his light on the leaves. He could see a couple sets of tracks. He could just make out what he thought were his boot marks, and a couple of other tracks heading in both directions. Those were probably Sarah's from when she came and went along the same route. He stood up, proud of his newfound skill. Sure, it wasn't tracking an animal through the woods so he could catch it for food, but it was a start. Something he could share with the kids the next time he was at the centre.

He walked back to the tree where Jonny was hanging. 'Where's that coroner?' he wondered, checking his watch. He looked at Jonny's shoes, bending down to have a look at the treads, wondering if he would be able to see which direction Jonny had come into the woods from. He backed a couple of feet away from the tree and repeated his earlier actions, getting down low before shining his light along the tops of the leaves. To his disappointment, he wasn't able to see any distinct tracks—just a jumble of impressions. He wasn't even sure they were footprints. He realized that he and Sarah had walked around the area several times earlier in the night, making one track over the other, probably erasing anything that had been left before. He moved back another couple of feet and tried again, hoping he hadn't already walked on the ground right in front of him. This time he was able to see some tracks appear, toes pointing towards the tree. Not quite as crisp as the tracks he had seen before, but they were tracks none the less. He got down closer for a better look, pretty sure they matched the treads of Jonny's shoes, or at least another pair of converse sneakers. It looked like Jonny, or whoever made the tracks, had taken a couple of steps towards the tree, before the tracks disappeared in the nondescript mess. As he was standing back up, Constable Grant thought he saw another track. He stayed down low, shining his light on the leaves to the left of Jonny's track. Sure enough, another print appeared, again fainter than those of Sarah and himself, but it was a track. He got down lower to get a better look. Definitely a different pattern than any of the others he had seen, and a bit larger than the ones made by Jonny. It looked like it was heading in the same direction, towards the tree. He moved his light around a bit and caught sight of the same print, this time moving away from the tree, back towards the path he and Sarah had come in on. He stood up, looking around. He knew a lot of people came through the woods—it was a good shortcut from town to the reserve. It was also a good place for someone to sneak a beer or cigarette without their parents knowing. There was no way of telling how old the track was, but he did find it interesting that it was there.

Suddenly, off to his right, he heard a large cracking sound, like a branch being broken in half. 'Hello? Who's there?' he yelled out, shining his light in the direction of the sound, hoping not to see a pair of eyes glimmering in the dark. Another crack and the sound of shuffling leaves. He moved around a bit, trying to see past the trees that were between him and the sound. 'Hello?' he called again, a slight quaver in his voice.

'Hello! Where are you?' a voice responded. It wasn't a voice he recognized.

'Over here,' Constable Grant said, holding his flashlight above his head, moving it side to side like a beacon. He could see another light shining back towards him. Two men appeared from behind a pine tree, the first carrying a flashlight and a large duffel bag, the second with a headlamp on, carrying a lightweight, orange stretcher. 'You must be from the coroner's office. Glad you finally made it.'

'Not the easiest place to find,' the man carrying the bag said. 'Would have been here earlier, but we've been wandering around for a bit.' He put the bag on the ground. 'Dr. Dickinson.'

'Constable Grant.'

'Shawn Enns,' the other man said.

'Pleasure,' Grant said, shaking both men's hands. 'So, here

he is. We didn't touch the body at all—figured we should wait for you.'

'Well, let's see what we got,' Dr. Dickinson said, shining his light on the body. 'Shawn, can you grab the ladder, please?'

Constable Grant looked around. He hadn't noticed either of the men carrying a ladder. Shawn put down the stretcher and walked over to the bag the doctor had been carrying. He opened it up, and pulled out a collapsible aluminum ladder. When it was folded down, it was only twelve inches tall, but when Shawn expanded it, it reached nearly six feet. 'Cool,' Grant said, admiringly.

'Makes life a lot easier when you got to get up into a tree to cut someone down. I'm getting too old to climb trees these days. It's not too bad getting up them, but my knees aren't a fan when I jump back down,' the doctor said as Shawn propped the ladder against the tree. 'Mind holding the bottom?'

Grant moved over and grabbed hold of the ladder as the doctor climbed up, rung by rung, until he was staring at Jonny's head. He moved the hair out of Jonny's face, leaning over to see his expression. 'Shawn, hand me the camera, will ya? I forgot to grab it.'

Shawn went into the bag again, pulling out a camera. He reached up and handed it to the doctor.

'Thanks,' the doctor said, as he leaned around again, taking pictures of Jonny's face. He took a few pictures of Jonny's neck, showing where the rope was digging into his skin, and of the rope tied around the limb above his head. 'Okay, that should be good for now,' he said, leaning down to pass the camera back to Shawn. 'Right, so here comes the tricky bit. I'm going to cut the rope and I need the two of you to hold onto him. I don't want him falling on the ground, if we can help it. Nice and gentle, okay?'

Constable Grant watched as Shawn moved to the side of the body and grabbed it around the leg. Constable Grant did the same on the other leg.

'Okay, so, once I'm almost through the rope, I'll let you know.' The doctor removed a large knife from a sheath on his belt. He grabbed the rope with his left hand and started sawing at the rope, leaning against the ladder and the tree for balance. One by one, the strands of the rope gave way under the edge of the sharp knife—each time, making the body drop slightly. 'Ready? He's going to drop.' Another strand gave way and the body fell with its full weight into the arms of Constable Grant and Shawn, who were taken by surprise despite the warning. Carefully, they held onto Jonny and lowered his body to the ground.

'Man, he's a lot heavier than he looks,' Grant said.

'They always are,' the doctor said, climbing down the ladder. 'Right, let's get him bagged up and on the stretcher.'

Shawn went into the duffel bag again and pulled out a body bag, laying it on the ground beside the body, unzipping it so it was splayed open. 'Mind giving a hand?' Shawn asked Constable Grant.

'Sure, what do you need?'

'You grab his feet, and I'll pick him up around his shoulders. We'll lift him up and Dr. Dickinson can slide the bag under him,' Shawn said, moving to Jonny's head, bending down and grabbing under his shoulders. Constable Grant squatted down and grabbed around Jonny's ankles, which were cold to the touch. He tried not to think about what he was lifting. 'On three. One, two, three,' Shawn said. The two of them lifted in unison as the doctor moved the bag under the suspended body.

'Good. Put him down,' the doctor said. Grant was all too happy to oblige. Dr. Dickinson felt around inside Jonny's front pockets. 'Empty. We'll check his other pockets and everything else more thoroughly once we have him back in town where there's more light. I'll let you know if we find anything, Constable. Go ahead and zip him up,' he said, standing up. Shawn did up the zipper on the bag, sealing it around Jonny's face. He and the doctor each grabbed an end of the bag and lifted it onto the stretcher. Shawn folded the ladder back up, put it in the duffel bag, closed it and put it on Jonny's stomach. He strapped Jonny and the bag to the stretcher.

'Well, that's it for us here. We'll bring him back to town for an examination before sending him to the morgue—just see if there's anything odd. Check his blood for drugs and alcohol. Once we're done, I'll send my report to the band office. You guys can let next of kin know.'

'Sounds good,' Constable Grant said. 'A death notice. My favourite,' he thought. Looking around, he noticed a hint of light trying to break through the trees. The sun had finally risen.

'You know the easiest way out of here?' Dr. Dickinson asked.

'Um, I think so. Pretty sure it's this way.' Constable Grant took a step to his left. He thought for a second and then turned back around to his right and started walking at a brisk pace. Dr. Dickinson and Shawn exchanged a look that was less than optimistic.

CHAPTER FOUR

ven though it had taken twice as long as it should have, Constable Grant was finally able to lead the three of them out of the woods. All the paths looked the same to him and they had taken a couple of wrong turns. But at least they made it.

'So, I'll try to get to the autopsy later today, maybe tomorrow. It's a bit busy back at the office right now,' Dr. Dickinson said, after loading the stretcher into the back of a van. 'It seems pretty straightforward, so I'm not expecting to find anything, but we'll let you know.'

'Perfect. Thanks again for coming out as quickly as you did,' Grant said, shaking the doctor's hand. 'If you're free this afternoon, you guys should come back. There's a powwow starting at noon. Should be fun.'

'Thanks. I'll see what the day has planned,' Dr. Dickinson said, climbing into the passenger seat of the van. 'We'll be in touch,' he said, before closing the door.

'Nice meeting you,' Shawn said, as he closed the driver's side door.

'You, too. Wish it had been under different circumstances.' Grant waved as they drove away. He looked at the sun peaking out over the horizon, a vibrant pink hue in the clouds. 'Going to be another hot one today,' he thought. 'Don't envy the dancers.' Checking his watch, he began walking towards the band's police station. Barry should still be there and it would be good to fill him in on the night's events. As he walked along, he could already hear children playing and laughing in the early hours. Life here was so different from in the city. At home, it seemed like kids didn't play outside as much as they used to, at least not as much as he had when he was young. When he was a kid, he would leave the house on his bike at the crack of dawn, sometimes not coming back home until dinner time. Or until he heard his mom yelling his name from the back door. Today, city kids seemed to stay inside more, surfing the internet or playing video games. Not here though. Sure, kids had access to games and computers, but they still seemed to prefer to be outside, playing with their friends. Or, maybe it was more that their parents wouldn't let them stay inside all day. Either way, it was good to see.

Grant climbed the wooden steps to the office and pushed the screen door open. He could hear Barry on the phone. It sounded like someone's dog had a run-in with a porcupine.

'Sorry, Ann. There really isn't anything I can do. I'm not a vet. No, you're going to have to bring Zeus to the city vet. Do you have the number? Okay, hold on, I'll grab it for you.' Barry put down the phone and started flipping through a binder that was on the desk, next to the phone. 'Right, got a pen? It's 613-67...'

Constable Grant waved to let Barry know he was there, then went to the kitchen to see if there was any coffee on. The pot was empty.

'Hey, Grant. How'd it go?' Barry asked, coming into the kitchen. Constable Grant was opening and closing various cupboard doors, searching for coffee filters.

'Well enough, I guess,' Grant replied over his shoulder. 'Not sure if Sarah told you much, but it was Jonny Two Bears. Know him?'

'Yeah, she let me know,' Barry said, opening a drawer and pulling out a package of filters. 'Good kid. Surprising really. He never seemed to have a care in the world. Did you want me to tell his mom? We're pretty close and it might be easier coming from me than...' He stopped mid-sentence.

'Than from the white, city boy?' Grant finished his thought, holding out his hand for the filters.

'Well, yeah. No offense.'

'None taken,' Grant said. He placed a filter in the basket, filled it with grounds and turned on the coffee maker. 'Anytime someone volunteers to do a death notice, I'm not going to refuse, no matter what the reason.'

'Are you going to open the drop-in centre today at some point?'

'I wasn't really planning to. I figured everyone would be at the powwow for most of the day and I didn't think anyone would want to stop by.'

'Might not be a bad idea, though. Some of Jonny's friends might want to talk,' Barry said, as he moved the pot out from the coffee maker, replacing it with his mug.

'Hey, what are you doing? That's the strong stuff!' Grant said.

'You're just jealous you didn't think of it first,' Barry said, smiling. When his cup was full, he moved it out of the way and put the pot back in its place.

'Unreal,' Grant said.

'Man, that's good. Nice and strong.' Barry made a show

of smacking his lips after his first sip. Grant just shook his head. 'Anyway, might not be a bad idea to ask around at the powwow. See how the kids are doing. If it looks like there's a need, we could call in a counsellor from the city. There's a good one who works at the hospital. We had her out a couple of years ago when three elders died on a hunt.'

'Three? What happened?' Grant asked, finally pouring himself a coffee.

'They were tracking a moose during the winter hunt. A storm rolled in at the end of the day and visibility was really bad. They ended up following the tracks out onto the ice and they must have hit a thin area—all three of their snow machines broke through. Water's pretty deep where they went down, and there's a strong current. They didn't have much of a chance.' Barry stopped, thinking about the friends he had lost. 'Divers didn't find the bodies until late the next spring. That was really hard on the community.'

'Man, I guess. I couldn't even imagine,' Grant said.

'The counsellor lady was really good. Almost the whole reserve showed up in the Great Meeting Hall, and we just talked, taking turns telling stories about them. It was really a good way to heal. She made sure everyone was doing okay at the end, talking to each one of us personally. Afterward, we had a meal and a drum circle. It was a good send off.'

'I'll make sure to ask around and see how everyone's doing. I'm sure the news will travel fast,' Grant said, finishing his coffee. He looked at his watch. 'I think I'm going to try to catch a couple hours of sleep. I don't want to miss the Arrival of the Clans ceremony.' He pointed at Barry. 'Don't forget you owe me a bannock.'

'Yeah, no problem,' Barry said. 'Thanks again for your help

last night.'

Constable Grant walked out of the office, squinting in the morning sun. The humidity was already making the air heavy and hot. 'Hope they have tents set up,' he thought as he started walking back to his room. In the distance, he could hear someone pounding on the ceremonial drum over at the fairgrounds. After the night he'd had, he was looking forward to a better day.

CHAPTER FIVE

Detective Terry Millar knocked, hesitantly, on the Captain's office door. It had been a few months since Millar had been back at the precinct. Even after he felt like he was ready to return to work, his therapist had recommended taking a little more time off. But sometimes Millar thought being home alone was worse than being around crime. He was feeling good. As good as could be expected anyways. He was still having a hard time coming to terms with what his daughter, Tina, had done. But, with the help of a good therapist, he had finally accepted that it had happened and he couldn't do anything about it. Life was different now, but he still had a life to live, no matter how hard it seemed to be some days.

The Captain looked up from his paperwork, smiling when he saw Millar. Privately, the Captain thought that Millar looked a bit rougher than he remembered, but that was to be expected. The man had gone through something no parent could even imagine. The fact that he was still walking around and willing to come back to work was a small miracle in itself.

'Terry, great to see you!' the Captain said, waving Millar into the room. 'How are things?'

'Hey, Captain. It's good to be seen,' Millar said taking a seat in one of the spare chairs. 'Things are pretty good, actually. Been getting more sleep over the last month or so. I wasn't sleeping very well at all for the first couple of months. Just couldn't turn my brain off, you know? My doctor prescribed some meds that really helped—just made things a bit quieter in my head.'

'That's good to hear. Take all the help you can,' the Captain said. 'Looks like you lost a bit of weight. Still eating?'

'Yeah, I've actually been eating a lot. But, being at home, I can eat real meals instead of sitting in my car or office eating whatever I can pick up at the closest fast food restaurant or convenience store. Mind you, I do kind of miss those microwave pizza pocket things from the convenience store on the corner.'

The Captain smiled. He remembered the days when he wasn't in his office all the time. Some days he was lucky if he ate any real food at all. Lots of chocolate bars and vending machine sandwiches. 'How's Tina doing, if you don't mind me asking?' He knew this was a touchy subject, but, if Millar was going to come back to work, he was going to be asked it a lot, so the Captain wanted to see how he reacted.

'She's getting by.' Millar's demeanor changed slightly as he started talking. 'She's still getting physio for her leg, which is good. I didn't know if that would continue once she was inside. Still walking with a limp, but it's not as pronounced now. Apparently it's not always noticeable.'

'Well that's good. Pain gone?'

'Mostly. Sometimes it flares up if she uses it too much, but for the most part she said she's been okay. She's started having tutoring sessions. There are two other girls that are at the same level, so they're working together. They all seem to get along, which is good. I was worried she was going to get picked on, but so far so good.'

'Glad to hear it. I was worried for her. I didn't think it was going to be an easy ride for her. Still a long time to go, but she's a strong kid. She should be fine,' the Captain said.

'I sure hope so, but not much I can do either way,' Millar said. Out of everything he'd said so far, this admission of helplessness seemed to bother him the most.

'So, what are your thoughts?' the Captain asked, trying to change Millar's train of thought. 'Thinking of coming back?'

'Well, I talked it over with my doctor and we think I'm ready. Maybe not ready to take the lead on any new cases, but to run support for Penner or someone else. How is Sue, anyways?' It had been a few weeks since Millar had spoken to Sue Penner. Before taking time off, he and Sue had been partners, investigating homicides and other major crimes in the city.

'She's doing well. Been teamed up with Detective Marks while his partner was on paternity leave. Lemieux's wife had a little boy around the time you went on leave. They seem to be working out, but I know she's ready to have you back. Apparently Marks won't let her boss him around like you will.' The Captain chuckled.

'Smart guy. I should have tried that years ago.' Millar smiled. 'She still working with Constable Grant?'

'At times,' the Captain said. 'He's been splitting his time as a liaison officer at a reserve about an hour south of the city. They've been really understaffed and needed the help.'

'Wow, really? That's a big step for him, isn't it?' Millar was surprised. Constable Grant hadn't been on the force for too many years. Usually a role like that would have gone to a more senior officer.

'Well, the band office got in touch looking for someone, and they actually asked about him, specifically.'

'Really. How did they know who he was?'

'When he was a paramedic, before joining the force, he attended several calls from the reserve. They don't have their own doctor out there, and people weren't getting the help they needed until they were really sick. By the time it gets to that point, they're often so poorly off that they need an ambulance to go to the hospital,' the Captain said, shaking his head. 'If the government would just commit the money to ensure they got the services they needed.' He stopped himself. Thinking about how the Indigenous communities in Canada were treated made him angry. 'Anyway, apparently he ended up building a good rapport with a lot of the community. Did you know he actually goes out there on his days off and helps with the youth drop-in centre?'

'I had no idea.' Millar was a bit taken aback. 'I guess I never really got to know much about him.'

'Came as a surprise to me, too. He never mentioned it to his Sergeant, either. I guess he likes to keep his personal life separate from his work life.'

'Don't we all,' Millar said, knowing that his personal life was way more out there now than he really would have liked.

'I'm all for a healthy work/life balance. So, speaking of which, are you sure you're ready to come back? There's really no need to rush,' the Captain said with concern. 'You can continue on long-term leave for another six months, I think. Why not take advantage of the time? Go do something for yourself?'

'I appreciate it, sir, I really do—but I'm kinda going stir crazy,' said Millar. 'I think I need some normalcy back in my days. Some routine. Like I said, maybe not full days or anything right away, but there has to be something I can do.'

The Captain thought about it, looking at Millar's face. It was riddled with concern, trepidation, fear and hope. He knew the best thing for Millar was to feel needed, to keep busy. Sitting alone at home wasn't doing either. 'Right. What if you help Constable Grant out at the reserve? It doesn't sound like it's high pressure stuff for the most part, just being an extra presence of authority, helping out when and where needed. Kind of being a goodwill ambassador.'

'Helping Grant?' asked Millar. 'I don't know, sir. Would I actually be reporting to him?'

The Captain smiled. 'Well, I guess you would be. It's his gig, so you would be doing whatever he wanted you to do. But,' the Captain added, 'I'm sure he would treat you fairly.'

Millar thought it over, drumming his fingers on the Captain's desk. He wasn't really sure he wanted a younger, lower ranked officer as his boss. 'I assume this is your best offer?' he asked, hoping it wasn't.

'I think so. For now, anyways,' the Captain said. 'Give it a try for a couple of weeks. If it's really terrible, go back on leave. Or, if you find you can handle the workload, we'll reconvene and get you back helping Penner with her cases here. Detective Marks's partner should be back within the month. Sound good?'

'Good? Not really. But I'll take it.' Millar wasn't sure if he was making a good choice, but at least he was making a choice. Mixing things up a little. 'He better not expect me to call him *sir* or anything.'

'I'll let him know,' said the Captain with a grin, standing up.

'It's really great to see you, Terry. I'm glad you're doing as well as you are. Again, if you need anything, let me know. We'll try to help you out as much as possible.' He extended his hand. Millar took it, giving it a strong shake.

'Thanks, sir. I really appreciate it.' Millar turned to walk out of the office. 'Guess I should try and find my new boss,' he added, shaking his head.

'I think he's actually at the reserve this weekend, but I'm not positive. Penner might know, if you can track her down.'

'Perfect. I'll see if she's in her office,' Millar said, opening the door.

'If you want to make a good impression, you should probably bring her a coffee—she still hasn't kicked the habit,' the Captain said, sitting back down and picking up his paperwork. He smiled, thinking how good it was to see Millar again.

***

Millar walked down the hall towards Penner's office. Even if he wasn't really back to full time duty, it felt good to be back at the precinct. It didn't matter if he was going to work one day a week or seven. Just knowing he was going back to work gave him a sense of purpose he hadn't felt for months. He passed a couple of uniformed officers who gave him a little nod hello. He nodded back and continued on. Everyone knew what had happened—and Millar knew that they knew. But what he didn't know was how people were going to treat him. His therapist had told him to hope for the best, but expect the worst. So far, things seemed pretty good.

At the end of the hall, Millar stopped and glanced in the kitchen, expecting to see Penner standing at the coffee maker, but she wasn't there. He grabbed two mugs out of the cupboard and filled them with coffee, finishing off the pot. He glanced around, checking to see if anyone was watching. Seeing no one, he poured a bit of coffee back into the pot from both mugs—just enough to say it wasn't empty so he wouldn't have to put on a new pot. 'Technically,' he thought to himself with a smile, 'I'm not working, so I'm basically a guest. You wouldn't expect a guest to put on more coffee.' Whistling to himself, Millar walked out of the kitchen, passing an officer on his way in. He avoided eye contact and picked up his pace, just in case the officer was looking for a coffee.

When he got to Penner's office, the door was closed. Trying not to spill the coffees, he knocked with his foot, kicking the base of the door. There was no answer. He maneuvered the mugs so he was holding both in his right hand, and tried the doorknob with his left. The door swung open, but there was no one inside. Millar decided to leave a note on Penner's chair, just letting her know he stopped by. He flicked on the light and walked over to the desk that was pushed up against the far wall. The top of the desk was littered with stacks of file folders. He put the coffees down and picked up one of the folders, opening it up absentmindedly. Paperwork was definitely one aspect of the job that he didn't miss. 'I wonder what ever happened to the paperwork I didn't finish before I left,' he said out loud.

'Your partner got stuck doing it, ya jerk,' Penner said from the door, making Millar jump and drop the file on the floor. 'Good to see you're making yourself at home,' she added, walking over and giving Millar a kiss on the cheek before picking up one of the mugs of coffee. 'It's great to see ya, stranger. You're looking good.'

'Likewise. I was just about to leave you a note—didn't think you were here. Keeping busy?'

'Yeah. As you can see, got a couple cases on the go,' Penner said, pointing to the folders on her desk. 'Nothing too interesting, but that's okay. At least I've been working almost normal hours for a change. Haven't had to come in at two in the morning for a couple of months now.'

'Sounds heavenly,' said Millar. He grabbed the other coffee mug and took one of Penner's chairs, sitting down and stretching his legs out. 'Don't remember the last time that happened when I was working. How's the new partner? The Captain said you were missing me?'

'Really? That's what he told you? He must have confused you with someone else,' Penner said, laughing. 'It's good. Different, but good. You coming back soon?'

'Maybe. For now, and don't laugh, I'm going to be helping out Constable Grant on the reserve.' Millar waited for a snide comment from Penner.

'Why would I laugh? I think that's great!' Penner said, to Millar's surprise. 'He was looking to move into a supervisory role.'

'There it is. Okay, get it out of your system,' said Millar, rolling his eyes. 'For the next couple of weeks or so, I'll be heading out to give him a hand. Not reporting to him, just helping, okay?'

'Are you going to have to salute him?' Penner asked, almost snorting out a laugh.

'Boy, am I glad I stopped by,' said Millar. He was glad—he missed this. 'Anyway, the Captain thinks it will be good for me to transition back into work. Take it easy with Grant, just be more of a presence than actually working on any major cases. Then, once your partner gets sick of you—which shouldn't be too long from now, I'm sure—I'll come back to show you how a real detective works.'

'How rude!' Penner said, smiling. 'So, when are you starting out there?'

'Don't know really. I was hoping to see Grant today—he doesn't even know about it. But, I guess he's already there this weekend, so I'll touch base next week sometime.'

'Hang on. Why don't we drive out there? It's only an hour away,' said Penner.

'What, now?'

'Well, I've got the weekend off with nothing to do. Other than paperwork, that is, but what's another couple of days. I'm sure the Captain's used to waiting by now,' Penner said. 'Grant was saying that there was a powwow this weekend—could be fun. I've never been to one and I've always wanted to. We can drive down this morning, see the dancing and art vendors. Have a bite to eat, check out the place. You can talk to Grant and see what it's going to be like. Whatcha think?'

'Could be fun,' Millar agreed. 'Alright, you're on. What time's it start?'

'At noon, I think. I'm pretty much done here for the day. How 'bout we stop at Joe's for breakfast, then hit the road.'

'Sounds like a plan,' Millar said with a smile. 'As long as you've got time.'

'For you, I got time.'

CHAPTER SIX

Two hours later, Constable Grant was awoken by someone knocking on his door. He rolled over and checked the clock. He did the math. He could sleep for another few hours and still make it in time for the opening ceremonies. He rolled over and pulled his blanket over his head, ignoring the knocking. Everyone would be at the powwow that afternoon, so if someone needed to talk to him, they could find him then. The knocking on his door continued—louder this time. 'Are you kidding me,' he muttered, popping his head out of the blanket. If he lay there quietly, maybe whoever it was would just leave. They pounded on his door again, more emphatically this time.

'Police,' a deep, booming voice called out from the other side of his door, making him sit straight up.

'Police?' he thought. It didn't sound like Barry, and Pete shouldn't be back from his hunt yet. Confused, he got out of bed, slipped on a t-shirt and headed for the door. 'Who's there?'

'Police. Open up, Mr. Grant,' the voice answered back.

Grant unbolted the lock on the door and slowly opened it, peering out. With surprise, he opened it fully. 'Detective Millar? Detective Penner? What are you doing here? You scared the crap out of me, ya know? I was having such a good sleep. Come in, come in,' he said, stepping out of the way, letting Millar and Penner into his small room. 'I'll put some coffee on. It's great to see you guys.'

Penner and Millar walked into the small apartment. There wasn't much to see. A sofa was pushed up against the wall to the left of the door, a small table with two chairs sat beside it. There was a kitchen. Well, there was a countertop with a microwave, a coffee maker and a two burner cooktop. In the corner was a bar fridge with some shelves above it. A small three-piece washroom and a tiny bedroom rounded out the place.

'So, Detective,' Grant turned to Millar. 'How've ya been? It's been way too long.'

'Been well, thanks,' Millar replied, sitting down at the kitchen table. Penner joined him, sitting in the only other chair.

'So, are you back at work now? How's Tina doing?'

'She's good, thanks,' said Millar. 'As good as can be expected anyway. As for me, I'm not back full time just yet. I met with the Captain this morning and we're trying to figure things out. What about you? How do you find it working out here?'

'It's really good, actually. Pretty different than being in the city, but it's good. Been helping out at a drop-in centre for kids for a while now. And, every now and then, I help out when the band police are short-staffed,' Grant said, bringing in three cups of coffee and placing them on the table. 'I'll show you around in a bit. I guess you came out for the powwow?'

'Yeah,' said Penner, taking a sip of coffee. She froze. Stared into her cup, and then looked up at Grant in awe. 'Wow! This is really good. What brand is it?'

'It's actually roasted here on the reserve,' Grant said. 'It's one of their recent start-up businesses and it's pretty cool. They buy the beans directly from Indigenous farmers in Peru, and then roast and package the coffee here. There's no middle man, so it's Indigenous people in North America working with Indigenous people in South America. The money helps kids in Peru go to school, and here, they're using the money to install water filtration systems in the reserve housing and to work on some of the other water issues they have. The Government isn't doing enough to make sure all the houses have clean water, so they're trying to help themselves.'

'That's awesome,' Penner said. 'Don't let me forget to pick up a couple of bags before we head home,' she said to Millar.

'I'll bring you by the roast house when we do our tour. They should be mid-way through a roast for the powwow right now, actually. Smells amazing in there,' Grant said.

'That would be great,' Penner said. She looked at Millar with a smug smile. 'Millar, don't you have some news to give to Grant?' Millar shot her a dark look before turning back to Grant.

'Yeah, so. Like I said, I was talking to the Captain this morning, and he thought it would be good for me to ease back into work,' Millar said.

'Probably a good idea. It's been a tough year for you,' said Grant.

Millar wasn't sure why he was finding this hard. Grant was a good guy—working with him shouldn't be too bad. But, working *with* someone and *for* someone were two completely different things. 'Anyway, the Captain thought it would be a good idea if I helped you out around here for a bit.'

'What Millar's trying to say is that he's going to come and

work for you,' Penner said, trying not to laugh.

'No, I'm going to help him out, not work for him,' Millar said.

'Either way, that would be great,' said Grant. 'We could definitely use the help at the centre—it's so understaffed there. I can't get half the programs up and running that I want.'

'Might only be for a couple of weeks. Just until the guy Penner is working with gets sick of her—which, let's be honest, it's kind of surprising it hasn't happened already,' Millar said.

'Jerk,' Penner said, punching Millar lightly on the arm. 'Make sure you boss him around real good,' she said to Grant.

'Don't worry, sir. I'm a pretty laidback boss.'

'Great,' said Millar with a grimace. 'And you can just shut it,' he said to Penner, who was stifling her laughter.

'I didn't say anything. I'm just sitting here quietly, enjoying my coffee.'

Grant looked at the clock hanging above the small table. 'We should go if we want to have a tour before the powwow starts.' He drained the last of his coffee and put his cup on the counter. 'Give me two minutes to get changed and we'll head out. I'm so glad you guys are here.'

'Glad to be back,' Millar said, with a deep sigh.

CHAPTER SEVEN

'Man, I can't get over how humid it is already,' Grant said, as he, Millar and Penner walked out of his apartment, into the heavy, stifling air. 'Sure glad I'm not dancing today.'

'Pretty sure everyone's glad about that,' Penner said, already starting to sweat. She pulled her hair up into a bun on the top of her head and fanned the back of her neck as they walked along.

The boom of the drum circle was louder now, as more and more drummers arrived and joined in. 'At the last powwow, they had ten people around the one drum. It's really something to see, all of them singing and pounding in unison. Such a cool thing,' Grant said. 'And then when the dancers start, it's really something else. Just wait until you see their traditional outfits. So colourful. And the beadwork is phenomenal! I have no idea how the beaders don't go cross-eyed working on the designs.'

'Should we head over and find somewhere to sit? Or stand, whatever the case may be?' Millar asked.

'We still have some time,' said Grant, checking his watch. 'I'll show you the band office and the police station first. Oh, then we'll go to the coffee roast house so you can see the set-up and buy some beans, if you want.'

'Oh, I want,' said Penner.

They continued walking down the street towards the small, square cinder block building used as the band's police station. It wasn't much, but it was all they really needed. Grant led the way up the wooden steps and pushed open the door, holding it for Penner and Millar. Inside, a desk stood against the far wall with a phone, computer and papers scattered about. There was a small kitchen, a bathroom, and a single cell.

'Isn't there anyone on duty?' Penner asked, looking around.

'Not always. Well, not during the day, anyway. There's always someone here overnight, just to make sure the phones are answered. But, during the day, all the calls go directly to the band office. Whoever's there takes the call, then gets in touch with the officer on-duty. There are only three full-time cops here, so they can't man the station all the time. And right now, one of them's on a hunt and another had a family emergency,' Grant explained. 'That's why they requested I come help out every now and then, just to help take the load off.'

'Big difference from home,' Penner said, thinking how many cops were on duty at any given time in the city. And Ottawa had three different forces, too—the RCMP, Ontario Provincial Police and Ottawa City Police. 'What happens if you have more than one person to lock up?' she asked, looking at the single cell.

'Doesn't happen too often, I don't think. But when it does, they share the one bed in there. Not the most comfortable, I'm sure, but maybe it acts as a bit of a deterrent. If it's really bad, they get in touch with the city police and bring them there.'

'Do you have a court house here, too?' Millar asked, looking around the small room.

'No. I think that's the biggest difference here,' Grant said. 'For major crimes, the perp gets sent to the city and is tried there. But for minor crimes, which make up the majority of the crimes here, they go before a Council of Elders.'

'What's that?' Penner asked.

'It's a really interesting approach. Kind of like restorative justice. The offender sits in the centre of a circle of Elders, or a group of respected members of the community, if you like. They discuss the crime that was committed and, based on the severity of the crime and the individuals involved, they decide on the appropriate punishment. It could be community service, going out on the land alone for a period of time, providing a moose for the community. It really depends.'

'Really? Does it work?' Penner looked skeptical.

'Seems to. There aren't a lot of repeat customers,' Grant said. 'At first, I had a hard time getting my head around it. Being a cop, you think someone should be punished the traditional way. Go to court—if you're found guilty, go to jail. But here, they don't see it like that. If someone committed a crime, why should that follow them around forever, defining who they are for the rest of their lives? A criminal record could end up being really detrimental for the person, making life harder than it needs to be. And it could actually lead to a life of crime out of necessity. If someone has a record and they can't get a job, they have to do something to get money.' Grant straightened a pile of papers on the desk and then continued, 'Getting a job here is hard enough already. Instead, the Elders take the opportunity to teach them some life lessons. Get them back on the land to reflect on what it means to be alive, to have respect for what the Maker has given them. The community takes it to heart.

Everyone here feels that if someone has strayed into crime, they're all partially responsible. It really is an interesting way of looking at things.'

'Interesting concept. But I don't know how well that would work back home.' Millar wasn't sure how he felt about this style of justice.

'I'm not sure it would,' Grant said. He checked his watch. 'We should get a move on if we want to see the coffee house before the opening ceremonies.'

Outside of the station, it was eerily quite. The drums that had been pounding all morning were silent. 'Must be taking a break before the big event starts,' Grant said. As they turned to walk down the street, a figure sitting on a bench next door raised a hand in greeting. A small dog lay at his feet. 'Oh, great,' said Grant. 'This should be fun.'

'Well, well, well. If it isn't Constable I-can't-play-cards-to-save-my-life Grant. Coming back asking for a rematch, are ya?' the man called out with a thick Jamaican accent.

Grant smiled and shook his head. 'You know, I'm pretty sure you guys only won because Barry was dealing off the bottom of the deck. There's no way the two of you are that good!'

'Calling me a cheat? Outrage!' the man said with a laugh. His little dog barked once at his raised voice.

'Yeah, you can save your outrage,' Grant said. 'Travis, I want you to meet a couple of friends of mine from Ottawa, Detectives Millar and Penner.'

Travis stood up, removing his straw gardening hat and revealing his freshly shaved head. 'Well, it's definitely a pleasure to meet you,' he said, taking Penner's hand, kissing the back of it. 'And what is a pretty lady like you doing being friends with a man like Grant?' he asked with a wink. Penner smiled. She couldn't figure out how old Travis was. His beard was swept with streaks of grey, but the rest of his features made him look young. There were no wrinkles around his eyes, but when she looked into them, she could tell his eyes had seen a lifetime of adventures.

'Alright, that's enough,' Grant said. 'Travis manages the band office. He's been working here for, what, five years?'

'Thereabouts,' Travis said.

'So, you're the band manager?' Millar asked with surprise.

'Yeah, I'm actually employed by the federal government, stationed here to help out. Kind of a middleman between the feds and the band. I help with getting funding for projects, running the day-to-day operations here. Lots of paperwork with not many results,' Travis said, pulling a pipe out of his shirt pocket. Taking a pouch out of his pants pocket, he filled the pipe with tobacco and tamped it down. He struck a match on the bench, holding the flame to the pipe's bowl.

'Interesting that they would hire someone from outside to do the work,' Penner said, leaning down to pet the dog, who had rolled over and was writhing around, exposing his belly.

'Well, it didn't used to be like that,' Travis said. 'Seems like Chewie likes you,' he said, watching his dog roll around as Penner played with him.

'He's a little cutie,' Penner said.

'He can be a handful at times. Likes to get out of his collar and take off on me,' Travis said, puffing on his pipe. He blew a cloud of smoke that wafted towards Millar. 'Sorry, my friend.'

'No worries,' Millar said, waving his hand to disperse the smoke. He had never smoked, but the smell of a pipe always reminded him of his dad.

'It used to be that the band ran their own affairs, but they complained to the feds that they weren't getting the resources they needed. There was too much red tape, too many hurdles. So, the Minister of Indigenous and Northern Affairs decided that hiring an outsider who knew how the government worked would be a good thing, make everything work much smoother,' Travis said, drawing on his pipe.

'Did it?' Penner asked.

'Nope. All it did was give me a job. I try, don't get me wrong. But bureaucracy works at its own pace. As long as the majority of voters aren't affected, it doesn't matter if a couple of thousand people can't drink their water. It's all about votes.'

The boom of the drums started up, filling the humid air again. Grant looked at his watch. 'If you want coffee, we'd better go. Things are going to start real soon.'

'It was nice meeting you, Travis. Are you coming to the powwow?' asked Penner.

'Gonna try. Especially if you're going to be there, my dear.'

'Give it a rest, old man,' Grant said. 'Good seeing you.'

'Likewise,' Travis said, having another puff on his pipe. 'Cards next week! Your turn to bring the snacks.'

'Sounds good,' Grant said, starting to lead Penner and Millar down the street.

'Hope you don't suck as bad as last time!' Travis called out, laughing to himself.

'He seems nice,' Penner said as they crossed the street.

'Yeah, he is. Bit of a handful at times, but he's pretty harmless. Likes to have fun, but he really does try to get the best for the band. When he started here, he couldn't believe the water wasn't drinkable. He said one of the reasons his family moved to Canada was because they always heard how great a country it was. He came from a very poor part of Jamaica, and they didn't have running water. They had to walk to the neighbouring village to fill jugs twice a day,' Grant said. 'Imagine leaving a poor country to come to a first world country, only to find out people here are living with the same types of issues.'

'I didn't realize it was that bad here,' Millar said. 'So, you can't drink the water at all?'

'You can, but it's not advisable,' Grant said. 'Sometimes it just smells really bad, but it isn't actually unsafe to drink. Other times it smells really bad *and* it's unsafe. Problem is, you never know what you're going to get. Plus, if the water smells like dirt, are you going to want to drink it, whether it's safe or not?'

'Probably not,' said Millar, thinking how lucky they were at home. He never gave something like water quality a second thought.

The smell of freshly roasting coffee hit Penner as they turned a corner. 'Oh man, that smells good!'

'Sure does. Wait 'til you go inside,' Grant said, opening the shop door. The smell was amazing. It was like the strongest, freshest pot of coffee one could imagine. Penner was in heaven.

'*Mino kigijebawan*,' a young girl greeted them, looking up as she took a scoop of coffee beans out of the roaster in the centre of the room.

'*Mino kigijebawan*,' Grant said. 'That means good morning in Algonquin,' he said to Penner and Millar.

'*Mino kigijebawan*,' Millar said, struggling with the pronunciation. The girl smiled.

'Welcome to *Makadewamik Gaapii*. That's Black Beaver Coffee. We just finished roasting a test batch. We're experimenting—trying out a new combination of three different beans. They're all from Peru, but they're from different locations, which gives them each a slightly different flavour.'

'Sure smells good. How often do you roast?' Penner asked, moving closer to the fresh beans.

'We've been roasting once a week, but I think we're going to need to add another day. We're having a hard time keeping up with demand,' the young girl said.

'I can see why,' said Penner. 'We had a pot of it earlier—it's delicious.'

'*Meegwetch*,' the young girl said. 'That's thank you.'

'How do you say you're welcome?' Penner asked.

'*Ka'n nigodizinon*,' the young girl said.

Penner tried to repeat the words but wasn't even close to successful, breaking into laughter. 'Sorry about that.'

'At least you tried,' the young girl said, giggling. 'Would you like to try a cup of the new blend? I have a pot just finished.'

'You don't have to ask her twice,' Grant said, seeing Penner's eyes light up.

The young girl poured three small cups of coffee and passed them out.

'It almost has a sweet smell,' Millar said, sniffing the steam coming out of his cup.

'That's the bean from high up in the mountains, it has a very distinctive taste and aroma. On its own, we found that it was a bit too different for most people. We're hoping it will be more popular, mixed with the other two beans. Please, enjoy,' the young girl said.

'Wow, now that's a cup of coffee!' Penner said, finishing her cup.

'No kidding. I could go for a pot of that,' Grant said. 'Is this one ready to be sold yet?'

'Not quite. The beans have to cool before we can package them—otherwise they'll continue to cook in the bag and get too bitter,' the young girl said. 'If you're going to the powwow, I'll be there later this afternoon. I can bring some then if you want.'

'Definitely. That would be great,' said Grant. 'I'll take a pound.'

'Me too,' Millar said.

'Put me down for two pounds,' said Penner.

'Two pounds? That's a lot of coffee. Are you sure?' the young girl asked with surprise.

'Trust me, that's not a lot of coffee for her—might not even last a week,' said Grant. He checked the time. 'We should go. We'll see you later?'

'For sure. Thank you for coming in,' the young girl said. An order for four pounds of coffee was a great start to the day.

'*Meegwetch*,' Penner said, making the young girl smile again. 'Say,' she added, 'any chance of getting a cup to go?'

CHAPTER EIGHT

By the time they arrived at the fairgrounds, there were already hundreds of people milling around. Millar looked around, taking in the sights and sounds. Under a pop-up canopy, eight men sat around a drum that was almost three feet in diameter, singing and pounding the drum in unison, causing a thunderous sound. Outside of the canopy, some young kids had gathered, dancing to the beat. Along the perimeter of the grounds, at least two dozen vendors had set up tables, each with an assortment of artwork and crafts for sale. There were half a dozen food trucks, selling everything from fresh walleye and bannock tacos to french fries and cotton candy.

'Do we have time to check out some of the vendors?' asked Penner.

Grant checked his watch. 'Sure. The official Arrival of the Clans should be starting soon, but we'll still be able to see from over at the tables.'

They walked through the crowd, mingling with people in traditional dress and some wearing their everyday street clothes.

'They're so colourful!' Penner said, admiring the women wearing brightly coloured garments adorned with beadwork and silver-coloured cones.

'Those are jingle dresses. When they dance, the sound of the jingling cones really adds to the experience,' Grant said as they approached the first table. A young woman stood behind it, greeting them with a big smile.

'Welcome!' she said.

'These are beautiful! Did you make them?' asked Penner, looking at the assortment of earrings that were spread across the table. She picked up a pair made of small beads woven into blue, red and yellow chevrons.

'Thank you,' the young woman said. 'I made them all by hand. That pair you have there are some of my favourites. I love how the colours work together.'

'I can see why they're your favourites,' Penner said, scanning the rest of the table. 'I'm going to take these and these ones here.' She picked up another pair with long, fringes of black and turquoise beads.

'Fantastic!' said the young woman. She took the two pairs of earrings from Penner and put them in a small paper bag. 'That will be forty dollars.'

Penner reached into her purse and pulled out two twenty dollar bills, handing them to the young woman in exchange for the bag. 'Thank you so much. I'm looking forward to wearing them.' She tucked the paper bag into her purse.

They walked past a table of tanned hides and Millar stopped to admire a pair of beaded gauntlet mitts. As they continued walking, a voice called out from behind them.

'Hey, City Boy! You made it!' Sarah said. Grant turned to look at her. She was wearing a yellow dress that fell just below her knees and tall, fur-covered mukluks. Her dress jingled as she approached.

'Hi, Sarah—love the dress. This the one your mom made?' Grant asked.

'Yup, she did a good job, eh? Better than the one she made for me last year,' Sarah said, spinning around. 'Should look good when I'm dancing.'

'You'll steal the spotlight for sure,' said Grant. 'I want you to meet two of my friends from back home. Sarah, this is Detective Sue Penner and Detective Terry Millar.'

'Nice to meet you,' said Millar, holding out his hand.

'Likewise,' Sarah said, shaking his hand.

Penner looked at her in awe. 'Your hair is so long! How long have you been growing it?'

'About this long,' Sarah said with a smile, indicating where her hair ended around her waist. 'Kidding. I haven't actually cut it since I was really young. Four or five, I think.' She gestured at Grant. 'So, you guys work with City Boy? Must be fun.'

'It has its moments,' Millar said. 'City Boy. I like that.'

Grant sighed. 'Just what I need, another nickname from you,' he said looking at Millar. 'Did you get a chance to talk to your brother about Jonny?' he asked, turning back to Sarah.

'Yeah, I saw him before I headed over here,' Sarah said. 'He was really surprised. Took it kinda hard.'

'He was surprised?' asked Grant.

'Yeah. I guess Jonny never seemed like he was depressed or anything,' Sarah answered. 'He was looking forward to heading out on a moose hunt this week. Been doing good at school—no problems at all. Sammy said it really didn't make any sense.' Her head tilted as she heard the rhythm of the drumming change. Looking over Grant's shoulder, she saw the dancers lining up to enter the Ceremonial Circle. 'Gotta go. See you later? It was nice meeting you two,' she said as she ran off to join the other dancers, her dress ringing out with every step.

'Have fun,' Grant called out. He turned to his guests. 'We should probably find somewhere to stand so we can see.'

'So, who's Jonny?' asked Millar as they walked to the edge of the circle, trying to find a spot amongst the crowd.

'Young local guy. Sarah found him last night. Hanged himself from a tree in the woods,' Grant said.

'That's awful!' Penner exclaimed. 'She doesn't seem too phased by it.'

'No, she doesn't. Not sure if it's an act or if she's really okay,' Grant said, surging forward as he spotted an opening in the crowd. 'We're going to get a counsellor in to talk to anyone who wants to talk.'

'Probably a good idea,' Penner agreed. The dancers began to enter the circle, each of the women wearing a different coloured dress, the men in colourful shirts and pants. Their regalia were covered in silver-coloured cones, beads, feathers and porcupine quills—sometimes all at once. Several of the men wore necklaces with a large medallion hanging around their neck. Each medallion had a different symbol beaded into the design. A raven, a crow, a bear, a wolf. Each represented the clan they belonged to.

'*Ladies and Gentlemen, welcome to the annual harvest powwow,*' a voice came over the speaker system. '*We would ask each of you at this time to remove your hat, unless it has an eagle feather in it.*'

Millar looked around the crowd as people, young and old, removed their hats. Several of the older men wearing cowboy hats with a feather in the hatband kept their hats on.

'It's a sign of respect,' Grant explained. 'The eagle feather is a sacred item.'

Millar noticed a young man in the crowd still wearing a baseball cap. He either didn't hear the message or didn't care. One of the dancers, a very large man, almost as tall as Millar but probably eighty pounds heavier, arms covered with Indigenous tattoos, pointed at the young man and motioned for him to remove his hat, which he did rather quickly.

As the last dancer entered into the circle, the drumming and singing stopped and the crowd applauded. The voice came over the speakers again.

'Thank you, dancers, for the grand entrance. We will be starting the individual dances in a minute, starting with the under sixteen girls, then the boys, and we will be ending with the over sixteens and the group dances. But first, I would like to call on Chief Ravenclaw to come up and say a few words.'

There was another round of applause as the large, tattooed dancer walked up to the podium, taking the microphone in his hand. Penner noticed he had matching tattoos on his forearms. A skull wearing a traditional headdress, with long, flowing feathers.

'Thank you, Noah,' the Chief said. 'I would like to personally welcome you all to our event today. This is an event that helps bring our communities together, and, hopefully, strengthens the bond between those of us who live here and those who have come to visit from outside of the reserve. Before we start, we have some sad, troubling news. Last night, we lost a member of our community. Jonny Two Bears was found dead.' There was an audible gasp from several people in the crowd. 'I would like each of you to take a moment to think about Jonny and remember him for the young man he was. Dancers,

I would ask that you channel your memories of Jonny while you dance. Remember Jonny's joy and how he shared it with us as he danced.' Chief Ravenclaw paused for a moment in silence, his eyes closed. Then he opened them and gestured to the circle. 'Drummers and singers, please welcome the first dancer.' The drummers started pounding the drum a little harder than before, singing louder and with more meaning as the first young girl started dancing.

'She's so cute,' Penner said. The girl was probably eight years old, her green dress hanging around her ankles. She was stomping her feet the best she could to the beat of the drum, trying to keep her oversized headband from falling over her eyes.

'That's my daughter,' a voice said from behind them. Grant turned to see who was talking.

'Barry, I didn't know Emma was dancing this year. I didn't recognize her at all. She's grown quite a bit since the last time I saw her.'

'Growing like a weed,' agreed Barry.

'Barry, these are my friends, Millar and Penner. They're from the force back in Ottawa,' Grant said. "Guys, this is Barry. He's one of the officers I work with here.'

'Nice to meet you,' Barry said as his daughter finished dancing. 'Great job, baby girl!' he yelled out. Emma smiled at him as she walked out of the circle, another young girl taking her place.

'So, did you get me my bannock?' Grant asked, smiling at Barry.

'Oh, you were serious?

'Of course I was!' Grant said. 'You think I'm going to work for free? Come on, you owe me a snack.'

'Fine, fine,' Barry said, turning to walk towards the food trucks. 'You guys want anything?'

'What's bannock?' asked Penner.

'It's a traditional fried flat bread. Really delicious when it's fresh out of the pan, smothered with butter and strawberry jam,' Barry said.

'Sounds like my kind of snack,' Penner said. 'I'll get one of those.'

'Yeah, me too,' Millar said. They followed Barry and joined him in the long line at the bannock truck.

'So, I went and saw Jonny's mom this morning,' Barry said. 'She didn't take the news too well.'

'Not surprised,' said Grant. 'No one would take it very well. Did she say if he'd been depressed recently or anything?'

'Not a care in the world, like usual,' Barry said as the line moved forward slightly. 'I checked out his room, too. Didn't find a suicide note or anything. Really seems so random. No idea why he would have done it.'

'Well, I guess people are pretty good at hiding how they're really feeling. Maybe he got in trouble at school or something. Was he into drugs or drinking?' Grant asked, shuffling forward as the line moved again.

'Not that I know of,' said Barry. 'Maybe he was. One of his friends might know better than me. Four bannocks, please,' he said as they finally got to the front of the line. He turned back and asked, 'Anything to drink?'

'I'll just get a coffee later. Thanks, though,' said Penner.

'I'm good,' Grant said.

'Same,' Millar said.

The young man in the truck handed them each a large piece of bannock wrapped in a piece of newspaper to soak up some of the oil. 'Butter and jam are on the side of the truck. That's ten bucks.'

Barry paid and they walked to the side of the truck where there was a container of butter and five different types of jam.

'Cheers, Barry,' Penner said, spreading butter on her bannock and adding a large dollop of blueberry jam. She took a bite and nearly burned the roof of her mouth. 'Wow!' She chewed a bit until she could talk again. 'That's delicious.'

'We've been making it the same way for hundreds of years,' Barry said. 'Well, we don't grind the flour by hand any more, but some of the Elders still do.'

'How did they used to cook it before having frying pans?' Millar asked, taking a bite.

'They would either heat up a rock in a fire and lay the dough over it,' Barry said. 'Or they would wrap the dough around a stick and cook it over an open fire. Kinda like cooking a marshmallow or a hot dog.'

'Bet that would be good. It would give it a nice smoky flavour,' said Grant, strawberry jam dripping down his chin.

'My mom still cooks it that way. Definitely one of my favourite ways to do it, but it's kind of hard to do at the powwow. Too big a risk of kids getting hurt,' Barry said, taking his last bite. 'How 'bout we go find some coffee.'

'Sounds good to me,' Penner said. 'I sure hope the coffee roaster brings our beans with her. Wonder if I should have got another pound.'

'I can always bring you some more anytime you want. I'm out here quite regularly,' Grant said. 'Plus, Millar will be out here for a while, too. Oh, that reminds me. Barry, Millar's going to be helping out for a couple of days a week.'

'Really,? That's perfect,' said Barry. 'We can definitely use the help. Welcome aboard. What about you, Detective Penner? Want to become a small town cop for a couple of days?'

'Sorry—don't think the Captain will let me,' Penner said. 'Mind you, I could get used to working somewhere where I could get bannock and that great coffee everyday. Beats the stuff we get back home.'

'Maybe something to consider for the future then,' Barry said as they spotted the tent where the coffee was being sold. The young girl from the coffee roast house sat behind a table.

'*Kwey*,' the young girl said, seeing them walk up to the tent. 'That's hello in Algonquin. I have your beans. I figured you would be stopping by for a coffee.'

'You're a good judge of character,' said Penner. 'Do you have any of this morning's coffee brewed?'

'I do,' the young girl said, grabbing a cup. 'We also have a nice dark roast and a medium bodied one too.'

'I'll go for the dark roast, if I could,' Millar said.

'Me, too. Thanks,' said Grant. 'Barry?'

'I'll go for the medium. I've already had a cup this morning,' Barry said.

'Only one? Amateur,' Penner said, smiling. 'I'll pay for all four.'

'Six dollars, plus the beans,' the young girl said, handing out the coffees.

'They can pay for their own beans,' Penner said, giving the young girl some money. 'Keep the change—put it towards the business.'

'Thank you so much!'

'No problem. You should really set up an online shop, or set up a subscription service with a different type of coffee every couple of weeks,' Penner suggested, sipping her coffee.

'I'd definitely be a customer.'

'It's actually something we're looking into. We just have a few logistics to figure out.'

'Well, when you do, be sure to let me know,' Penner said, digging through her wallet and pulling out a business card for the girl.

'Make sure you do,' Millar said paying for his beans. 'She'll buy enough on her own to keep you in business.'

'I'll remember that,' said the young girl, passing a bag of beans to Grant, who also gave her some money.

'Thanks,' Grant said. 'Did you know Jonny Two Bears by chance.'

'Not really—seen him around all the time, but I didn't really know him,' the young girl said. 'Pretty sad news.'

'That it was,' Grant said. 'We're going to bring a counsellor in sometime in the next couple of days, so if you feel like you need to talk to someone, make sure you come down to the youth centre. Thanks again for the coffee.'

'I'll keep that in mind, thanks. Enjoy the rest of the powwow,' she said, turning to serve another customer.

CHAPTER NINE

Sarah was just entering the circle when they got back with their coffees in hand. As the drumming started, she began to dance, turning in such a way that the bottom of her dress flared to the beat, the jingling cones playing a complementary tune. After a couple of turns, she danced to the edge of the circle and picked up half a dozen white plastic hoops, each the size of a small hula hoop. As her stomping feet kept the rhythm going, she started manipulating the hoops across her back, outstretching her arms to simulate the wings of an eagle.

'That was cool,' Penner said to Millar as they both clapped along with the rest of the crowd. Sarah continued to dance, picking up more hoops as she went. She made several more shapes with the hoops, telling a story as she danced along. By the time she was done, she had gathered more than two dozen hoops in her hands. When her turn was over, she took a bow, exiting the circle as the next girl entered.

'Never seen a hoop dance before. That was really neat,' said Millar. 'Must take quite the coordination to keep dancing while trying not to drop the hoops.'

'You can probably give it a try down at the drop-in centre during the week, if you want,' Barry said.

'If he does, make sure to film it. I'm sure the guys back in Ottawa would love to see that!' Penner said, chuckling.

'Fat chance that's going to happen,' Millar said.

'You really should give it a try while you're here—see what our culture is really about,' a deep voice boomed from behind them. Millar turned to see Chief Ravenclaw standing just a few paces away.

'Chief Ravenclaw, I would like to introduce you to my friends from back in Ottawa. Detectives Sue Penner and Terry Millar,' Grant said.

'Pleasure to meet you,' Penner said, with a smile. 'I'm so glad we made the drive to see the powwow. It's such an experience.'

'I'm glad you're enjoying yourself,' said the Chief. 'And that the weather held out. It rained pretty good yesterday.'

'So, if it had rained today, what would have happened?' asked Millar.

'You would have gotten wet,' the Chief said, letting out a booming laugh and slapping Millar on the shoulder. 'No, we would have set up a couple of other tents and tried to stay as dry as possible, but the show would have gone on. We don't let the weather dampen what we have planned, no pun intended. We try to teach our youth that the weather is a part of life that you can't change, and you respect it but still go on with your plans. When our ancestors were living in shelters off the land, they didn't have a choice to sit around inside when it was raining. They still had to hunt and gather food. Life went on. You just got a little wet while living it.'

'Are the kids here receptive to learning about the ways of their ancestors?' Penner asked, looking around. 'I can see some of them are, based on the number of dancers today, but are all of them?'

'For the most part,' the Chief replied. 'Some of them more than others. During school, the young kids all take part in various forms of dance and, one day a week, they have a history lesson, learning what it was like before the Europeans came to Canada. The older kids can choose to study dance, learn basket weaving or take a tracking course. That one seems like it's one of the most popular. They also study history, too, but we try to have a more balanced curriculum—one that's not just focussed on the European view of past events. For instance,' the Chief continued, 'we study the impact of the Indian Act and we include more recent history, like when our children were taken and put into Residential Schools. We think that's really important because it affected a lot of our kids' grandparents, and some of their parents, too.'

'That should really be taught to every kid, not just the Indigenous kids. I don't think enough people know exactly what happened and the repercussions that still linger,' added Grant.

'Well, thankfully, the Canadian government is starting to make it mandatory to teach about the Residential School system in every school. And federal employees have to take mandatory training on Indigenous issues, so it's a start.' The Chief paused before continuing thoughtfully, 'Could they do more? Probably, but anything is better than nothing, right?'

'So, what's the tracking course all about?' asked Penner.

'Well, the hunt is still really important for us—to make sure we connect with the land on a regular basis. So, we teach the youth how to identify different animal tracks and how to follow them in all kinds of conditions,' the Chief explained. 'It's important that they can identify the difference between a moose track and a deer track. You don't want to be tracking a bull moose for a day just to find out you've been following a young deer.'

'Makes sense,' Penner said. 'I would love to try my hand at something like that.'

'Well, you should stick around for another day—you could join up with one of the classes tomorrow,' the Chief said. 'Not sure when you were planning on heading back to Ottawa.'

'I was planning on heading back tonight, but I don't report back to the office for another couple of days. I could always come back tomorrow,' Penner said, warming to the idea. 'If you wouldn't mind, that is.'

'Not at all,' said the Chief. 'If you want, we can set you up for the night, so you don't have to drive back and forth. There's an extra room in the band house, next to where Constable Grant's staying. You're more than welcome to spend the night there, if you want. We can get you a change of clothes and some toiletries. Bedding's already there.'

'That would be fantastic. I would really like to stick around and learn some more about your culture,' Penner said. 'Oh, but where will you stay?' she asked, turning to Millar.

'I have a sofa bed in my place,' Grant offered. 'He can stay there for the night, then he can move into the other room when you head back. Well, I assume he can move in there—if it's okay with you,' he quickly deferred to the Chief.

'Sounds good to me. We don't have anyone looking for a room right now, so it's better to use the space than to let it sit empty.' The Chief grinned and rubbed his hands together. 'So it's set. This evening, we're having a moose roast and I'd like you all to be my guests. I'll send over a change of clothes to your room and we'll see you all in the Great Hall around six o'clock. Now, if you'll excuse me, I should go mingle with the crowd.'

'We'll see you later. Thanks for the invite,' Grant said.

'My pleasure,' the Chief said as he was walking off into the crowd.

Millar looked thoughtful. 'You know, he really reminds me of someone. You know, that wrestler that became an actor? Can't think of what his name is now.'

'I think I know who you mean,' said Penner. 'He seems nice.'

'He really is,' Barry said. 'He's done a lot of good for the community since he became Chief five years ago. He's really trying to improve life here for everyone. To be honest, Jonny's death has probably affected him more than he let on. We had a couple of teen suicides last year, including someone really close to the Chief, and we thought we had turned a corner—feels like a setback for the whole community.' He pulled out his phone and checked the time. 'I should probably head home for a bit. I've gotta man the phones again tonight, so I should get some sleep before the feast starts.' Barry put his phone back in his pocket and reached out to shake first Penner's hand and then Millar's. 'It was really nice meeting you two. Looking forward to working with you, Detective Millar.'

'Likewise. Thanks for the bannock,' Millar said.

'So,' Grant asked, 'what do you guys feel like doing? We've got a bit of time to kill before tonight's feast.'

'Can we check out the drop-in centre where you work?' asked Penner.

'Sure,' Grant said. 'Probably be a good idea to open up for a bit, just in case anyone wants to talk about Jonny.'

'Perfect,' Penner said. 'And…maybe we can get another coffee for the walk over.'

'Good to see you haven't changed while I was gone,' Millar said, smiling. 'I'll get this round.'

***

'Back again?' the young girl from the roast house asked when she saw Penner, Millar and Grant.

'Thought we'd get another couple of cups for the road, if you still have any left,' Penner said.

'I just put on a new pot, if you don't mind waiting a minute.'

'For that coffee, I'd wait as long as needed,' Penner assured the teenager, picking up a pamphlet from the table and reading it. She turned when a phone suddenly rang beside her.

'Excuse me a sec,' Grant said, taking his phone out of his pocket and walking a few steps away before answering.

'So, how was business today?' Millar asked the young girl, turning his attention back from Grant. 'Make many sales?'

'Almost sold out of fresh beans—only have one pound left. And I got several orders for some blends that I didn't bring with me. All in all, I really don't think it could have been any better,' she said, picking up some disposable cups and lids. 'All three of you having one?'

'I think Grant's having one,' Millar said to Penner.

'If not, I'll have his,' Penner said. 'And I might as well take the last pound of beans you have—I'd hate for it to go to waste.'

'You might just be my best customer!' the young girl said. 'I really appreciate it. You're helping lots of people.'

'My pleasure,' said Penner, taking out her wallet. 'I'll pay for the beans—he's getting the coffees,' she said, pointing to Millar.

'You never forget when someone offers to pay for something,

eh?' Millar said.

'Free is free,' said Penner as Grant joined them.

'Sorry 'bout that,' Grant said, grabbing one of the cups the girl had poured. 'Thanks for this.' He nodded at Millar.

'Enjoy the rest of the day!' the girl said, putting the money in her lock-box. She couldn't believe she had sold out of beans as early as she had.

'So, which way to the drop-in centre?' Millar asked as they started walking back through the crowd. Grant didn't respond. 'Grant, you okay?'

'What? Oh, sorry. Yeah, I'm fine,' Grant said. 'Just got a call from the coroner who took Jonny last night.'

'Did they find something?' Penner asked, sipping her coffee. 'Did you ever find a note?'

'Yeah, apparently he had one in his back pocket. The coroner is going to courier it to the band office—should probably get it later today or tomorrow,' Grant said.

'What'd it say?' Penner asked.

'In a nutshell, it said he couldn't face living on the reserve anymore. That he hated the fact that they didn't have the basics, like fresh water, to live a decent life. And that he'd had enough,' Grant said. 'He said he was sorry and that's about it.'

'Such a shame that living conditions would be so bad that someone would do that. Especially someone so young,' Millar said, shaking his head.

'Yeah, but...' Grant said.

'But, what?' Penner asked.

'Well,' said Grant, 'the coroner said that Jonny's hyoid bone was broken.'

'His what?' Millar asked.

'Exactly, right?' Grant said. 'I vaguely remember hearing its name back when I was a paramedic, but I always thought it was called hynoid. Probably a good thing I switched careers. Anyway, he said the hyoid bone is a horseshoe-shaped bone in the neck.'

'So? You said he hanged himself, right?' Penner said. 'With the pressure of the rope, wouldn't you expect something in his neck to break?'

'Yeah, I would. But according to the coroner, it's pretty rare for the hyoid bone to break when a young male hangs himself,' Grant said. 'Apparently it only happens in about six percent of cases.'

'Really? That seems pretty low.' Penner frowned. 'So, what did the coroner think?'

'Well, he said it could be nothing, but that particular bone usually only breaks as a result of manual strangulation. So, bottom line is he thinks it's something worth looking into. Unfortunately, he really can't say either way,' Grant said. 'The bruising on his neck is more or less consistent with hanging.'

'Wait. More or less?' Millar said. 'Either it is or it isn't.'

'Well, he said there were a couple of marks on the side of his neck that could be bruising from an individual's fingers grabbing his neck. Or, they could be from something else. Maybe hickies.'

'Hickies? Like, from someone sucking on his neck? Do kids still do that?' Penner asked, surprised.

'Maybe. I really don't know,' Grant said. 'But, the coroner recommends we find out if Jonny had a girlfriend. Or a boyfriend, I guess.'

'So what are you getting at? It might not have been suicide after all?' Millar asked. 'What about the note?'

'I don't know. I'm thinking that as soon as we get it, I'll

ask Barry to bring it to Jonny's mom. See if she can confirm that it's his handwriting,' Grant said. 'If it is, then there's probably a good chance it's a suicide and the bruising came from something else. But, I'll still ask around.'

'And if it's not his handwriting?' Penner asked.

'Well, then I guess Millar and I are gonna have to be more than just figureheads,' Grant said. 'I should give Barry a call and give him a heads-up.'

CHAPTER TEN

As they approached the drop-in centre, they saw that two teenagers and a young girl were hanging out outside. The boy was bouncing a basketball against the side of the building, while the girls chatted. Grant recognized Sarah, still in her dress from earlier, and the boy was her brother, Sammy, but he didn't recognize the young girl.

'Hey, City Boy. I was starting to think that you weren't going to open up today,' Sarah said as Grant unlocked the door.

'Hey, Sarah. Great job dancing earlier! That was really cool,' Grant said, stepping inside and turning on the lights. 'I didn't realize you were dancing with the hoops this year—you're getting pretty good with them.'

'I thought I recognized your dress,' said Penner. 'I had never seen anything like that before. I don't know how you kept the beat while manoeuvring the hoops around like you did. I'm sure I would have either dropped them all or fallen flat on my face!'

'Lots of practice,' Sarah said. 'That, and the thought of my instructor lecturing me next time I saw her. Fear is a pretty good motivator,' she said with a smile.

'Well, whatever it was, it worked,' Penner said. 'I think your dance was the highlight of the powwow for me.'

'Wow, even over the coffee?' Millar said. 'That's a pretty huge compliment!' Penner gave him a friendly shove.

'I didn't see many other girls doing that type of dance, though,' Penner said. 'Mainly just guys.'

'Traditionally, only boys and men danced with the hoops, but that started to change recently,' Sarah said. 'A few of the Elders still think it should just be males that do it, so some of the other girls here don't want to try. They don't want to upset anyone.'

'You're not worried about that?' Penner asked.

'Me? Hardly,' said Sarah with a trace of scorn. 'If they don't like it, they don't have to watch. I'm going to do what makes me happy, not what makes someone else happy.'

'Now that's a good way to live,' Penner agreed.

'If you want, I can show you some moves,' said Sarah, grabbing Penner by the arm, leading her to one of the back rooms.

Grant turned his attention to the other two kids. 'So, how're you doing, Sammy?'

'Okay, I guess,' Sammy said, dribbling his basketball with one hand. 'It's weird. I'm really not sure how to feel.'

'Well, that's understandable in situations like this,' Grant said, grabbing some chairs that were stacked along one of the walls. He placed eight of them in a circle, just in case anyone else decided to show up, and sat down. Millar sat in the chair beside him, while Sammy and the girl sat down across from them. 'This is my friend from Ottawa, Detective Terry Millar. He's going to be helping me out here for a while.' Millar nodded at Sammy and the girl. 'And what's your name? I don't think I've seen you here before,' Grant asked, looking at the young girl. She was probably around nine or ten, with long black hair flowing over her shoulders.

'This is Ella. She's our cousin from Peterborough. She came down for the powwow with my auntie and uncle,' Sammy said, as Ella tried to hide her face behind his back. 'She's pretty shy.'

'Well, nice to meet you, Ella,' Grant said in a soft, parent-like tone. Ella gave a little wave, still hiding behind her cousin. 'Would you like to do some colouring?' he asked. Ella moved her head back into view and gave a nod. 'Perfect,' Grant said, getting up. He went over to a closet that was beside the stack of chairs and pulled out a colouring book of animals and a box of pencil crayons. He handed Ella the book, putting the box on the chair beside her.

'So, Sammy,' Grant started as he sat back down. Ella was busy colouring a bear green. 'When was the last time you saw Jonny?'

'Saw him the day before yesterday,' Sammy said. 'We went out biking in the woods, then decided to go for a dip down at the old pond cuz it was so hot.'

'What time was that?' Grant asked.

'Not too sure,' Sammy said. 'I don't wear a watch. But maybe three or four in the afternoon.'

'How did Jonny seem to you? Had he been upset about anything?' Grant asked, glancing down at Ella as she searched for a different colour in the box.

'Seemed like Jonny,' Sammy said. 'He always just seemed the same. Never really sad or anything, always real happy. He was looking forward to next week's hunt. He loved being out hunting.'

'Was he dating anyone?' Grant asked. Millar sat quietly, just taking in the way Grant worked. He hadn't really seen Grant questioning anyone before.

'No, he wasn't seeing anyone,' Sammy said, breaking eye contact and looking around the room. 'Not since last year. He took it really hard when Amanda died.'

'Amanda?' Grant said.

'Yeah, the Chief's step-daughter,' Sammy said. 'Jonny and her had been dating for a long time—maybe six months before they broke up.'

'I didn't know the Chief had a daughter,' Grant said. 'So, what happened to her?'

'She hung herself,' Sammy said. 'Really shook Jonny up. When he broke up with her, she told him that she was going to kill herself, but he didn't think she really would. No one took her seriously. No one thought she'd really do it.'

'She hanged herself?' Grant said, looking over at Millar. 'Do you think Jonny was still upset?'

'I know he missed her,' said Sammy, thoughtfully. 'He kind of felt guilty for not believing her, but he had come to terms with the fact that she was gone. After a month or two, he was back to himself.'

'Something to keep in mind,' Grant said to Millar. 'So, when you guys were swimming, did you notice any bruises on Jonny?'

'What kind of bruises? You think someone beat him up?'

'No,' said Grant, 'nothing like that. More like…a hickie, maybe? Or any other kind of bruises on his neck.'

'I'd remember a hickie…cuz I would have teased him about that. That's lame.' Sammy shook his head in disgust. 'But, I didn't notice any marks at all. And he didn't mention anything. Like I said, he was just his normal, happy self.'

'Right.' Grant straightened up in his chair, 'So, do you think it would be good to have someone come in and talk to you and your friends?'

'Why? We're talking now, right? Why would we want someone else to come in?' Sammy asked, furrowing his brow.

'Well, if you have any questions about death, or you just want to talk about how you're feeling. Anything, really,' said Grant.

'I'm good,' Sammy said, standing up and picking up his basketball from the floor. 'Maybe some of the other kids might have questions or something, but I'm cool. Death happens—nothing we can do about it, right?'

'You're definitely your sister's brother,' said Grant.

'Well, d'uh,' Sammy said, not understanding the expression. 'I'm going to head out back and shoot some hoops. Mind looking after Ella until Sarah's back?'

'Yeah, no problem,' Grant said, standing up. 'Thanks for chatting, Sammy. If you do need to talk, just let me know, okay?'

'Will do, City Boy,' Sammy said with a wave as he walked out of the room.

'You, too? Great,' Grant said.

'Seems like they really respect you,' Millar said with a chuckle.

'Yeah, tonnes of respect,' said Grant, sitting back down in a chair beside Ella. 'Wow, a purple moose. Does he have a name?' She didn't answer and just kept colouring.

'No, I'm actually serious,' Millar said. 'The fact that he sat here and talked to you shows he has a level of respect for you. And giving you a nickname, well, that helps, too.'

'Glad you think so,' said Grant. 'Sometimes I really feel like an outsider here. There's a lot of mistrust of anyone who's not from here. I can understand it—they've been screwed over a lot over the years. But, slowly, I think things are starting to change.'

A loud crash sounded from the room Penner and Sarah had gone into. Sarah poked her head out of the door. 'Sorry about that! I think we need a little more practice.'

'Everything okay?' Millar asked, walking towards the room. He looked in past Sarah and saw Penner laying on the floor, laughing hysterically, hoops strewn all around her.

'It's all good, but my career as a dancer may be over,' Penner said, slowly getting to her knees, still shaking with laughter.

'Not sure it ever really started,' Sarah said, picking up the hoops.

***

Grant checked his watch. He had hoped some more of the kids would have shown up to talk, but he wasn't too surprised they hadn't. With the powwow and the feast, there was a lot going on to distract them from whatever they might be feeling. Tomorrow was a different day. 'Well, we should probably head out if we want to get cleaned up before dinner.'

Grant and Millar stacked the chairs back against the wall while Sarah and Penner helped Ella put away the pencil crayons. They walked outside into the bright, humid air and waited for Grant to turn off the lights and lock the door. They could hear Sammy still playing with the basketball around the side of the building.

'You and your family coming to the feast?' Grant asked Sarah, who was admiring Ella's colouring job.

'Yup, we'll be there for sure. Never turn down a moose roast,'

Sarah said, taking Ella's hand. 'Guess I'll see you there later. Thanks for opening up, City Boy. Good dancing, Sue.'

'Maybe I'll get another lesson before I head back home,' Penner said.

'That can be arranged,' Sarah said over her shoulder, as she and Ella walked around the building to get Sammy.

'She seems like a good kid,' Penner said as they started heading back towards their rooms.

'She is,' said Grant. 'Most of the kids here are good. Well, the ones I've met, anyway.'

'Do the rooms here have air conditioning?' Millar asked, wiping his forehead. 'This has to be one of the hottest, most humid weeks of the summer.'

'Well, technically they do—but they're really only good at making noise,' Grant said. 'They don't seem to cool down the rooms too well.'

'Excellent,' said Millar. 'Maybe I'll have to try and find that swimming pond Sammy was talking about before trying to sleep tonight.'

'I think it's supposed to rain most of the night,' said Grant. 'So, with any luck, the heat will break a bit.' He looked up at the cloudless sky. 'Well, according to the weather report it's supposed to rain.'

'And that's never been wrong before?' Penner asked sarcastically.

'Touché,' said Grant. Looking down the street, he saw Barry walking towards them. 'Hey, Barry! Up already? I thought you were heading home to sleep.'

'Yeah, I managed to get a bit, but not as much as I would have liked,' Barry said. 'Got a call earlier from the band office that the courier had dropped off the suicide note from the coroner in town. Figured I'd bring it over to Jonny's mom and get her to have a look at it.'

'Oh, yeah?' Grant said, intrigued. 'What'd she say?'

'Well, when she finally stopped crying enough to be able to actually read the note, she gave it back to me and said Jonny didn't write it,' Barry said.

'Really? Was she sure?'

'I asked her and she said there was no way Jonny wrote this note,' Barry said. 'She said it looked nothing like his writing.'

'Well, if he was distraught, is it possible that there might be a difference in how he wrote?' suggested Penner. 'Maybe she's just in denial?'

'That was my thought, too,' Barry said, nodding. 'So, I asked her if she had anything he had written recently. She got me one of his book reports. Kind of lucky—he usually used a computer for his assignments, but his printer was out of ink when he had to do this one.' He took the report and the letter out of a large manila envelope. 'See. Looks like the slant of the letters is wrong…and the way he loops certain letters. I'm no handwriting expert, but to me, they look really different.'

Grant took the two documents to have a look. The suicide note was in a clear, plastic cover. 'You put it in here?'

'No, that's how it was when it was sent over,' Barry said. 'Guess in case we wanted to check for prints.'

'We should definitely give it a dust. See if there's anything to see,' Grant said, checking out the documents. 'You know, I think you're right. Look at how the r's are done—in the note, they're more like script, but in his report, everything is printed. Look at the word sorry,' he said, passing the letter to Millar.

'Anywhere in the report where he wrote double r's? Maybe it's just how he wrote when the r was doubled,' Millar said, looking over the rest of the letter.

Grant scanned the book report. 'Okay, here. He wrote hurry. All the letters are printed, the r's are very different,' he said, looking up at Millar.

'Hmm, did he use double r's anywhere else?' Millar asked. Penner could see his wheels turning.

'Yeah, here he wrote burry,' Grant said, pointing to the page.

'Like, a plant had a lot of burrs, so it was burry?' Penner asked.

'Probably meant bury, based on the sentence,' Grant said. 'But again, the r's are printed. Nothing like the note.' He passed the report to Millar, who held the two side by side. 'What do you think?'

Millar scanned the two documents for a minute without saying anything. 'I think we need to get these checked out,' he finally said. 'There are definitely differences between the two. But, just because there are differences doesn't mean he didn't write both of them. We have to look at the differences and the similarities to be able to tell for sure.' He looked up at Penner. 'Didn't one of the guys working with fraud take a handwriting analysis course?'

'Yeah, what was his name?' Penner thought hard. 'Waters maybe?'

'No, it was a Scottish name, I think. McCoy?'

'McGee!' Penner exclaimed, happy she thought of it before Millar did.

'Yeah, that's it. I'll give the Captain a call—see if we can fax these over to him to have a look. See what McGee thinks,' Millar said, passing the documents back to Barry. 'Do you mind if I use the phone in the office here?'

'No problem,' said Barry. 'Fax machine's here, too, so we can send them off as soon as you get the go-ahead.'

'Perfect. I'll take care of this, then I'll meet you back at your place,' Millar said to Grant. 'I think I can find my way back from here.'

'Sounds good,' Grant said, turning to Penner. 'I'll show you where you'll be staying. See if the Chief dropped off a change of clothes for you, yet.' He turned back to Barry and Millar. 'By the way—that was some good policework, Barry.'

'Thanks. See you later at the dinner,' Barry said, holding the door to the band office open for Millar. Inside, Travis sat at a desk behind a mound of paperwork, his straw hat hanging on a hook behind his chair and his dog, Chewie, laying asleep in a small bed beside the desk.

'Looks like my desk back at the precinct,' Millar said. 'Don't think I've actually seen the surface of my desk for at least a year now.'

'This ain't even the half of it,' Travis said with his Jamaican drawl. 'There's another stack on the desk over there,' he said pointing to the back of the office. 'Sometimes I feel like all I do is fill in forms, and for what? Can't get approval from the government for anything.'

'Well, we appreciate you trying,' Barry said. 'You can use the phone over here, Detective.'

'Thanks,' Millar said, sitting at a desk Barry was motioning too. He pulled a sheet of paper out from his wallet to look up the Captain's phone number. 'Really should know these numbers by now,' he said to Barry, shaking his head. It was like his home phone number. He almost never called it, so he could never remember what it was when he needed it. He dialled the number and waited while it rang. 'Hi, Captain? It's Millar,' he said when the Captain finally picked up.

'*Terry, how are you? Didn't expect to hear from you so soon. Don't tell me you got into it with Constable Grant already?*'

'No, nothing like that. Things are good. Got a favour to ask.'

'*What's up?*'

'Well, we have two samples of handwriting that we want to have compared—see if they came from the same person. I was wondering if we could fax them over to you so McGee could have a look and we could get his opinion.'

'*I don't see an issue with that. Pretty sure McGee's working nights this week, so he should be in the office in a couple of hours. I can send them down to his office and get him to look into it when he gets a chance. Already working a case out there? That didn't take long.*'

'Well, we're not too sure right now if we have a case to investigate or not.'

'*Oh?*'

'Yeah. Young lad was found hanging from a tree. There was a suicide note, but his mom is adamant that he didn't write it. We want to try and do a comparison with a known sample of his writing.'

'*That's gotta be tough on her. Right. Send them over. I'll get back to you as soon as I can. Anything else?*'

'No, that's it,' Millar said, knowing the Captain's cue that a conversation was done. 'Thank you, sir.'

'*No problem.*' The Captain hung up.

'Right, we're good to send them over,' Millar said, hanging up the phone. 'Here's the fax number.'

CHAPTER ELEVEN

Penner and Grant were sitting on the sofa, having a cup of coffee, when Millar finally arrived.

'Any trouble finding your way back?' Grant asked. 'Coffee?'

'Thanks,' said Millar, pulling out a kitchen chair and sitting down across from the sofa. 'Got here more or less okay. Only took two wrong turns.'

'Really?' Grant said, getting up to grab a coffee for Millar. 'How's that even possible? It's almost a straight line.'

'You'll learn that Millar can get lost walking from his office to the washroom,' Penner said, chuckling. 'Some would say he's a little directionally challenged.'

'True, true, but I made it and that's all that matters. Thanks,' Millar said as Grant passed him a cup of coffee. 'So, we faxed off the note and the book report. Captain said that McGee's working tonight, so he would send it right down. Hopefully he gets a chance to look at them tonight, but apparently he's working a case right now, so no guarantees. Barry and I dusted the suicide note for prints, but we didn't find any.' He took a sip of coffee before continuing. 'Which is really strange, when you think about it. Why aren't Jonny's prints on the note?'

'Do you really think someone here would kill a teenager and

cover it up like a suicide?' Penner asked, finishing her coffee. She put the cup down with a rattle to get Grant's attention.

'Want another one?' Grant asked, grabbing the cup and standing back up before Penner could answer. 'To be honest, I don't know what to think about the whole situation. On the one hand, hiding a murder as a suicide is a pretty good idea,' he said, pouring a coffee and passing the cup back to Penner.

'Cheers,' said Penner.

'But, on the other hand, I just can't see why anyone here would kill him. From what I've heard, he was a good kid with no cares in the world. Didn't seem to have a problem with anyone,' Grant said, sitting down on the edge of the sofa.

'Could it have been someone off of the reserve? How are relations with the closest communities?' Millar asked.

'You know, that could be a possibility,' Grant said. 'Some of the kids have said they've been harassed when they go into town. Unfortunately, racism's all too real out here.' There was a knock at the door and Grant stood up again to answer it. 'I guess we'll just have to wait and see what McGee has to say,' Grant said as he opened the door. 'Oh, Chief Ravenclaw, come in. Can I get you a coffee?'

'No, thanks. I can't stay. I have to head right over to the Great Hall to see how everything's coming for the feast,' the Chief said, entering the room. 'I just wanted to bring these clothes for Detective Penner. Hopefully they're the right size. They're my wife's,' he said, handing Penner a bag.

'This is beautiful,' Penner exclaimed, pulling out a bright blue dress that had colourful flowers embroidered down the front. 'Is this done by hand?' she asked, looking closer at the fine thread work.

'It is,' the Chief said. 'Took my wife quite some time to do, but it was a good winter project. Better sitting on the sofa sewing than being outside during an Ontario winter, eh?'

'I've got to try this on,' Penner said, getting up and heading to the washroom. 'My new earrings will go perfect with this.'

'I stopped by Jonny's mom's place on my way over here,' the Chief said, taking a seat at the kitchen table next to Millar. 'She was saying she didn't think Jonny killed himself. Something about a note that Barry brought over. You know anything about that?'

'Yeah, the coroner in town found a note in Jonny's pocket that he couriered to the office,' Grant said. 'Barry brought it to her, but she doesn't think he wrote it.'

'Really?' said the Chief. His attention turned to Penner as she walked out of the washroom. 'Well, that fits like it was made for you.'

'I know, right?' Penner said, admiring the dress hanging just so from her body. 'It's so comfortable, too. I can't thank you enough for letting me borrow this. You'll have to thank your wife for me.'

'She'll be there tonight, so you can thank her yourself.' The Chief turned his attention back to Grant and asked, 'Did you see the note?'

'We did. Jonny's mom also gave Barry a book report he had written,' Grant said. 'Gotta say, there were definitely differences between the penmanship. I'm not an expert, but I would say someone else wrote the note.'

'We faxed a copy of both back to Ottawa to have one of the detectives there have a look, see what he thinks,' Millar said. 'He has a lot more experience with handwriting than we do. Hopefully we'll find out soon.'

'Right,' the Chief said, standing up and walking towards the door. 'Until we find out for sure, let's try and keep this under wraps. People like to talk. If we're not careful, before we know it, everyone will be talking about how Jonny was murdered. We really don't need that type of gossip going around. Keep me in the loop.'

'Will do, Chief,' Grant said. 'We'll see you at the feast in about an hour or so.'

'Perfect. Make sure you bring your appetites. Ever have roast moose before, Detectives?' the Chief asked. Both Millar and Penner shook their heads no. 'You're in for a real treat then. See you soon,' he said, closing the door behind him.

'That dress really does look nice on you,' Millar said as Penner twirled around the living room, the ribbon bands on the skirt rippling as she moved. 'Going to make me look like a right old bum!'

'Not too hard, really,' Penner said, reaching into her purse and putting on the earrings she had bought earlier at the powwow. 'Grant, do you have your nice, baby blue suit here?' she asked with a laugh.

'No, I got rid of that and bought a new one. Dark grey,' he said. 'Much more up-to-date that the blue one.'

'I think anything would be more up-to-date than that was,' Millar said. 'Well, if we're going to head over in the next hour, I think I'll have a shower, if that's okay.'

'No problem,' Grant said. 'There's an extra towel on the shelf over the toilet. Don't be too alarmed by the smell of the water. Or the colour. It might be a bit brown—you never really know what you're going to get.'

'Still blows my mind that the water can be so bad here,' Penner said. 'The coffee tastes fine. Do you use tap water when you make it?'

'Depends. Sometimes I'll use bottled water, but I usually boil a big pot of water as soon as I get here and keep it in the fridge,' Grant said. 'I'll use that for coffee and I keep the bottled water for drinking. Even after boiling the water, it still has a bit of a taste. And the colour's always going to be there. It may be safe to drink, but it's not the most appetizing. At least the coffee masks it. It's really noticeable when you just have a glass of water.'

'Crazy. Okay, I think I'll go to my room and freshen up, too,' Penner said. 'I'll be back in about, say, half an hour?'

'Sounds good. It only takes about ten minutes to walk over to the Great Hall from here,' Grant said. 'Want another coffee ready for when you come back?'

'You know, I wouldn't say no,' Penner said.

'Figured as much. See ya in a bit,' Grant said, heading into the kitchen to start a fresh pot.

CHAPTER TWELVE

'Wow! This is beautiful,' said Penner as they entered the great hall, admiring the artwork that adorned the walls.

'The majority of the pieces are by local artists,' Grant explained. 'But there are a few pieces from artists across Canada. They're mostly gifts given to the different chiefs over the years by other chiefs. A few times a year, the different chiefs get together for a weekend retreat where they discuss the various issues they're each facing in their region. Sometimes there are representatives from the Federal Government there, too. But most of the time they don't show up. Or they're not invited. Some of the chiefs feel it's easier to discuss topics among themselves first before presenting them to the government.'

'I love the masks,' Millar said, pointing to six masks hanging on the wall. 'Are they carved from wood?'

'They are,' Grant said, walking over to the wall of masks. 'Each one is carved from a single piece of softwood, usually cedar, and then painted. They were originally for ceremonial use, or to be used by a shaman. Now, the majority of masks are carved for decoration, but they still have a lot of meaning and symbolism.'

'Are there any carvers still working in the reserve? I would love to see how they're done,' Penner said, admiring the craftsmanship.

'There's at least one that I know of. This one here was done by the Chief's nephew, Les,' Grant said, pointing to a large mask of a stylized human face—mouth open, so you could see its teeth. The wood was largely natural and unpainted, but accents of red and black had been painted around the eyes, cheeks, mouth and hair. 'Most of the local masks are painted using only red and black. Some of the artists will use a turquoise colour, but it's less common. Red and black are traditional colours that were used hundreds of years ago when paints were made from different plants and insects. Tradition is very important.'

'You'll have to introduce us to Les. Maybe we can check out where he works,' Penner said. She looked around the rest of the Great Hall, which was filling up quickly. Round tables, each seating ten people, had been set up around the room. Along the back wall, a dozen chairs had been placed behind a long table decorated with different flowers and plaited reed decorations. Across from where they were standing, several long tables holding plates and cutlery lined the side of the Hall. 'Do we just sit anywhere?'

'You sit up front with us,' a deep voice spoke from behind Penner and caused her to jump. 'I told you that you were my guests, and guests sit at the head table.'

'Chief Ravenclaw,' Penner said, turning around. The Chief was wearing a long-sleeved shirt covering his tattoos. The shirt had flowers embroidered down the length of the sleeves, in the same style as the dress he had lent Penner. Over top of the shirt, he wore a green suede vest that had an embroidered bison on each of the breast panels. 'Love your outfit!' she said.

'Thank you, Detective.' The Chief grinned. 'I'd like to introduce you to the designer, my wife, Sooleawa,' the Chief said, signalling to the woman standing beside him.

'Such a pleasure to meet you,' Penner said, shaking the woman's hand. The two were so similar in stature that, from behind, the only way to tell them apart was the hair. Penner's vibrant red hair, which owed its colour more to a box than to nature, was tied in a tight bun on the top of her head. Sooleawa's long black hair, with the slightest hint of grey, was worn in a sleek, single braid hanging half way down her back. 'I have to thank you for lending me this dress for tonight,' she added. 'It is absolutely lovely. And it fits better than anything I've ever bought at a store.'

'*Ka'n nigodizinon,*' Sooleawa said.

'That's you're welcome, right?' Penner said with a smile.

'Wow, I'm impressed,' the Chief said. 'Seems like you are learning about our culture.'

'Trying,' said Penner. 'Now, whether I would have remembered the word if I had to say it instead of hearing it is another story.'

'Either way, it's still impressive,' Sooleawa said. 'I'm glad you like the dress. It was one of my first attempts at embroidering such a large piece, and I'm pretty happy with how it turned out. Since then, I don't know if I've made any piece of clothing without a bit of embroidery. It's kind of my signature now.'

'Sooleawa is getting a bit of a following online for her clothing designs. Last year, the Prime Minister's wife wore one of her scarves at a big to-do,' the Chief said, smiling with pride. 'How many orders did you get as a result?'

'More than I could keep up with,' said Sooleawa. 'I still get requests for pieces because of that event.'

'So, you sell your clothing?' Penner asked.

'I do. I have a little shop I run out of our living room. I used to work as a computer animator, but it was time for a change. I got tired of commuting to work, sitting in an office all day. I felt like a trapped animal and knew something needed to change,' Sooleawa said. 'You should stop by and have a look while you're here. If that dress fits, then I've got lots of pieces in your size. I'm good at making things that fit me, but I find it harder making things that fit other people,' she said with a smile.

'Probably took you, what, five attempts at making a shirt that would fit me?' the Chief said.

'Well, Machk, you're not exactly a typical off-the-rack size, are you? No matter what pattern I bought it needed to be adjusted.'

'Machk?' asked Millar. 'What's that mean?'

'That's my name,' the Chief said. 'It's Algonquin for Bear. Well, when it's used as a boy's name. An actual bear is *makwa*. Most people just call me Mac.'

'And what does Sooleawa mean, if you don't mind us asking?' asked Grant.

'Not at all. It means silver,' Sooleawa said. 'The day I was born, the light was shining off of the frozen lake, making it shimmer like silver. My father thought it was a sign.'

'Did your parents see a bear the day you were born?' Grant asked the Chief.

'Well…not exactly,' the Chief said, his wife giggling.

'No, he was such a chubby baby when he was born. And apparently he snored so loudly when he slept, it sounded like a bear. Or a hippo, but his parents didn't think *Sibi Kokosh* was a good name, so Machk it was,' explained Sooleawa, between fits of giggles.

'Pretty sure it was for my power more than anything,' the Chief added, mildly embarrassed.

'Yeah, you keep telling yourself that, dear. Oh! Looks like they're bringing out the food. We should probably take our seats. You have to do your welcoming speech, too,' Sooleawa reminded her husband.

'Right. Well, the three of you can join us at the main table. Take the seats to the left of Sooleawa in the centre. I'll be up in a minute—I just have to see if I can find Travis.'

As the Chief wandered into the crowd of people, a heavenly scent wafted over towards Millar. 'What is that smell?' he asked, his stomach rumbling.

'Ah, that's the moose,' Sooleawa said. 'Have you ever had it before?' she asked as they walked towards the head table.

'Never,' Millar said, looking over at the table along the wall where the food was being set up.

'Well, you are in for a real treat then,' she said as they got to the table. 'Please, have a seat.'

Millar took the chair between Grant and Penner, who was sitting next to Sooleawa. 'I can't get over how many people are here,' Millar said, looking around the room. 'Is there going to be enough food?'

'Have you ever seen a moose?' Grant asked, leaning in to make sure Millar could hear over the din of conversations. 'A single bull moose, depending on its size, is going to give around three to four hundred pounds of boneless meat. I think they're expecting around a hundred and fifty or a hundred and seventy-five people, so should be plenty. Not everyone is going to eat a couple of pounds of meat, not with everything else they usually serve.'

'How on earth do they cook four hundred pounds of meat?' Millar asked, his stomach rumbling louder than before.

'It turns into a very communal affair,' said Grant. 'Probably a third of the people here have been helping out cooking for the last two days. People will take home portions of the moose and cook them different ways, either in their ovens or barbeques. I think one family took an entire half of the moose and cooked it in a traditional fire pit.'

'How's that done?' Penner asked, joining the conversation.

'Well, they dig a big pit, big enough to fit in the moose meat, and about three feet deep,' Grant said. 'They line the pit with large rocks, which helps to regulate the heat. Then the fun begins. Several large fires are set so they can get a really good amount of coals, they need to make a bed in the pit that's about a foot thick.'

'That's gotta take a lot of wood,' Millar said, envisioning the size of pit required to fit half a moose.

'That's for sure. People have been chopping wood for the last week or so,' Grant said. 'Once they have all the coals in the pit, they wrap the moose in damp burlap. Several men lower the moose into the pit and bury it with the dirt they removed when they were digging the pit. Once it's buried, they keep a fresh layer of coals over top of the pit while the moose cooks.'

'How long's it take to cook?' Millar asked.

'About twelve to sixteen hours. It's not a quick process, but boy is it good,' Grant said. 'You guys really chose a good weekend to come for a visit.'

'Seems like it,' Penner agreed. 'This has been such a cool experience. It definitely won't be the last time I come for a visit.'

'I hope not,' said the Chief from behind her, giving her a start.

'You really have to stop sneaking up on me like that,' Penner said. 'I don't know how someone your size can be so quiet when they walk.'

'Lots of time in the woods tracking animals,' explained the Chief. 'If you walk with a heavy foot, you'll starve to death.'

'He's not always that quiet,' Sooleawa chimed in. 'Especially when he's coming home late from one of his meetings. Or his card games.'

'Cute,' the Chief said. 'Right, should we get started?' he asked, standing behind his chair. Sooleawa stood up beside him.

'Are we supposed to stand, too?' Penner whispered to Grant.

'Don't think so,' he whispered back, looking up at Sooleawa and the Chief. Neither looked back so he assumed they were okay sitting.

The conversations in the crowd petered out as people noticed the Chief and his wife standing at the front of the hall.

'Welcome!' the Chief called out with his powerful voice over the quieted assembly. 'Welcome to our friends, those from near and far who have joined us tonight to celebrate together. Welcome to our special guests that join us here from Ottawa. Welcome to our ancestors who look over us and help us live our lives on a daily basis.' There was a cheer from the crowd of people when the Chief paused. 'Thank you to the Creator for helping those who hunted the moose for us this evening. And for the moose for giving of himself. When we feast tonight, I ask that you remember those who cannot be here tonight, whether due to distance, illness or death.' There was another cheer. 'Now I know you didn't come here to listen to me ramble on, so please, let's eat and enjoy each other's company!'

With that, several young people rose from various tables around the room and walked over to where the food was waiting. In turn, each one filled a plate with food and brought it back to one of the Elders. They gave the Elder a kiss on the cheek and returned to their seats.

'Wow, don't see that all the time,' Penner said, thinking of her own family gatherings where it seemed to be every one for themselves. Instead of saying 'let's eat', the host might as well just say 'save yourselves'.

Another set of young people, slightly older than the last, got up and went to the food table. Again, in an orderly fashion, they each filled plates with food and brought them to all the women sitting around the room. Each of the women held the youth by their cheeks and gave them a kiss on the forehead.

Millar watched in amazement as the youths returned to their seats, sitting down quietly—still no food in front of them. 'I'm in shock,' he said to Grant.

'There is so much respect for Elders in their culture. It's something that's taught from a very young age,' Grant said. 'Youth are taught that they should help take care of the Elders in the community, whether they're related or not. Everyone's part of the same community, and a community should look after one another.'

'That's a good lesson that everyone should learn,' Millar said as a dozen men stood up and walked to the side table, each grabbing a plate, filling it with moose meat and vegetables. They walked up to the head table, each standing before one of the people seated at the table. Millar looked down the line of people holding plates. He recognized Barry standing in front of the Chief and Travis standing in front of Sooleawa. All at once, at some unheard cue, the plates were put down on the table. '*Meegwetch*,' Millar said to the man standing in front of him. He smiled and gave a little nod before turning and returning to his table.

This time the men didn't sit back down. They stood in place as all of the young people in the room and the remaining men stood up. Everyone moved towards the food, getting in line. It was as though everyone knew their place. At the front were the youngest girls, each with an older girl behind them to help get their food. Once all the girls had their plates full, the youngest boys grabbed a plate, with an older boy helping them. Finally, the men grabbed their plates, taking their food and returning to the tables, sitting down.

'It's like a well-choreographed dance or something,' Penner said to Sooleawa.

'Everyone knows their role in the community and likes to help those who need it,' she said with a smile. 'We are very proud of the way people treat each other here.'

The Chief stood up. 'Brothers. Sisters. Family and friends. I invite you all to partake in this wonderful-smelling meal. *Niwìdòpandimin*. We eat together.' With those words, the noise in the room started up again, everyone eating and talking. The Chief sat back down. 'Please, enjoy,' he said to the members at the head table.

Millar looked down at the plate in front of him. There were several slices of roast moose meat, a moose meatball, a chunk of barbequed moose steak, roasted carrots, parsnips and potatoes. On the side was an ear of roasted corn, slathered in butter, and a piece of bannock. 'Man, that's a lot of food!' he said, looking over at Penner.

'But it is so good,' she said. 'You have got to try that roast moose. That has got to be some of the most tender, tasty meat I have ever eaten.'

'Wait until you try the corn,' Grant said, butter dribbling down his chin. 'Not sure how this was cooked, but it has a real nice smoky taste. Almost like it was put right into a fire or something.'

'It was roasted on the coals that cooked the moose in the fire pit,' the Chief explained, overhearing their conversation. 'No point in letting good embers go to waste. Easiest way to cook two hundred ears of corn.'

'How can you afford to put on such a huge dinner? Doesn't it cost a fortune?' Penner asked, taking a bite of her meatball. She closed her eyes as she chewed and swallowed. 'Okay, this may be my new favourite food!'

'How can we afford not to put on such a dinner,' the Chief countered. 'We don't have a lot here on the reserve, and there isn't much for the youth to do. If we want to keep people happy and build that sense of community, we have to put on events like this. Cost wise, it really isn't that much. The Creator provided the moose. And, of course, the wood for the fire we used to cook it. Members of the community provided their time to help prepare the food. The only thing that cost us any money was the corn and other vegetables. We got these ones from three different farmers in the surrounding communities. The carrots, parsnips and potatoes are all considered "ugly vegetables".'

'What are "ugly vegetables"?' Penner asked, looking at her plate.

'That's when a carrot or parsnip isn't quite straight, or a potato has too many nooks and crannies. It's produce that the grocery stores won't buy because it doesn't look pretty. Usually, the farmer would keep some of these for his own use, but the rest would just get plowed into the ground,' the Chief said, shaking his head. 'Imagine. We live in a world where people can't get enough nutritious food, or sometimes any food at all, and we're destroying almost forty percent of all that's grown because it doesn't look perfect.'

'You've got to be kidding,' Millar said. 'How does that make any sense at all?'

'Now, that's the million-dollar question, isn't it,' the Chief said. 'Works well for us, though. The farmers are willing to sell us the produce for a fraction of its normal cost, because at least they're getting something. In exchange, we get nutritious food. And it's another bond we can build with the outside community. If you look over there, fourth table from the wall,' he said, pointing in the direction of a table where a white man in a plaid shirt, a woman and two blonde kids were sitting with a family from the reserve. 'That's one of the farmers and his family. Until we started buying from them, they had never been to the reserve. Their farm's only five minutes down the road and their family has lived there for three generations. Now, their children come and play with our children a couple of times a month.'

'So, this type of gathering is building bonds within the reserve and with the communities around it, too,' Penner said, spearing a parsnip on her plate and popping it in her mouth. 'Man. Ugly or not, that's one sweet parsnip.'

'Good, right?' the Chief said. 'So, you see, hosting this type of event is really important. Important for us as a people and a community. Important for the businesses around us and important for the local families, too. Hopefully, each year, we'll have more and more local families come out and enjoy the event. There's still a lot of uncertainty about different cultures and races in the world. Anything we can do to alleviate that, even just a little, we're going to try.'

'Well, I can tell you that I'm going to be here next year,' Penner said, finishing her moose meat with a flourish of her fork. 'Damn, I'd be here every weekend if you had food like this!'

The Chief laughed, almost choking on his food. 'I can't guarantee a moose feast every weekend, but you're always welcome as our guest.'

'*Meegwetch*,' Penner said. A buzzing sound caught her attention. She looked over at Millar.

'Sorry, I thought I turned this thing off,' Millar said, taking his phone out of his jacket pocket. Before turning it off, he looked at the number. 'It's the Captain,' he said to Penner.

'You should probably answer it,' said Penner. 'Don't need to get on his bad side as soon as you're back at work.'

'That'd be kind of rude, don't you think,' Millar said, trying to keep his voice down.

'More rude not to answer when your boss calls,' Sooleawa said, smiling. 'Answer the phone—there's a room just behind you, if you want to hear better.'

'Thanks,' said Millar, standing up and pushing his chair back. 'Sorry about this.' Excusing himself from the table, he walked into the room Sooleawa pointed out, answering the phone as he went.

Penner looked at his plate, spearing his last piece of meat with her fork. 'No point in letting this get cold.'

***

When Millar returned to the table, the youths were picking up all the empty plates, clearing off the tables. He sat back down and looked at his plate, then over at Penner. 'Really?'

'What?' Penner said, trying not to smirk.

'Well, I hope you enjoyed it at least,' Millar said, popping the last potato in his mouth.

'That I did,' Penner said, reaching over and grabbing his last parsnip. 'So, what did the Captain have to say?'

'Well,' Millar started. 'Oh, thanks so much,' he said to a young girl who picked up his empty plate. 'So, McGee had a chance to look at the two documents we sent over.'

Grant and the Chief leaned in a bit closer so they could hear better. 'And?' Grant asked as his plate was taken away.

'As far as he can tell, the two documents were not written by the same person,' Millar said, keeping his voice low. He didn't want anyone else overhearing. He figured he would let the Chief decide how and when to tell the community.

'Well, that's not good,' the Chief said.

Sooleawa looked between him and Millar. 'What's going on? What documents?'

'Looks like Jonny Two Bears may not have killed himself after all,' the Chief said.

'What do you mean? I thought you said he was found hanged?' Sooleawa asked with concern.

'He was, but it looks like his suicide note was written by someone else,' Millar said.

'Is it possible his report was written by someone else and he actually wrote the note?' Penner suggested.

'Don't think so. Didn't Barry say Jonny's mom knew right away the note wasn't his handwriting?' Millar said. 'She said the book report was written by him, so I think we can safely say that was a good sample.'

'Alright,' the Chief said with a sigh. 'Let's keep this quiet for now. I'd like to meet with the three of you later, if we can. We'll get Barry there, too. See what our next step is going to be.'

'Sounds good,' Grant said. 'I'll let Barry know. Should we meet at the police station or the band office?'

'Let's meet at the band office. There's more room there,' the Chief said. 'They should be bringing out the dessert shortly. Let's eat that, then meet up in about, say, forty-five minutes? I've got to mingle for a bit before I can leave.'

'There's dessert, too?' Penner said, her eyes growing large. 'If you say there's going to be coffee as well, you may end up with a new resident after all.'

CHAPTER THIRTEEN

'Make yourselves comfortable,' Barry said, unlocking the front door of the band office and turning on the lights. Millar and Penner wandered in and sat on a couple of tattered chairs. 'Sorry,' Barry glanced over to where they were sitting, 'Those are probably not the most comfortable chairs. Travis put in an order for some new furniture, but it hasn't arrived yet.'

'They're not too bad,' Penner said, shifting around, trying to get comfortable. 'I've sat in worse.'

'Barry, did you leave the note and report in here, or did you bring them back to the station?' Grant asked, opting to stand.

'They're at the station. I locked them in my top drawer,' Barry said. 'The note was either going to be evidence, or Jonny's Mom was going to want it, so I figured I should make sure it was kept safe. Why?'

'I just figured the Chief may want to see them when he gets here,' Grant said, looking at his watch. 'He'll be a few minutes yet. Mind passing me your keys? I'll go grab them real quick.'

'Catch,' Barry said, tossing his ring of keys over to Grant. They bounced off of his left hand, falling to the floor. 'Nice one.'

'I lost them in the light,' Grant said, bending over to pick them up. 'Plus, it wasn't a very good throw.'

'That's right, blame the other guy,' Barry said. 'Anyone want a coffee? Not sure how long this meeting's going to go.'

Penner perked up, but waited to see if anyone else would say anything first.

'I don't know if I need one,' Grant said, winking at Millar.

'Yeah, it's getting kinda late,' said Millar. 'Don't know if I could sleep tonight if I had another coffee.'

Penner looked at Grant, then at Millar. They both tried hard to keep a straight face. 'You both suck,' she said as they started to chuckle. 'Barry, I would love a coffee. Tweedle dum and Tweedle dumber here can go without.'

'I'll put some on,' Barry said. He went into the kitchen and started filling the coffee machine with water.

'I'll go grab those papers,' Grant said, heading for the door. 'Be back in a minute.'

Penner glared at Millar.

'What?' Millar said, still laughing.

'You're a jerk,' Penner replied. 'You sure you want to come back to work? Maybe you should take some more time off. You know, another fifteen years, or so—just 'til I'm ready to retire.'

'You would miss me way too much,' Millar said. 'Couldn't do that to you. Imagine how boring your career would be if you only had to work with people like Grant all the time.'

'Sometimes I think I could get used to that real quick,' Penner said, throwing a cushion at Millar, hitting him in the head.

'Just what I needed. Thanks,' he said, putting the cushion behind his back and stretching out. 'Much more comfortable.'

'You really are a piece of work,' Penner said. Hearing the door handle turn, she looked over to the main door to the office.

'Somebody here?' Travis said, poking his head around the partially opened door. Chewie ran inside, yapping to announce his arrival. 'Oh, Detectives. What are you doing here?'

'Hey, Travis,' Penner greeted him. 'The Chief wanted to have a word with a few of us. We're just waiting for him to show up. Hi, Chewie,' she said, scratching the dog enthusiastically behind its ear.

'I was just passing by on my way back from the feast and I saw the light on,' Travis said. 'Figured either I left it on or we was getting robbed.'

'Sorry about that, Travis,' said Barry, coming out of the kitchen. 'I wanted to let you know we were going to be here, but I couldn't find you at the feast before I left.'

'Must have been in the washroom,' Travis said. 'Or out back having a pipe. I don't like to smoke it around the little ones, if I can help it. They don't need to see that.'

'Got some coffee on the go. Want one for the road?' Barry asked, heading back into the kitchen.

'Nah, that's good thanks,' Travis said. 'Just make sure you lock up when you're done. Ya'll have a good night. Let's go, Chewie.' He patted his leg as he called his dog over.

'Will do,' Barry called out. 'See ya in the morning.'

Travis opened the door to walk back into the night air, almost bumping into the Chief. 'Sorry about that, Chief. Almost got ya.'

'Travis? What are you doing here?' the Chief asked. 'You know, doesn't matter. I actually need to talk to you for a minute, if you've got time.' He looked into the room. 'Give me five minutes, I'll be right back.'

'No problem,' Penner said as Travis and the Chief left. 'More coffee for us.'

'You and your coffee,' Millar said. 'I'm sure if you ever donated blood, it would actually be black.'

'It would help give the recipient a nice little boost,' Penner said. 'Thanks, Barry,' she said as Barry handed her a cup.

'Did you want any?' Barry asked Millar.

'Please,' Millar said, taking a cup.

'And here I thought you didn't want any because you wouldn't be able to sleep,' Penner mimicked Millar as the door to the office opened.

'What's going on out there?' Grant asked, closing the door behind him.

'What do you mean?' Barry asked as he walked over to the window and peered out from between the blinds.

'Seems like the Chief and Travis are having an argument or something,' Grant said. 'When I was coming back I could hear the Chief yelling at him. Couldn't make out what he was saying, but he seemed pretty mad.'

'No idea,' Barry said, trying to see into the dark night. 'The Chief seemed fine when he popped in just now. Probably something to do with finances or something. I think the latest payment from the Feds was supposed to be delivered last week. Pretty sure I heard Travis saying yesterday it was delayed again.'

'That's three months in a row now, isn't it?' Grant asked. 'I can see why the Chief would be mad.'

'Oh, he's coming,' Barry said, moving away from the window as the door opened and the Chief entered the room.

'Sorry to keep you guys waiting,' the Chief said, settling his large, bulky frame in one of the chairs. 'Any more coffee,

Barry?'

'Yup, give me a sec,' Barry said, going back into the kitchen. 'Anyone else?'

'Please,' Grant said, looking over at Penner.

'I'm still good, thanks,' she said, everyone looking over at her. 'What? Sometimes I take my time drinking.'

***

'Okay, so…where are we at?' the Chief asked. 'Thanks, Barry,' he said, taking the cup of coffee Barry brought over to him.

'Well, like I mentioned earlier, according to our contact in Ottawa, the suicide note found on Jonny and his book report were not written by the same person,' Millar said. 'Grant, you have the copies you can show the Chief?'

Grant gave the papers to the Chief, who read over the suicide note, then looked at the report. Glancing up at Millar, he asked, 'And we're certain Jonny wrote the report?'

'According to his mom, it's definitely his writing,' Barry said. 'We may be able to get more examples from either his mom or maybe the school, if you want.'

'How sure was the Detective in Ottawa that they were written by different people?' the Chief asked, flipping between pages. 'Because they look pretty similar to me.'

'He said he was about ninety-five percent sure,' Millar said.

'So, there's still a chance Jonny wrote them both, then,' the Chief said, looking at Millar.

'A very slim chance, yes,' Millar said. 'With this type of analysis, it's very rare for there to be a one-hundred percent certainty, but ninety-five is pretty much a sure thing.'

'And the Detective who did the analysis, he's good?' the

Chief asked.

'Best on the force,' Millar said, a bit defensively. 'If he says he's that certain Jonny didn't write the note, I would take it to court.'

'Right,' the Chief said, still looking at the pages. 'Do we have anything else that may indicate Jonny was killed? I don't want to seem like I don't trust your expert, but I just don't want to think he was murdered.'

'Well, when I spoke with the coroner after he did the autopsy, he did find some indications that Jonny may not have died by hanging,' Grant said.

'Really? Like what?' the Chief asked, putting the papers down on a table beside his chair.

'Well, for one, he had a bone in his neck, called the hyoid, which was broken,' Grant said. 'Apparently, it's extremely rare for this type of bone to break in cases where young men have hanged themselves. It's much more indicative of manual strangulation.'

'Rare, but not impossible?' the Chief asked.

'Maybe six percent of cases, so very rare,' Grant said. 'Also, there was some bruising on his neck that didn't seem to match up with the rope—it may have been from someone's hands wrapped around his neck.'

'May have been, but not definitive?' the Chief asked.

'You could say that, yes,' Grant said.

'Anything else?'

'Well, I spoke with Sammy Greycrow—the two were best friends,' Grant started.

'I know Sammy. Good kid. He must be pretty upset,' the Chief said.

'More confused, I think,' Grant said. 'He had spent the day

with Jonny, so he may have been one of the last people to see him. Said Jonny seemed normal. Just his normal, happy-go-lucky self. At the time, Sammy didn't notice any marks on his neck, which is another reason we think it may have happened at the time of death.'

'And there's no way they were made by the rope?' the Chief asked.

'According to the coroner, no,' Grant said.

'So, Barry, what are your thoughts?' the Chief turned to Barry, who had been quiet up until this point.

'Me? Well, if it was just the note, or just the broken bone, or just the marks, I could overlook it. One of them would have been an anomaly. Two, a coincidence. But all three? I think we have to go where the evidence is pointing, and I say it's pointing to murder.'

'Gotcha,' the Chief said, rubbing his temples. 'Definitely not what I wanted to hear. So, how do we figure this out? Do we even have any suspects? Any chance Sammy did it?'

'I really doubt it. Not by himself, anyways. There's no way he would have been able to get him up in the tree. I helped take Jonny down from the tree and he was a lot heavier than he looked,' Grant said. 'Don't even know if Sammy would have been able to hold him down and strangle him. Sammy's not the biggest kid out there. When I talked to him, I didn't notice any defensive marks on him. I would assume that Jonny would have tried to fight back if he could.'

'What if Sammy was straddling his chest, pinning Jonny's arms under his knees?'

'Maybe, but like I said, Sammy isn't all that big. When someone's getting strangled, they're going to be fighting with all their worth. I would think Jonny could have thrown Sammy off pretty easily.'

'So, you're thinking it was either a couple of people at least, or someone really strong,' the Chief said. 'So really, that doesn't narrow it down at all.'

'Unfortunately not,' Grant said. 'The only thing that may help is where it mentions the water issues in the note. Someone would have to know about the problems with the quality of water on the reserve, so that should help.'

'Problem is, everyone around knows about the water issues,' the Chief said. 'I've been so vocal about it over the years. I've done countless interviews for both the news and the papers. CBC ran a story on the national news just two months ago.'

'I still think that may be our best lead right now,' Millar said.

'Why's that?' the Chief asked.

'Well, why would someone kill someone else, and try to make it look like a suicide?' Millar said.

'Cover their tracks?' Penner said.

'Sure. But I think there are easier ways to do that,' Millar said. 'Just make it look like an accident. That'd be easier—especially out here. Plus, if you kill someone in the woods, like where Jonny was found, why take the extra time to tie him into a tree? The chances of someone coming by would have been pretty high, so it was pretty risky. I think staging it as a suicide was about more than trying to cover up a crime. I think whoever did this was trying to send a message.'

'Send a message?' the Chief said. 'What type of message?'

'Well, as twisted as this may sound, I think whoever killed Jonny was trying to get sympathy for the conditions here in the hopes that the reserve would finally get the aid it needs,' Millar said. 'It's still not much to go on, but I think the content of the note and the reason behind writing it is our best lead. If I were leading this investigation, I would start looking at people on the reserve before I looked at the outside communities.'

'Now hold on a sec,' the Chief said, anger rising in his voice. 'I can't see anyone here killing someone, let alone one of our own kids, to try and send a message. That just doesn't make sense.'

'I know how tight-knit everyone here is. I saw it myself tonight,' Millar said, as both Penner and Grant squirmed uncomfortably in their seats. 'I'm just telling it like I see it. There has to be a reason this was made to look like a suicide, and there has to be a reason that water conditions were mentioned in the note. I really don't think an outsider would care enough to mention it. Someone from outside the community may have killed Jonny. They may have tied him in a tree to make it look like a suicide. And they may have left a note. But I really don't think the water conditions would have been mentioned. This is more personal than a complete stranger murder. At the same time,' Millar added, 'Jonny may not have been chosen because of who he was—he may have just been an easy target. It's personal and it's not personal. He was chosen because he lives on the reserve, and whoever killed him did so to make a point.'

'Detective,' the Chief said slowly. 'I don't really like the way you are looking at this. However, I will admit that some of what you've said seems to make sense. Barry, what do you think?'

'As much as I don't want to think he was murdered, especially by someone from the reserve, it really does seem like the most logical explanation,' Barry said. 'Like Millar said, why would an outsider mention the water. They don't care if we have clean water or not.'

'That's all too apparent,' the Chief said. 'Alright. So let's say he was killed and it was done by someone or several people from the Reserve. How are we going to figure out who's involved?'

'Well, when I was waiting for the coroner the other night, I did some looking around, trying to keep myself occupied,' Grant spoke up. 'There are way too many strange sounds in the woods at night. Anyway, I was able to make out some tracks on the leaves and stuff. It wasn't much, but I definitely saw shoe prints. I could make out my own and Sarah's, who had found the body, and I think Jonny's, too. But there were others. I have no idea if they were involved or not, but they were there, around the tree that Jonny was hanging from. Maybe they're still visible? If we get someone out there with better tracking skills than I have, maybe, I don't know, we could see where they came from or went? Or at least what type of shoe they were wearing?'

'Hasn't rained yet since that night,' Barry said. 'There's a chance we may be able to see something.'

'I guess it's worth a try,' the Chief said. 'Unless anyone has any other ideas?'

'Right now, I don't have anything else. I kinda feel like it's going to be like searching for a needle in a haystack,' Penner said.

'Unless someone talks,' Millar said. 'Which is always a possibility.'

'I guess that's one problem with being a dry community. People aren't getting drunk and confessing things to a bartender anymore,' the Chief said wryly. He glanced up at the clock on the wall. 'Well, if there's nothing else, why don't we call it a night. Barry, you manning the phones tonight?'

'I am.'

'So you'll probably want your sleep first thing in the morning,' the Chief said. 'The rest of us can head out to where Jonny was found, see if we can see anything. Let's plan on meeting up at six, unless that's too early. First light's usually pretty good for tracking—the sun hits the ground at a good angle.'

'Works for me,' Penner said. 'I'm usually up pretty early. I can head over to Grant's for a coffee at half five, then we can all meet up.'

'Perfect,' the Chief said, getting up and heading for the door. 'Looks like you'll get your tracking lessons after all.'

CHAPTER FOURTEEN

The sound of knocking woke Millar from a broken sleep. 'What time is it,' he murmured to himself, looking at his watch. After a moment of trying to get his eyes to focus, he was able to read the time. 5:35. 'Penner,' he said, swinging his feet out of his makeshift bed. He didn't find sofa beds to be the most comfortable at the best of times, and this apparently wasn't even close to the best of times. He walked over to the door, trying to find his way in the half light of the morning. He felt around for the light switch and turned it on, causing a fluorescent light above his head to flicker to life. Rubbing his eyes, he unlocked the door.

'Took you long enough,' Penner said. 'Nice boxers.'

'Morning to you, too,' Millar said, shutting the door and walking back to his bed. 'Grant's not up yet,' he said, slipping on a t-shirt and pair of pants.

'I'm up,' Grant said from his bedroom. 'Hope you guys slept better than I did. Coffee?'

'I slept like a log,' Penner said. 'The air conditioner in that room works like a charm. Pretty warm in here, though, isn't it?' she observed, fanning herself.

'Just a little,' Millar said. 'I could have wrung out my pillow last night, I was sweating so much.'

'That's a lovely visual,' Penner said. 'There's actually a bit of a breeze out this morning—you should open a window. Might help air the place out. Smells a bit in here.' She wrinkled her nose.

'What are you talking about? Smells fine,' Millar said, defensively.

'That's what people with pets think, too,' Penner said. 'So, any more thoughts on what we can do to figure this case out?'

'Honestly, I have no idea,' Millar said. 'Hopefully we can find something in the woods this morning. If not, I don't know what we can do. Someone knows something, so maybe they'll talk.'

'Definitely not a lot to go on right now,' Grant said. 'Maybe I should have tried to get a cast of the tread marks I saw the other night. Don't know if I would have been able to or not, but I should have tried.'

'Why would you have? At that point, you thought a kid had hanged himself,' Penner said. 'There was nothing pointing to murder, so no reason to collect evidence.'

'True, but still. Kinda kicking myself now,' Grant said, pouring three cups of coffee. 'With any luck, the Chief will still be able to find the tracks. If I was able to find them once, I would think a hunter should be able to find them, too.'

'Looking forward to seeing how he does it,' Penner said. 'The only time I did anything with tracks was when I was in summer camp. We were out on a hike once and we came across a deer track. We mixed up some plaster of paris, filled the track with it and let it dry. After about ten minutes, we were able to gently dig out the hardened plaster, revealing the hoof. Pretty cool.'

'Did you guys always go on hikes with plaster of paris?'

Millar asked, with skepticism.

'Well, I guess the camp counsellor hoped we were going to come across a track, so she happened to have some with her,' Penner said.

'Pretty lucky you guys found the track,' Millar said.

'You know, now that you mention it, there was only a single track,' Penner said. 'And it was right in the middle of a pretty wide path. Probably should have been several others. I don't think it was really a deer track after all. She lied to us. Thanks a lot, Millar.'

'Me? I wasn't there.'

'But you took away my one tracking experience. Jerk.'

'Well, hopefully the Chief can point out some tracks for you today,' Millar said, pulling the curtain aside to look out the window. 'Speaking of the Chief, what's he doing?'

Penner and Grant crowded around the window to see what Millar was looking at. The Chief was standing amongst a group of people, some holding cameras, some holding voice recorders. Two were holding TV cameras.

'Is he giving a press conference or something?' Penner asked.

'Sure looks like it,' Grant said. 'Wonder what's going on.'

'One way to find out,' Penner said, chugging the last of her coffee. 'Let's go have a listen, shall we?'

***

'As I have said many times before, these are very difficult times for us here on the reserve. And two nights ago, things got even worse. One of our young family members was so distraught over the conditions here, especially the lack of clean water, he decided to end his life. He could not bear the thought of continuing to live in a community where he didn't know if he could safely drink the water. Whether he would get sick if he did.' The Chief paused, looking around at the reporters. 'I ask you. Should this ever happen in this great province of Ontario? Or anywhere in this great country of Canada? Again, I reach out to the politicians that are supposed to work for the people. Please, send us the resources we so desperately need so our people can live in humane conditions and our children can feel like they have a future here. Thank you.' The Chief turned from the reporters and started walking over towards the band office, leaving the media to check their recordings, making sure they caught all the information they needed to run the morning story.

'What was that?' Penner asked, breathlessly, as she caught up with the Chief.

'A news conference,' the Chief said, opening the door to the office, holding it for Penner before entering himself. 'I needed to get the information out so something can be done.'

'But, it's not really true,' Penner said in confusion. 'He didn't kill himself.'

'We still don't know that definitively, do we?' the Chief said. 'All we know for sure is one of our youth is dead, and there was a note in his back pocket stating he killed himself because of the water issues here. Technically, I didn't lie.'

'Technically, no. But...' Penner started.

'Look. I understand what you're saying. But look at it from my point of view. I've been working for five years, trying to get the government to give us money to fix our water problems. Five years. And you know what we have to show for it? Nothing. Not a single penny. Not a single person from the government has even come out here to look at the water to see what's going on. Nothing. So, you can think what I did was wrong, but I have to do something. I didn't lie. I just told them what I needed them to hear.'

After a long pause, Penner finally spoke. 'It must be frustrating. But don't you think the truth would be better?'

'And say what? Someone killed a young man on the reserve, made it look like a suicide and we don't know who did it, or why?' the Chief asked, looking at Penner like she was the crazy one. 'What would that get us? We don't get a lot of sympathy from people in the first place. And if we announce a murder covered up as a suicide, a lot of people will just think it's another death on the reserve and go on about their day. At least this way, until we figure out what really happened, maybe some good will come out of Jonny's death.'

As much as Penner didn't like it, she realized the Chief made a valid point. She had seen the news about missing and murdered Indigenous people. There was never as much coverage as there should be, and way too many cases were left to go cold. Out of sight, out of mind. 'I'm sorry, I should have kept my opinion to myself. The things you have to deal with on a daily basis are so foreign to me. I have to realize you're just doing what you feel is best for the community.'

'I wish it wasn't like this, but unfortunately, it's one of the realities of life,' the Chief said. 'So, we'll give the media a couple of minutes to leave, then we'll head into the woods to see if we can see anything. If you're still up for going.'

'If it helps solve this case,' Penner said, 'I'm up for anything.'

***

From her post at the window, Penner watched the reporters

begin to disperse. 'Should be good to go in a minute or so,' she said. She could see Millar and Grant standing together talking at Grant's front door, when a girl suddenly ran up to them. 'Looks like something's going on.'

'Like what?' the Chief asked, moving to the window next to Penner. 'That's Sarah Greycrow. She looks pretty upset.'

'Yeah, she does,' Penner said. 'I'm going to see what's going on. Come out and join us when you feel enough of the reporters have left.'

Penner hurried out of the office and over to where Millar and Grant were talking to Sarah.

'Okay, Sarah, calm down,' Grant said. 'What happened to Sammy?'

'He never came home last night,' Sarah said. 'Mom said she didn't see him when she left the feast last night, and this morning, it didn't look like his bed had been slept in.'

'When was the last time you or your mom saw him?' Grant asked, as Penner joined their group. 'Sammy seems to be missing,' he told her.

'We all went to the feast together. Before the dessert was served, he said he was going to go and shoot some hoops,' Sarah said. 'He doesn't have much of a sweet tooth.'

'So, after the feast, did you and your mom just head home?' Grant asked.

'First, I went over to the drop-in centre to get Sammy, but he wasn't there,' Sarah said. 'I figured he had headed home. When we got there, he wasn't around. But at that time, mom wasn't too worried—it was still pretty early. We just figured he went for a bike ride with one of his friends, or went down to the pond for a swim. I had to work the late shift at the restaurant last night, so I got changed and headed out. I got home around two this morning, I think, and went right to bed. Mom just woke me up and told me Sammy never came home.'

'Could he have stayed over at a friend's house?' Penner asked.

'Not without calling to let mom know,' Sarah said. 'He always makes sure she knows where he is. If he wasn't going to come home, he would have either called or sent her a text.'

'We should probably check with them anyway,' Grant said. 'Can you write down a list of his friends? We'll give them to Barry to start calling around.'

'Yeah, I can do that,' Sarah said.

'Good,' Grant said. 'Go into the station and get some paper from Barry. Let him know what's going on.' Sarah ran over to the station.

'So, we should probably start a search while he's making the calls,' Millar said.

'Agreed, but where do we start?' Grant said.

'I guess we can head to the drop-in centre and see if there's evidence he was even there last night,' Penner said. 'Do you know where the pond is that Sammy likes going to?'

'I know where it is,' the Chief said as he walked up behind her. 'Something wrong with Sammy?'

'He didn't come home last night after the feast,' Grant explained. 'His mom's worried—it's not like him not to come home without letting her know. Sarah's giving Barry a list of names to call, see if any of his friends know where he is.'

'Do you think he was upset enough about Jonny that he did something to himself?' the Chief asked.

'It's possible, I guess,' Grant said. 'He seemed fine when I talked to him yesterday, but maybe it was an act.'

'He seemed pretty genuine to me,' Millar said. 'He really didn't seem too bothered by death at all.'

'A lot of young guys aren't keen on showing their emotions, but losing his best friend had to have shaken him up,' the Chief said. 'Maybe he thought he was doing okay, then started to think more about Jonny during the day. Then it hit him hard during the feast and he couldn't deal with his feelings anymore.'

'Let's hope that's not the case,' Penner said. 'Should we get going?'

'Why don't you guys head over to the centre, start having a look around the basketball nets,' Grant said. 'I'll just go in and talk to Barry. Hopefully he doesn't mind making the phone calls before he heads home for the day.'

'Sounds good,' Millar said. 'We'll wait there for you.'

CHAPTER FIFTEEN

'Do you know Sammy very well?' Penner asked the Chief as they started making their way to the drop-in centre.

'Well enough,' the Chief said. 'I'm not sure if you're aware, but my step-daughter, Amanda, killed herself last year. She had been dating Jonny Two Bears, and sometimes the three of them would hang out at our home.' The Chief paused before continuing, 'Jonny's death brought so many memories of grief back for Sooleawa—that's why she didn't attend the powwow yesterday. But to go back to your question, yes, I know Sammy a little. As Chief, I also try to make a point of visiting with everyone at least once a month. Not always the easiest thing to do, but I make an effort. The role of Chief is an elected position, so if the people aren't happy, you're not going to last long. Getting to know the people in the band and ensuring I listen to their needs and wants is very important to me. If it wasn't for them, I wouldn't have a job. And without the Chief and the rest of the band council, things wouldn't run as efficiently as they do,' he said as they turned a corner, the drop-in centre becoming visible at the end of the street.

'So, do you go to everyone's house each month then?' Millar asked. 'That would never happen in the city. To be honest with you, I'm not really sure I would want it to. I can't imagine the mayor or my city councillor stopping in for a coffee to chat every month.'

The Chief laughed. 'Things are different here. But, yeah. Sometimes I just stop in for a quick chat or a coffee. I usually invite the Elders over for dinner. Or, if they can't get out, Sooleawa and I will make some food and bring it over to their house. I also stop in at the school and sit in on each class. A lot of times when I visit their houses, the kids aren't home, so I want to make sure they get a chance to express their concerns, too.'

'Even the kids? That's surprising,' Penner said as they arrived at the drop-in centre.

'Why?' the Chief asked. 'Children can be rather insightful, when they're given the opportunity to talk. Plus, what we are building today is for their use tomorrow. Why shouldn't they get the chance to tell us what they think?'

'I guess,' Penner replied. 'I'm just thinking of my nephews. I'm sure they would say they need more ice cream and cookies and less homework.'

'Trust me, I get answers like that, too,' the Chief said. 'But, we also opened the drop-in centre because some of the teens had mentioned that there was nowhere they could gather and talk. If we hadn't listened to them, this would never have been built.'

'I think there's a lot we could learn from how you operate here,' Penner said, as they walked around the side of the building to where the basketball court was.

'We're definitely not perfect,' the Chief said. 'But we try to do what we can to make everyone's lives a little better, while respecting each other and Mother Earth.'

'In the city, seems like everyone is more interested in making their own lives better. Doesn't really matter what happens to anyone else along the way,' Millar said.

'Change can begin with one person's attitude,' the Chief said. 'Remember that for when you get back home. Alright, how do we begin, Detectives? I can track an animal through the densest forest, but looking for clues in an urban setting is definitely not my forte.'

'Well,' Millar said, looking around. 'First thing we want to see is if there's any sign of Sammy here, which, there doesn't seem to be. I thought maybe he may have left his basketball, or a hoodie, or something.'

'Nothing that obvious,' the Chief said. 'Do we know if he had his bike with him last night?'

'He did,' Sarah said as she walked up to them with Grant. 'He biked over to the feast last night and I didn't see his bike at home this morning.'

'Any luck with the phone calls?' Penner asked.

'Barry was just starting when we came over,' Grant said. 'Sarah gave him ten names, so once he's done calling around, he'll give me a shout—let me know if he found out anything.'

'Is your mom still at home, in case Sammy goes back there this morning?' the Chief asked Sarah.

'She is. She has my number, so she'll call if he shows up. I sent her a text to let her know we're looking for him,' Sarah said.

'It might be best if you go home and wait with her,' the Chief said. 'She's probably worried sick. You can help keep her calm.'

'I think I'd be more help out here,' Sarah said. 'No point in everyone sitting around. Besides, she called my Auntie. She's going to head over this morning.'

'Well, make sure to check in with her from time to time. Make sure she's okay,' the Chief advised.

'So, if Sammy was here last night playing basketball and didn't go to one of his friends or back home, you said you think he may have gone to the pond?' Grant asked.

'That'd be my bet,' said Sarah. 'Either went for a swim or to do some fishing. Not sure if his rod was still at home or not—I didn't think to look. Should I call my mom?'

'We can just head over and check the area. See if he's there,' Grant said. 'Maybe he was fishing, had some good luck, got tired and fell asleep.'

'It's possible,' said Sarah, doubtfully. 'He has done that before, but he usually lets mom know he's going to be late.'

'Anywhere else we should be checking?' Penner asked. 'We can split up, save some time.'

'Honestly, if he's not with one of his friends or out at the pond, I really don't know where he would be,' Sarah said. 'He likes riding his bike through the woods, so maybe he fell and got hurt.'

'Well, we have to head into the woods to get to the pond,' the Chief said. 'So we can all head in together and fan out to search. If he was in there biking, there's only really three paths he could have taken, and they all lead to the pond. I assume he would have stuck to the paths?'

'Depends on how many logs he could see to jump,' Sarah said. 'He's a bit of a dare devil when it comes to biking.'

'Well, let's see what we can find,' the Chief said, and with that, the group started walking towards the forest entrance.

***

'Definitely some bike tracks here,' Grant said, looking down at the first path leading into the woods.

The Chief squatted down on one knee, looking at the track in the dirt. 'Looks pretty fresh. Within the last twenty-four hours,' he said.

'How can you tell?' Penner asked, leaning down next to the Chief to have a better look.

'Well, it's hard to tell exactly how old it is, but it was made between now and the last rain, which was two nights ago,' the Chief said. 'If it had rained since this track was made, the edges wouldn't be quite as crisp. With age and weather, the edges start to fall in on themselves, so you would see some dirt on the bottom of the track and the edges would be rougher.'

'So you can narrow down the window, but not to an exact time?' Penner asked.

'Not exact, no,' the Chief said. 'It's a bit easier at different times of year, especially later in the fall or early spring when we get a good dew cover in the morning. Then the track itself and the ground around it may be different colours because of the water content, but this time of year, with the humidity that we've been having, it's not so straight forward. Oh, but look at this,' he said, pointing a bit further in front of himself. 'The bike rode over this foot print, so we can tell the bike came in after the person who walked here did.'

'And that helps how?' Millar asked, looking at the print.

'Doesn't really,' the Chief said. 'Just making an observation, I guess.'

'What type of bike does Sammy have?' Grant asked Sarah.

'Mountain bike. I don't know what the make is or anything, though,' Sarah answered.

'So, his bike could have made this track,' said Grant. 'The

tread pattern looks like a mountain bike tread. It's wide enough, too.'

'A lot of kids on the reserve have mountain bikes,' the Chief said. 'But it's somewhere to start.'

'Well, let's see where it goes,' Millar said, starting to walk in front of the others. 'Keep your eyes peeled for anything.'

'Like what?' Sarah asked, catching up to Millar.

'Look to see if it seems like a bike rode off of the trail, or someone walked off the path,' Millar said. 'Broken branches or turned over moss. Anything that doesn't fit in.'

'Gotcha,' Sarah said. 'Little less scary in here during the day, eh, City Boy?' she said over her shoulder to Grant.

'It was fine the other night,' Grant protested. 'Just a new experience was all.'

'Right,' Sarah said, looking back at the ground, following the tire tracks.

'They're getting harder to follow the further in we get. A lot more ground cover here, covering the dirt,' Millar said.

'Don't look right at your feet,' the Chief advised. 'Look about six to ten feet in front of where you're walking.'

Millar looked further along the path. Like magic, the impression of the tire tracks began to appear on top of the leaves covering the ground. 'Would ya look at that.'

'The light has to be at the right angle to see the tracks on this type of covering,' the Chief said.

'It's like the other night when I was out here,' Grant said. 'I tried looking around for tracks and couldn't see them until I squatted down and used my flashlight at just the right angle.'

'Exactly the same,' the Chief said. 'Different times of day you have to track differently. Sometimes it's easier than others, but it's almost always possible.'

As they continued along the path, the canopy got thicker, changing the way the light hit the ground. The sun was getting higher in the sky, too, making it harder to see the tracks.

'I'm not too sure, but it almost looks like there are foot prints crossing over the tire tracks here,' Sarah said, leaning down, moving side to side trying to make out what she thought she was seeing.

The Chief walked over beside her, training his eyes to where she was looking. 'I think you're right,' he said. 'Seems like someone was walking back towards the way we came in after the bike came through here.'

'I guess you can't tell how long ago, eh?' Penner asked, knowing the answer.

'Nope. I'm good, but not that good,' the Chief said, scanning the ground for more tracks. 'It looks like the tire tracks went off the path just up ahead. See there, just beside that large maple,' he said pointing. 'There are scuff marks on the moss covering the tree roots. Seems like they went off to the left of it.' He walked up to the base of the tree, squatted down and surveyed the ground ahead of him. 'I can definitely make out the tire tracks still. I don't see the foot prints though.'

'They had to have come from somewhere,' Grant said, looking around the ground to see if he could see anything. He wasn't even sure he could see the tire tracks where the Chief was looking. He leaned over, trying to see what the Chief had seen, moving up and down slightly, hoping to catch the light just right. At one point, he thought he saw the track going off in the near distance, but as soon as he saw it, it disappeared again. 'Don't know if I'd ever make it if I had to rely on my tracking skills to eat.'

'It takes years of practice to train your eyes to see what wants to be hidden,' the Chief said. 'You saw tracks the other night, which is pretty impressive. Tracking at night is much harder than tracking during the day.'

'Well, I think I'll keep buying my food at the grocery store, otherwise I'd starve,' Grant said, looking at the ground around the base of the tree. A glint of light caught his eye. 'A quarter,' he said, bending down to pick up the coin. Laying beside it was a wooden match. 'Guess some kids were probably out here smoking,' he said, pocketing the quarter.

'You can put that towards your next grocery bill, City Boy,' Sarah said. 'Come on, let's follow the bike tracks.'

'Before we get too deep in the woods, I'm just going to give Barry a call—see if he's found out anything. We'll probably lose the cell signal soon,' Grant said, pulling out his phone. 'Looks like he already tried calling. Guess I didn't have the volume turned up.' He dialed into his voice mail and listened to the message Barry had left. 'So, Barry called all the numbers Sarah gave him. No one saw Sammy after he left the feast. Barry also said he called your mom. Sammy hasn't come home, yet.'

'Sarah, why don't you take Detective Penner to the pond—check around that area,' the Chief said. 'The three of us will keep searching in this area. Try to figure out where the bike went. No point in all of us following the bike without even knowing if it was Sammy who rode through here. Like following deer tracks when you're hunting a moose.'

'Okay. Come on, Sue. It's this way,' Sarah said, grabbing Penner by the arm.

CHAPTER SIXTEEN

'Sarah, can you think of any reason why Sammy wouldn't have come home last night?' Penner asked as she and Sarah walked along the path, scanning the scrub on each side for any signs of Sammy.

'Only thing I can think is that he fell asleep fishing or he fell off his bike and got hurt,' Sarah said.

'Does he have a cell phone? I assume you tried calling him if he does.'

'Yeah, he does, but it went right to voice mail. Service out here isn't the best, if you haven't noticed,' Sarah said, taking out her cell phone. 'See, no service.'

'So, he wasn't too upset about Jonny?' Penner asked as they continued along the path. The morning humidity was starting to creep in.

'Don't think so,' Sarah said. 'If he was, he didn't mention anything. Like I told City Boy, death's natural. We all die, so there's no point in getting too upset about it. When we die, we're greeted by our ancestors and our second life begins. Why would you get upset about that? That's what my mom always taught us, anyway.'

'That's a good way of looking at things,' Penner said.

'That it is,' Sarah said in agreement. 'Come on, the pond's

just up around the bend,' she said, running up ahead of Penner.

'Wow, it's a lot bigger than I thought it was going to be,' Penner exclaimed. The trees opened up to reveal an expanse of water, surrounded by bulrushes and cattails. She could see a small beaver lodge on the far side. 'When you said it was a pond, I was thinking the type of pond someone has in their backyard with koi fish in it. This is like a small lake.'

'We've always just called it the pond,' Sarah said. 'Maybe it is a lake. Don't know really.'

'So, if Sammy was here fishing, where would he usually set up?'

'Usually over there, by those rocks,' Sarah said, pointing to the other side of the pond. 'Watch your step, lots of snakes and snappers around.'

'Snappers?' Penner asked, looking with dismay at the tall grass surrounding the water's edge. 'What are snappers?'

'Snapping turtles. They'll probably get out of the way before you even see them. They feel the vibrations through the ground when you walk. But still, keep your eyes out for them.'

'And these snakes, are they poisonous?' Penner asked.

'Nah, no poisonous snakes around.'

'That's a relief,' Penner said, feeling a bit better.

'Snakes are venomous, not poisonous,' Sarah said with a laugh. 'But don't worry, no venomous ones here either. Used to be a venomous rattle snake in this part of Ontario, but no one's seen one for years.'

'Just because no one's seen one doesn't mean they aren't here though, right?'

'I guess. Come on! We've gotta find my brother,' Sarah said, picking her way carefully around the pond. 'Just stay behind me. My footsteps should scare anything in front of us out of the way.'

'Just don't scare them backwards and I'll be just fine.'

'You're just like City Boy,' Sarah said. 'Don't worry—I'll protect you.'

'Saying I'm like Grant is okay. As long as you don't compare me to Millar.'

'He seems nice enough.'

'He is,' Penner said. 'I just like razzin' him.'

'I feel the same way about City Boy,' Sarah said as they got to the rocks. 'Pretty easy to get under his skin.'

'Same as Millar. Alright, let's have a look around.' There was no obvious sign of Sammy—neither he nor his bike was there.

'There's some broken fishing line here,' Sarah said, picking up a handful of clear fishing line that looked like a bird's nest. 'Whoever was fishing here had one heck of a snarl with their line.'

'Could it have been Sammy? Or is he too experienced for something like that to have happened?' Penner asked. 'I've never fished so I really don't know. I know you put your line in the water and hope a fish hops on your hook, but that's about it.'

'Hops on your hook?' Sarah said. 'You are like City Boy. That's something I'd expect him to say. Could have been Sammy. Stuff like this can happen to the best of fishermen.' She bent over again. 'Probably not Sammy, though. There's another wooden match here. Sammy doesn't smoke,' she said, picking up the match.

'You sure he doesn't come out here to sneak smokes?'

'No way. He knows mom would whoop his ass if she ever caught him.'

'Pretty good deterrent?'

'Let's just say mom has a favourite wooden spoon,' Sarah said. 'She's never used it, but boy, the threat has been there many a time.'

'Sounds like my mom,' said Penner. 'Sometimes the threat is much more powerful than the action. Hey, check this out,' she said, pointing to an area behind the rocks. 'Doesn't this look like the same bike tread we were following earlier?'

'It does,' Sarah said, looking at the marks left in the dirt. 'Looks like it goes off around the pond the other way. Think we should see where it goes?'

'Might as well. Sammy's not here,' Penner said. 'You lead the way. Make sure you walk with a heavy foot—scare off all those snakes and turtles.'

'Will do, City Girl,' Sarah said with a laugh.

'And here I was thinking we were hitting it off,' Penner said, shaking her head.

***

'I've lost the trail,' Sarah said after ten minutes of following the tracks through the trees. The trail had started out being rather easy to follow—the trees weren't as dense here as earlier so there were fewer leaves on the ground. But, as the trail continued, the forest started to close in around them, making it difficult to see the path, never mind to follow the bike tire tracks. 'I think it heads over in this direction, but I really can't tell.'

'Well, it definitely got to this point, so it could've only gone one of two ways,' Penner said. 'It could have continued down the path we're on, or it could have veered off to the right, away from the water.'

'Makes sense,' Sarah said. 'Doubt anyone would have ridden into the water. Okay. You stay on the path—I'll see if I can see anything in the woods. I'll meet up with you in five minutes or so if I don't find any more tracks.'

'Sounds good,' Penner said. 'Be careful. Call out if you find anything—I should be in earshot.'

Sarah turned off of the path, into the trees. Penner listened for a minute, the crunch of leaves getting quieter. 'Let's see if I can pick up the trail again,' she said to herself, starting to walk along the path, stomping her feet harder than before. Every ten steps she stopped, bending down, looking at the path in front of her. Truth be told, she hadn't seen any sign of the bike tracks in quite some time—she had just been following Sarah as they went. She started walking again, scanning the path in front of her, not seeing anything but leaves. A loud cracking sound ahead made her stop dead in her tracks. Standing frozen, her mind raced, trying to figure out what would have made the noise. It sounded like a branch breaking, probably being stepped on—she had heard similar sounds as Sarah walked on sticks in front of her. But Sarah should be off to her right, and this sound came from in front of her. She turned her head so her ear faced the direction she thought the sound came from, hoping to hear something that would help identify what made the sound, but all she could hear was the pounding of her pulse. There was another crack, and rustling of leaves. 'Whatever that is, it sounds big,' she thought, wishing she had her gun. She tried to think of her time at summer camp. Are you supposed to play dead if you see a bear? Talk to it? Run? 'Running's probably not right,' she said out loud. She slowly started backing up the path in the direction she had come, away from whatever was coming through the woods. It was getting closer. 'Maybe it's just a deer,' she thought, trying to calm her nerves. It wasn't working—her mind just kept envisioning a bear coming out of the woods, looking for an easy meal. 'Bears don't like people, do they?' she said, still backing up, nearly losing her footing. 'Back off, bear!' she yelled. The sound kept getting closer. 'Go away!' She screamed.

'I thought we were friends,' the Chief said as he stepped out of the woods.

'Chief! You scared the crap out of me.'

'I can tell. Sorry about that, I didn't realize we were so close to you guys,' the Chief said as Millar and Grant came out of the trees. Millar had a big smile on his face.

'Real funny, Millar. Jerk,' Penner said, not sure if she was more annoyed or relieved. 'I guess you didn't find anything?'

'Not really,' the Chief said. 'The tracks seemed to lead here. You?'

'No. We found some tracks back down the trail a bit. They started at the edge of the pond where Sammy usually fished, but we lost them just back there,' Penner said, pointing to where Sarah had lost the tracks. 'Sarah went into the trees to see if she could find them again, and I was looking out here.'

'Before you started cowering?' Millar said.

'Okay, tough guy. I'd like to see you out here by yourself, instead of with Grant and the Chief,' Penner said. 'You wouldn't last five minutes.'

'Maybe not but...' Millar said, a scream stopping him mid-sentence. 'Was that Sarah?'

'Must have been,' Penner said. 'Let's go.'

CHAPTER SEVENTEEN

'Sarah! Where are you?' Penner called out as they ran into the heavy undergrowth, ducking under low hanging limbs and trying to keep their footing on the uneven ground.

'Over here,' Sarah yelled back. 'I found him. Hurry!'

'It sounds like she's over this way,' Penner said, turning towards the direction she thought the cries were coming from. 'Yell again so we can find you!' she shouted, trying to keep her breath as she ran.

'I'm here!' Sarah called back. 'I think you're getting close—I can hear you running.'

'Look, there's a bike,' Grant said, passing Penner and pointing to his left. Laying in the brush was an older mountain bike. 'Sarah!'

'There she is,' Penner said, seeing Sarah crouched down beneath a large maple tree. As she got closer she could see Sammy lying facedown on the ground. A rope was around his neck, tied to a large branch that lay on top of his back.

'I think he's still breathing, but not much,' Sarah said, fumbling with the rope around her brother's throat.

'He is?' Chief Ravenclaw asked.

Grant immediately crouched down next to Sarah and took

a pocket knife out of his back pocket. Opening up the largest blade, he began sawing at the rope, trying to relieve the pressure on Sammy's throat. He could see Sammy's lips were blue. 'Get the branch off him,' he said as Millar and Penner got to his side. 'I'm almost through.'

Millar grabbed the branch and pulled it off Sammy's back, as Grant cut the final strand of rope. 'Don't move him yet—he may have broken his back or neck when he fell. It's a pretty heavy branch that fell on him.'

'Sarah,' said Penner. Sarah seemed oblivious to her voice. 'Sarah, I need you to listen to me,' she said, grabbing Sarah by the shoulders. Sarah stood up, almost in a daze. 'I need you to run to the edge of the woods or until you get a signal on your phone. You can run faster than us and you know your way back better than us. Call 911 and get an ambulance out here as soon as possible. Once you've done that, call your mom and Barry, let them know we've found Sammy. Have you got that?'

'Yeah,' Sarah said, staring down at Sammy. 'Is he going to be okay?'

'We're going to do everything we can, but I need you to go and call the ambulance, alright? If we can, we're going to get Sammy to the edge of the woods. Once you've told Barry and your mom, stay there and wait for the ambulance. If we're not there, you're going to need to bring the paramedics to us. Alright?'

'Alright. Please, take care of him,' Sarah said, looking up at Penner.

'We will,' Penner said, giving Sarah a kiss on the forehead. 'Go.'

Sarah seemed to gather her wits about her and she took off running through the trees, leaping over any roots in her way.

'How's he looking?' the Chief asked, leaning over Grant's back.

'He's breathing, but he's not conscious,' Grant said, looking over his shoulder. He was holding Sammy's head steady, a hand on either side of his face. 'Penner, I need you to hold his head. I want to check his back and see if it's broken.'

Penner knelt down beside Grant. 'What do I do?' she asked.

'Put your right hand over top of mine,' he said. 'I'm going to slowly pull my hand out from under yours. I want you to keep some pressure—we don't want his head to move. Okay, ready?'

'Ready,' Penner said, her hand pressed against Grant's. Grant slowly pulled his hand out from against Sammy's face. 'Good,' he said as his hand was completely out. 'Now, same thing with the left. Once you have hold of his head, try not to move it. If his neck or back are broken, things can get much worse with even the slightest movement.'

'Great, no pressure,' Penner said. 'Okay, when you're ready.' Grant slowly pulled his left hand out, leaving all the weight in Penner's hands.

'Perfect,' Grant said, standing up and moving behind Sammy. 'I'm just going to gently feel around. Watch his face, see if he reacts at all. Even though he isn't conscious, he may react to pain.' Penner got even lower and tilted her head sideways so that she could watch Sammy's face.

'Anything we can do?' Millar asked, standing with the Chief and helplessly watching what was going on.

'Yeah. We're going to need to find a way to get him out of here, if he's okay to move. Take the rope and see if you can find some tall, but thin trees, or something that we can make a stretcher out of. Couple inches thick and about six feet long.

A bit shorter's okay, but we want his entire body on it.'

'Gotcha,' the Chief said. He turned to Millar. 'Look for stuff laying on the ground. It'd be too hard to break a live tree that size with our bare hands. But we don't want anything too old or brittle.'

'How do you know if it's too old?' Millar asked, scouring the forest floor around the area.

'Pick it up and lean on it,' the Chief said. 'If it cracks or breaks, it's too old. But try not to put all of your weight on it,' he quickly added. 'If you do and it breaks, you'll end up on your face and I don't want to carry two people out of here.'

'You still alright holding him?' Grant asked Penner as he felt down the length of Sammy's back, feeling for any abnormalities.

'I'm fine,' Penner said. 'Bit of an awkward angle but not too bad. So far his expression hasn't changed, so I guess he's not noticing what you're doing.'

'That could be good or bad,' Grant said. 'He either has no pain, or no feeling. I'm not feeling anything out of the ordinary, so that's a good thing, at least. I'm going to feel around his neck now. I'll try not to move your hands.' Grant moved Sammy's hair out of the way from his neck, revealing a streak of blood. 'Looks like he was cut pretty good when the branch fell on him. We'll have to wrap this before we move him. I'm not feeling anything broken, so I think we should be able to roll him onto his back. Millar? Chief? Can you give us a hand?'

Millar arrived carrying a long, gnarly looking branch that was barely an inch and a half thick and not remotely straight. The Chief had found four six-foot long branches that looked like they had been expertly turned on a lathe. 'What can we do?' Millar asked, looking at the pieces the Chief dropped next to his.

'Millar, I want you at his feet. Grab hold of his ankles. Chief, come over beside me and put your right hand under his thighs and your left hand under his butt. I'll be at his back. Penner, you keep your hands on his head. On the count of three, we're going to roll him so he's flat on his back. We want to try and keep everything in line, so we're going to go slow and together, okay? Any questions?' Grant asked as everyone moved into position. 'Okay, ready? One. Two. Three.' Slowly, they rolled Sammy onto his back, trying to make sure his neck, midsection and legs all turned at the same speed, staying in line. 'Perfect,' Grant said with obvious relief. 'Millar, Chief, keep working on the stretcher. We should be able to get him partway out of here before the paramedics show up.' He grabbed his knife again and pulled off his shirt. He stabbed the knife into his shirt and cut a 3-inch-wide strip off the bottom of it. 'Help me lift his head a bit,' he said to Penner. 'Slowly! Just lift it a little bit. Just enough so we can slide this over his wound.'

Penner carefully lifted the back of Sammy's head off of the ground, allowing enough clearance for Grant to slide the makeshift bandage into position. 'Good, put it back down,' he said, tying the cloth off across his forehead.

'Think he's going to be okay?' Penner asked, looking down at Sammy's expressionless face.

'I hope so,' Grant said. 'Hard to tell how long he was hanging before the branch broke. It's a good sign he was breathing when we got here, and the colour's returned to his lips. But really only time will tell. If he was without oxygen for even a couple of minutes, he could have suffered irreversible damage. Right now, out best bet is getting him to the hospital. Guys, how's the stretcher coming?'

'This should be the last piece we'll need,' Millar said, bringing another branch over to the Chief, who had started tying them all together. 'Not to be the bearer of bad news, pun not intended, but I'm pretty sure I saw a bear track just ten feet from here—think we're okay?'

'Must be old,' the Chief said, tightening a knot. 'A bear's not going to stick around with the noise we've been making. Might have been walking around last night, or before we got here this morning. Pass me that last branch, would ya?'

'Here,' Millar said, choosing the straightest of the leftover branches and handing it to the Chief. 'Pretty lucky for Sammy if he was laying out here all night with bears wandering around.'

'For the most part, bears don't approach people in the woods—they don't like our smell,' the Chief said, pulling the last of the rope between two of the branches. 'It does sometimes happen, but not too often. Okay, all done. Now what?'

'Bring it over here and put it right up against his side,' said Grant. 'Yeah, that's good. Alright. Millar, come around beside me. Penner, up by his head again. Millar, we're going to tilt him towards us, nice and easy. Try to keep everything in line again. Chief, when he's up enough, slide the stretcher under him, then we'll lay him back down. Alright, ready. Tilt.' Again, they slowly turned Sammy so that there was enough clearance between his back and the ground for the Chief to push the makeshift stretcher partway under his back. 'Okay, put him down, but try to support him a bit, he's not entirely on yet. Now, this is going to be a bit tricky. We need to pick him up and get him entirely on the stretcher. I think what we'll do is, Penner—you stay at his head. Chief, can you move over to his feet—see if you can grab around his knees from there.'

The Chief moved into position and reached out. 'Shouldn't be a problem.'

'Perfect. Millar, you scoot up a bit, I want you to have one hand under his butt, the other under his shoulders. I'll do the same on his other side.' Grant moved to the other side of Sammy, putting his hands in position. 'Okay, real slow on this one. Ready? Lift.' They lifted Sammy in unison, making sure no part of his body moved out of alignment. 'Put him down,' Grant said and his body was centred over the stretcher. 'Great work guys. Is there any more rope left?'

'No. I used it all tying the branches together,' the Chief said.

'Okay, no problem,' Grant said. 'Good thing I didn't like this shirt,' he said, starting to cut more strips off of it. He passed one to the Chief. 'Tie his ankles to the branches. Not too tight—you don't want to cut off his circulation. Just tight enough to keep him in place.' He handed one to Millar and kept one himself. 'Do the same around his waist, I'll tie one around his chest.'

After a bit of struggling to get the strips of fabric in the right places, Sammy was secured well enough to his temporary transport. 'Okay, Chief. Can you grab the stretcher at his feet? I'll grab up by his head. If you need to put him down, let me know. I want to take it slow walking out—last thing we want to do is drop him. Penner, Millar, walk either side of us to make sure he stays in place. If we need to, we'll switch out with you. I don't think he's too heavy so it shouldn't be too bad. Alright, ready, Chief?'

'I am,' the Chief said as he grabbed onto the two longer branches he had tied in as handles. 'On your count.'

'One. Two. Three.' Grant and the Chief lifted Sammy into

the air, his body staying motionless on the stretcher. 'Alright, let's head out. Let me know if we're wandering off the path. I'm not too sure of the way out.'

'Just head to your left and we should be able to follow the shore of the pond most of the way,' the Chief said as they started walking. 'Hopefully we meet the paramedics partway. I'm sure this isn't the most comfortable for his back.'

'That would be ideal,' Grant said. 'They'll have a proper backboard and stretcher. Mind you, the less we have to manipulate him, the better. If we can get him all the way to the ambulance on this, I think it would be best. I didn't feel any breaks but even a hairline fracture could be bad if it's moved the wrong way.'

They continued to the edge of the pond where the path narrowed, forcing Penner to walk in the tall grass. 'Um, should we be making more noise?'

'Why?' Grant asked.

'To scare off the snakes and snapping turtles,' Penner said, paying more attention to her feet than to Sammy.

'Only turtles around this pond are painted turtles,' the Chief said. 'They're harmless as a dragonfly. Well, except to dragonflies, I guess.'

'Really? I was told to look out for snappers,' Penner said. 'You sure?'

'Sure as I can be,' the Chief said. 'Whoever told you that was having a bit of a laugh at your expense, I think.'

'She is just like Millar,' Penner said.

'What? What did I do?'

'Nothing. Just keep walking,' Penner said. 'If Sammy's okay at the end of all this, I'll get her back.'

'Get who back? Are you actually plotting against a kid?'

Millar asked.

'This doesn't involve you,' Penner told him. 'Do you guys hear sirens?'

'Ambulance must be getting close,' Grant said, picking up the pace a bit. 'You doing okay, Chief, or do you need to switch out?'

'I'm fine,' the Chief said. 'Let's just get him there as quickly as we can.'

As they arrived at the edge of the woods, they saw an ambulance and two paramedics removing a stretcher from inside. A small, curious crowd had started to form nearby. They could see Sarah standing next to her mom, her back to the woods, telling the paramedics to hurry up. Someone in the crowd called out, 'There they are,' and Sarah turned around. She ran up to Sammy's side. 'Is he okay?' she asked.

'I don't think he's any different than when you last saw him. He's breathing and doesn't seem to be in any pain, but he hasn't woken up yet,' Grant said as the paramedics brought the stretcher to them.

'Put him on here,' one of the paramedics said. Grant and the Chief gently put their homemade stretcher on top of the stretcher from the ambulance, and then shook out their arms, relieved to be done carrying the weight. The first paramedic put a blood pressure cuff around Sammy's arm and put his stethoscope to his chest while the other paramedic started strapping Sammy and the branch stretcher down.

'So, what exactly happened? We got a call of a possible hanging?'

'Yeah, he was found unresponsive in the woods,' Grant said. 'He was lying on the ground, rope around his neck, with a branch across his back. He has a slight laceration on the back of his head. Other than that, no obvious trauma. He's been unconscious since we found him.'

'Pulse and B.P. are low,' the first paramedic said. 'We should roll.' They wheeled the stretcher to the back of the ambulance and loaded it in, while the crowd of onlookers tried to see inside.

'Is there room for his mom and sister to ride with you to the hospital?' the Chief asked as they were locking the stretcher in place. Sooleawa appeared from the crowd and stood beside the Chief. She put a hand on his arm and watched the proceedings with eyes wide with shock.

'Only room for one back here,' the paramedic said. 'But whoever it is has to get in now.'

Chief Ravenclaw stepped forward, out of earshot of the crowd, and spoke quietly to the paramedic, 'Make sure his clothing is checked thoroughly. There may be a note.' After a split second, the paramedic nodded in understanding. 'Mrs. Greycrow, get in.' The Chief turned around and ushered Sammy's mom forward. 'I'll bring Sarah back to our place. Sooleawa can make her some soup, and then we'll come check on him.'

With the help of two of the men in the crowd, Mrs. Greycrow climbed into the back of the ambulance and sat in a little seat next to Sammy. She wiped the hair off his forehead and started to cry.

'Stay strong, Sammy!' the Chief called out as the paramedic started to close the door.

The doors closed and the ambulance pulled away, lights flashing and sirens blaring.

'Are you okay, Sarah?' Sooleawa asked, giving Sarah a hug.

'I'm fine,' Sarah said, watching the ambulance leave. 'I'm not really hungry, though. Can we just go right to the hospital? I think my mom's going to need me with her.'

'Of course, dear,' Sooleawa said, looking at the Chief.

'Yeah, no problem,' he said, looking around the crowd. 'I just have to talk to a couple of people. Go back home, and get the car ready. I shouldn't be too long,' he added, spotting Travis at the back of the crowd, smoking his pipe.

'Okay, but don't take too long.' Sooleawa followed his gaze and noticed Travis raising a hand in greeting at the Chief. 'Ten minutes and we're leaving without you,' she said, taking Sarah by the hand.

'I'll be quick,' the Chief said as his wife and Sarah walked away. Turning, he faced Penner, Millar and Grant. 'Good work out there, officers. I hope we got to him in time. Now, if you'll excuse me,' he said, pivoting away to walk towards Travis.

'Chief?' Penner said. The Chief stopped and turned to look back at her. 'Why'd you tell the paramedics to look for a note?'

'Pardon?' the Chief said.

'We already have one murder disguised as a suicide. It's not unreasonable to think this might be a second. But you specifically told them to look for a note—like you already knew one would be there for them to find,' Penner said, a hint of suspicion in her voice.

'Did I?' the Chief said. 'Honestly, I was just thinking how Jonny had a note in his back pocket. I don't know. I guess it's still easier for me to think that we might have a couple of depressed kids on our hands than a murderer. Sorry, I have to go. Thanks again.'

Penner watched the Chief as he walked off towards Travis.

'Everything okay?' Grant asked, walking up to her side.

'I'm not sure,' she said, still watching the Chief. She couldn't tell, but it seemed like he started yelling at Travis as the two walked towards the band office. 'Something doesn't sit right with this. I don't know what it is, but something's off. Hey, Millar! How thick was that branch across Sammy's back?'

'What? I don't know. Six, seven inches maybe? Big enough. Why?' Millar said.

'If it was that thick, how'd it break?' Penner said.

'What do you mean?' Millar asked. 'I assume it broke because of Sammy's weight.'

'But when you and the Chief were looking for branches for the stretcher, didn't he say it would be hard to break a tree that was just a couple inches thick?' Penner said. 'If you couldn't break a tree that was two inches thick, why would a branch that was three times that size break from the weight of a hundred-pound kid?'

'Maybe the branch was rotten?' Grant suggested. 'Did the tree seem dead?'

'I wasn't looking that closely at the tree or the branch, to be honest with you,' Millar said. 'What? Are you thinking this was all staged?'

'I really don't know,' Penner said. 'But I do think we should go back and have a look at that tree.'

CHAPTER EIGHTEEN

'Well, the tree looks pretty healthy to me,' Grant said looking up at the tree where Sarah had found Sammy. 'Lots of leaves—branches don't look dead. Does the break look right to you?' he asked, looking where the branch had broken. He took out his phone and took a photo of the break.

'Now that you mention it, something about it doesn't look quite right,' Millar said looking up. 'Top two thirds of the break looks way too uniform. The bottom third is kind of splintered, but the top almost looks like it's been sawn.'

'Where's the branch?' Grant asked. Looking around, he saw where Millar had moved the branch earlier. 'That's a big branch. No way I'd be able to break this, even if I was hanging off of it, and I'm a lot heavier than Sammy. Look how thick it is.'

'That's almost seven inches across,' Penner said. She looked at the end that was connected to the tree. 'That break really looks too clean. I know I haven't seen a lot of broken tree limbs, but I don't think they would break like this. Take a picture of this, too,' she said to Grant.

'One way to find out,' Millar said. He looked around some of the nearby trees, checking out the low hanging limbs. He found one where the branches were only a few inches thick and around six feet from the ground. He reached up and grabbed onto one of the branches. 'Here goes,' he said, lifting his feet of the ground. There was a large cracking sound as the branch broke and Millar landed on his feet.

'The break definitely looks different,' Grant said, examining where the branch was still attached to the tree by a small strip of bark. 'So, it looks like it broke at the top, then kind of peeled back along the branch. It's not a straight up and down break like Sammy's branch.'

'Hey, check this out,' Penner said, kneeling down by the original tree. 'Is this sawdust?'

Millar bent down, looking at a small area of dirt covered with wood dust. 'Now, that's weird,' he said. He moved over to the tree he had just broken and examined the ground under the branch. 'Nothing like that here.' He looked around at the trees in the immediate area as Grant took more pictures as possible evidence. 'Let's have a look around—see if there are any trees that have had branches cut with a saw. Maybe someone was out here looking for firewood, and for whatever reason, they started cutting that branch and left before they were all the way through.'

They wandered around for several minutes, checking out the trees in the area. 'None seem to have been cut, either partially or all the way through,' Grant said. 'So, either Sammy just happened to choose the only branch in the area that had been mysteriously sawn or...'

'Or this was staged,' Penner said.

'So, what are we thinking?' Grant asked.

'Well, maybe someone lured Sammy out here, bashed him on the head, knocking him down to the ground. Once he was down, they tied the rope around his neck, laid the branch over his back and that was that,' Penner said. 'They figured he was dead and left.'

'Okay, I'll buy it. But why try to kill him and make it look like a suicide?' Millar said.

'My guess is, the same reason they killed Jonny. Publicity. Using a local tragedy to get national attention for the poor conditions here.'

'But, if that's the case, why cut the branch first?' Grant said. 'Why not actually hang him like they did with Jonny? That would make it more believable, wouldn't it?'

'What if there were two of them the first time? I think we can agree that a single person wouldn't have been able to get Jonny up in the tree after strangling him,' Penner said.

'I'd say that's a fair assumption,' agreed Grant. 'When I helped get him out of the tree, it was shocking how heavy he was.'

'So maybe, for whatever reason, there was only one person who attacked Sammy last night,' Penner said.

'Pretty much everyone from the reserve was at the feast last night,' Millar said. 'So maybe we are looking for someone from one of the neighbouring communities.'

'Hopefully Sammy pulls through and he can fill in some of the blanks, because, if not, I really don't know what else we have to go on,' Grant said, walking around the tree with the cut branch. 'You smell something?' he asked, looking around. 'Oh, great,' he said, looking at the bottom of his shoe. 'I stepped in crap.' He started rubbing his shoe on the ground, trying to clean off the sole.

'Bear?' Millar asked, looking around, worried. 'Remember I found a print just over there when I was gathering branches.

'No, too small for bear,' Grant said, looking down. 'And it's not just a pile like bear scat. It looks like dog crap. Look at this,' he said, reaching down.

'Eww, are you picking it up?' Penner said. 'That's gross.'

'No, this,' Grant said, holding up a wooden match after photographing it. 'This is the second match I've found today out here.'

'Sarah and I found one when we were over by the pond, too,' Penner said. 'Coincidence?'

'Maybe. But I'd say it's one of the best clues we've got right now,' Grant said, picking up a stick and trying to dig out the feces from the tread on his shoe. He suddenly stopped. 'You don't think. Nah, couldn't be.'

'Think what?' Penner said. 'You really need to finish your thoughts if you want us to follow along.'

'Well, the wooden matches and dog crap,' said Grant. 'You think Travis could have had something to do with this?'

'Travis, the band manager?' Penner asked, surprised. 'Why would he try to kill kids from the reserve?'

'Well, what if he's trying to garner attention for the water problems here,' Grant said. 'He has said that he finds it frustrating that he can't get any assistance from the government. The note found on Jonny mentioned the water. Plus, when Travis lights his pipe, he always uses wooden matches. And he has that dog. Maybe he followed Sammy out to the pond, then told him Chewie had gotten loose. Sammy went with him, helping him look for the dog. Once they got around the tree, he whacked him on the head and made it look like an attempted suicide.'

'You really think he would do something like that?' asked Penner. 'He seems so nice.'

'He does. Well, he is. But…' Grant stopped, starting to doubt himself. 'It doesn't make any sense, does it?'

'Right now, we really don't have anything else to go on,' Millar said. 'Is there any way to compare the matches? Can we tell if they're the same brand as he uses or anything?'

'Maybe, but I kinda doubt it,' Grant said, looking at the match stick. 'There's no writing or marks on it at all. I would think all wooden matches are pretty much the same, no? Pretty uniform in length and size. Would one brand of match differ from another?'

'Maybe not,' Millar said. 'Let's say it was Travis that did this. Wasn't he at the feast last night? He served Sooleawa her meal, didn't he?'

'He did. But after dinner, Barry looked for him and couldn't find him,' Grant said. 'Remember when he came to the band office last night, Barry said he looked for him for quite some time with no luck.'

'Right, he said he was out having a smoke,' said Penner.

'Okay, so there's a chance he may have had time to do it. And a possible, though flimsy motive. But we don't really know for sure a crime was committed.' Grant paced as he spoke. 'I'm ninety percent certain one has been, but, until we get a chance to talk to Sammy or see if he wrote a note, we can't be one hundred percent sure.'

'So, we should head to the hospital, then,' said Millar. 'First, though, I think you have to try and clean your shoe better. You really don't smell very good,' he said to Grant.

CHAPTER NINETEEN

Penner, Millar and Grant walked through the doors of the hospital emergency ward and looked around for anyone they might know. They saw Sarah and her mom sitting in the waiting room. Nearby, Sooleawa leaned against the wall, talking on her phone. When she saw them, she motioned them over, hanging up her phone and putting it in her purse.

'How's Sammy doing?' Penner asked.

'He's stable, but still unconscious. The doctors have him on some oxygen and they have an I.V. in his arm. He's hooked up to some other machine, too. Checking his vital signs, I think. It's been a bit much for Mrs. Greycrow. She was in his room earlier but she didn't like seeing him like that.'

'Do you know if they found a note on him?' Millar asked, glancing over at Sarah and her mom. Sarah saw them and waved.

'They did. It was folded up in his back pocket. I think Mrs. Greycrow has it.'

'I guess the Chief was right,' Penner said.

'Pardon?' Sooleawa said, looking over at Penner.

'Nothing,' Penner said. 'Where is the Chief?'

'He decided to stay back at the reserve. He said he had some things to take care of. I think he wanted to contact the media again. Always working.'

'How are you doing, Sarah?' Grant asked, placing an arm around her shoulders as she walked over to them. 'Your mom okay?'

'We're alright, all things considered,' Sarah said. 'Mom's been crying off and on, but she's holding up pretty good.'

'Are you hungry? Thirsty?' Grant asked. 'There's probably a cafeteria here somewhere.'

'I could go for a pop, thanks,' said Sarah. 'It's been a long day.'

'Anyone else?' Grant asked. 'I assume you want a coffee?' he said to Penner.

'If you wouldn't mind,' Penner said. 'Want some money?'

'I got it,' Grant said. 'Sooleawa? Millar?'

'Coffee would be great, thanks. One cream,' Sooleawa said.

'I'll get a coffee. Actually, I'll come give you a hand,' Millar said. He turned to Sarah's mom. 'Would you like anything from the cafeteria, Mrs. Greycrow?'

'Tea would be lovely, thank you.'

'Right, be back in a bit,' Grant said, leading Millar and Sarah in search of a cafeteria.

'I'm just going to chat with Mrs. Greycrow,' Penner said.

'No problem. I have to make another phone call,' Sooleawa said. 'I'll just be over here.'

Penner sat down next to Mrs. Greycrow. 'Mrs. Greycrow, I'm Detective Sue Penner. I work with Constable Grant in Ottawa.'

'Nice to meet you. Sarah's told me a lot about you already,' said Mrs. Greycrow, patting Penner on the leg. 'Thank you for finding my boy'

'You're welcome,' Penner said, squeezing Mrs. Greycrow's hand. 'I hope he makes a full recovery. Sooleawa said that Sammy had written a note?'

Mrs. Greycrow opened her purse and pulled out a folded up sheet of paper. She handed it to Penner, who unfolded the page and read over the note.

'Mom, Sarah, I am sorry for doing this, but Johnny's death really got me thinking. I just can't continue living, knowing our conditions here are never going to improve and no one seems to care. I hope you forgive me as I go to my second life with Dad, my grandparents and all our other relatives. And I hope to see Johnny again. Love you. Sammy'

'Does this look like it was written by Sammy?' Penner asked, looking back over the note.

Mrs. Greycrow looked at Penner. 'It was in his pocket. Who else would have written it?'

'I don't know,' Penner said, carefully. 'I just want to make sure you think it looks like his handwriting.'

'I think so,' said Mrs. Greycrow. Her brow furrowed as she considered what Penner had said. 'Sammy didn't write too much, but he did write me this poem. I've carried it with me since he wrote it last year.' She opened her purse again, moving around some of the contents, pulling out another sheet of paper. She handed it to Penner. 'It's really not a very good poem,' she said with a smile. 'But it means a lot to me. He wrote it for my birthday.'

Penner looked at the poem, smiling when she finished reading it. 'It's cute,' she said. 'They do look pretty similar, don't they?'

'I think so, but my eyes aren't as good as they used to be. I have a hard time seeing small print these days,' Mrs. Greycrow said.

'Happens to all of us as we age,' Penner said. 'Do you mind if I hold onto these for a bit? I'd like one of my colleagues to have a look at them.'

'Okay,' Mrs. Greycrow said hesitantly. 'Please be careful with them.'

'I promise—nothing will happen to them,' Penner said. 'Do you mind excusing me for a minute? I just have to make a phone call.'

'Of course. I should just run to the washroom,' Mrs. Greycrow said, standing up and stretching her back. 'If you see Sarah before I'm back, can you let her know where I am?'

'Sure thing,' Penner replied as Mrs. Greycrow walked off to find the washroom. Penner pulled out her cellphone, checking to see if she had a signal. 'Finally,' she said, dialing.

'Yes?'

'Captain, it's Penner.'

'Hi, Sue. What's going on? I thought you were off today.'

'I am, sir. I'm still out at the reserve with Grant and Millar. Actually, I'm at the local hospital right now.'

'You alright?'

'Yes, sir, I'm fine. We found one of the local boys unconscious in the woods this morning. Possible hanging, but we're not sure. Well, truth be told, we're pretty sure it wasn't, but we need to be positive.'

'Possible hanging that isn't a hanging? I don't follow.'

'The boy was found with a rope around his neck and the other end of the rope was attached to a broken branch, but, well, we're thinking it may have been staged. Which is why I'm calling, actually.'

'I'm listening.'

'I was wondering if we could send another couple of notes over—have McGee take a look again.'

'You know, your timing is actually pretty impressive. He's here right now. Just a sec. McGee, if Penner sends you a couple of documents to compare, how long do you need to go over them? I'll ask. How long are they?'

'Not long—maybe half a dozen lines?'

'Half a dozen lines each. Twenty minutes? So, there you go. Send them over and he can get you an answer in the next half hour.'

'Thanks, sir. And thank McGee for me. I'll go find a fax machine.'

'Anything else?'

'That's it for now. Thanks, sir,' Penner said, hanging up the phone. She surveyed the waiting room and noticed a hall that seemed to lead to a reception desk. Mrs. Greycrow hadn't come back yet, and Sooleawa was occupied on her phone, so she quickly stood and walked down to the desk. An older nurse, wearing scrubs covered in cartoon cats, sat behind a computer.

'Can I help you?' the nurse asked, continuing to type.

'Do you have a fax machine here I can use?'

'Sorry, dear. We're not a stationary shop. There's a place down the road.'

Penner reached into her purse and pulled out her badge. 'Police business,' she said, holding up her badge. She didn't like playing the cop card, but it wasn't a lie.

'Around back here,' the nurse said, not looking up from the computer screen. 'But stay out of the way. Things can get hectic in a hurry.'

'Thanks,' said Penner, walking around the desk.

'No problem.'

Penner looked around until she saw the fax machine sitting on a shelf. She placed the two pages on top of the machine and typed in the fax number. The machine sucked the pages in, made some odd sounds, and sent the pages out the other side. She watched the display on top of the machine until it changed from 'sending' to 'received'. She grabbed the papers and walked back around the desk again. 'Thanks again,' she said to the nurse who just ignored her. 'Friendly,' she said under her breath as she walked back to the waiting room, noticing that the others had returned.

'Coffee?' Grant said, passing her a Styrofoam cup.

'Cheers,' Penner said, taking a sip. 'I appreciate it—but, man, that's awful.'

'Well, I guess hospital cafeteria coffee isn't quite the same as the fresh roasted coffee you got used to over the last couple of days,' Grant said. 'I can get you something else, if you want.'

'No, I'm still going to drink it. It's just not very good is all,' Penner said.

'You're something else,' said Grant shaking his head.

'I try,' Penner said. 'So, I just sent McGee the suicide note and another example of Sammy's writing. We should have an answer in the next half an hour as to whether Sammy wrote the note or not.'

'Can I see them?' Millar asked, taking the two pages from Penner. He looked at the two side by side. 'These kinda look the same, you know. With the note that was found on Jonny, you could definitely tell he didn't write it, based on his book report. But these? I'd be inclined to say they were written by the same person.'

'Really?' Grant said. 'Let's see?' Millar passed him the two papers.

'Look at how he writes his y's and g's,' Millar said. 'He does quite a large flourish in both. Same in the note and the other page.'

'They do look alike.' Grant sounded disappointed. He read over the note again. 'Maybe he did try to kill himself.'

'Well, once we hear back from McGee, we should have a better idea. But right now, I'm really confused,' Millar said.

'Wait,' Grant said, eyes scanning over the note. 'Sarah, does Sammy know how to spell Jonny's name?'

'What? Of course he does. He's not stupid,' said Sarah. 'They've been best friends forever.'

'So he wouldn't spell it J-O-H-N-N-Y?' Grant asked, looking back at the note.

'No way,' Sarah said, shaking her head. 'Jonny got really pissed if you put an H in his name. He liked the fact that his name didn't have an H—made him feel special.'

'Look at the note,' Grant said, passing it back to Millar.

'Well, I'll be,' said Millar. 'Good catch.'

'Still, maybe if he wasn't thinking clearly, he could have spelled it wrong,' Grant said. 'At least, that's what could be argued in court. We really need to talk to him. Or hear back from McGee. When's he supposed to call?' he asked Penner.

'Another ten or fifteen minutes, so we've got a while to wait,' Penner said. 'Anything we should be doing? This sitting around is killing me. Are we missing anything?'

'I guess one of us could stay here, in case Sammy wakes up. The other two could head back to the reserve and try to talk to Travis. Maybe he can tell us exactly where he was last night between dinner and the time we saw him at the band office,' Grant suggested.

'Travis—that reminds me,' interrupted Sarah, 'I remember

one time he was helping out down at the drop-in centre. He had each of us write a short story,' she continued. 'Jonny had written a story about going hunting or something. Anyway, at the end of the day, we all gave Travis our stories, so he could go over them that night and give them back to us the next day. The next day, he gave each of us our story back, and on the front he wrote some notes. On Jonny's, he wrote "Great job, Johnny", but he added an H. Jonny got so mad, he threw his paper on the ground and stormed out. I think that was the last time he went to the centre.'

'I forgot you said Travis helped out down there from time to time,' Millar said to Grant. He turned back to Sarah, 'Did your brother ever do any writing with Travis when he was there?'

'Yeah, quite a bit,' said Sarah. 'I think he's helped out five or six times that Sammy was there. He actually kept one of Sammy's stories a couple of weeks ago—said he really liked it and wanted to send a copy to his granddaughter back in Jamaica.'

Millar looked at Grant and Penner and raised his eyebrows. Pulling them aside, he said, 'So, Travis had access to Sammy's writing. Could have used it as a sample when writing the suicide note. I think you're right—we need to find Travis and ask him a few questions.'

'Why don't the two of you head back to the reserve,' Penner suggested. 'I'll hang here with Sarah and her mom—see if Sammy wakes up. If I hear anything from McGee, I'll give you a ring.'

'Sounds good,' Millar said. 'Hopefully you hear from him soon.'

CHAPTER TWENTY

'What the hell's going on?' Millar said to Grant as they pulled into the reserve. 'There's got to be a dozen different news stations here,' he said, seeing all the media trucks parked along the side of the road outside of the band office.

'Isn't that the reporter from Ottawa, Arden Wall?' Grant asked, as they found a spot to park behind a news van. 'Why on earth would he be here?'

'I have no idea,' Millar replied, getting out of the car and walking towards the scrum of reporters surrounding the Chief. 'Must be doing another press conference.' They nudged their way into the mix of reporters and residents who had converged to hear the Chief speak.

'Sammy Greycrow was a great, young member of our community and he will be dearly missed,' the Chief said. 'Once again, this is the second young member of our reserve that has killed himself, in just the past two days, because of the deplorable conditions here. Our youths' eyes have been opened. They have seen that the government isn't willing to help our people in our time of need and they don't see any other way out. All we are asking is for the government to send aid as soon as possible, so we can correct our drinking water issues before any other member of our community decides death is the only solution. Thank you all for coming.'

'Did he just say Sammy was dead?' asked Grant in disbelief as he watched the Chief start to walk away, followed by a few reporters who were anxious to ask questions and get their shots for the six-o'clock news.

'Sure sounded like it, didn't it? He knows he isn't dead, doesn't he?' Millar said. 'Oh great.'

'Detective Millar? I didn't expect to see you here,' Arden said, approaching with his camera man in tow.

'Arden,' Millar gave him a wary nod. 'What brings you out here?'

'The station got a call from the Chief. He told us that two young men had killed themselves because of the water conditions on the reserve,' Arden said, his camera man focusing on Millar to capture his expression. Millar remained stone-faced—he knew better than to give Arden anything. 'My boss figured it would be a good story. And hopefully some of the politicians back home will see the report and pay attention. If nothing else, could be good for ratings.'

'That sounds more like it,' Millar said.

'And what are you doing out here?' Arden asked.

'Just visiting.' Arden didn't need to know he was here helping Grant, who was helping out because the band police were understaffed. The less information given the better.

'Penner here, too?' Arden asked.

'Don't see her, do ya?' Millar said. 'Excuse us, we have to have a word with the Chief.'

'Chief Ravenclaw must have called every news team in a two-hundred mile radius,' Grant commented as they turned their backs on Arden and walked after the Chief.

'Yeah, no kidding. It's like his own little propaganda machine,' Millar said. 'I can't believe he would tell the media that Sammy died to try and get sympathy. What if one of Sammy's family or friends sees this?'

'Well, lets go ask him,' Grant said, seeing the Chief walk into the band office. Entering quickly behind him, they saw Travis at his desk. Chewie sat at his feet, gnawing on a bone.

'What was that all about?' Millar asked, barely containing his anger. 'You're actually reporting that Sammy died?'

'Didn't he?' the Chief asked, feigning innocence. 'I thought he had passed away at the hospital.'

'Not at all—he's very much alive,' said Millar. 'Why would you have thought he died? Where did you hear that?'

'Sooleawa called me earlier. I must have misunderstood what she said,' the Chief said, staring down Millar. 'Anyway, no harm, no foul.'

'Really? What if one of his family members sees the report on the evening news? Don't you think that could cause some harm?' Millar asked.

'If that happens, I'll apologize,' the Chief offered, leaning back against a desk and crossing his arms. 'Besides, if Sammy pulls through, then his relatives will be too relieved to get upset, right? And if he doesn't, then I didn't do anything wrong. Look, Detectives,' he uncrossed his arms and pointed first at Grant, then at Millar, 'I'm just doing my job, and my job is to get the best for the reserve. If two boys died or tried to kill themselves and they have notes in their pockets saying it's because of the water, well, I think the public has a right to know, don't you?'

'How do you know what Sammy's note said?' asked Grant quickly.

'Pardon?' the Chief said, looking over at Grant.

'The note. How'd you know what it said?' Grant repeated.

'Sooleawa told me when I was on the phone with her earlier,' the Chief said. He stood up and moved towards the kitchenette. 'If there's nothing else, I need a coffee. Can I get you one?'

'I'm fine,' Millar said. 'Actually, we just have a couple of questions for Travis.'

'For me?' Travis looked up from the papers he had been shuffling as he pretended not to listen.

'Last night, after the feast, where'd you go?' Millar asked.

'What? I, I left the feast and stopped by here because I saw the lights on—remember? I saw you guys. After that, I went home,' Travis said, looking over towards the Chief who was listening from the coffeemaker.

'Before you came here, where were you?' Millar asked.

'At the feast. Why?'

'After you served Sooleawa and before you came here, where were you? Barry looked for you and couldn't find you,' Millar said.

'I don't know, probably talking with people. Part of my job is to build relationships with the residents, so I was probably talking with some of the Elders. Barry probably just didn't see me.'

'Didn't you tell him last night that you were out having a smoke on your pipe?' Grant chimed in.

'Yeah, that's probably right,' Travis said. 'Takes a while to smoke a pipe, so I was outside smoking.'

'Have you been in the woods recently?' Millar asked.

'No, not recently,' Travis said, shifting in his seat.

'Excuse me,' Millar said as his phone rang. 'Millar. Hey, Penner. He is? Alright, we'll head back. See you in a bit.'

Millar put his phone back in his pocket. 'Grant? We've gotta go. Sammy woke up.'

'What?' Chief Ravenclaw looked back and forth between Millar and Travis. 'Is he able to talk?'

'Seems like it,' Millar said, raising one eyebrow at the Chief before turning to look at Travis. 'Don't leave town—we may want to talk again.' He walked over to where Grant was holding the door open. 'And, Chief? No more news conferences—unless you want to retract your earlier statement about Sammy dying.'

CHAPTER TWENTY-ONE

'So, what are your thoughts on this?' Grant asked Millar as they drove back to the hospital.

'Well, I'm kind of liking Travis for this, but I'm not too sure. What's his motive? How would he benefit by killing Jonny and trying to kill Sammy?' Millar said. 'Plus, if it was him, there's no way that he would have been able to kill Jonny by himself. He seems like he's in decent shape for his age, but he couldn't have strangled him and then hoisted him into the tree by himself. He had to have been working with someone.'

'What about the Chief?' Grant asked, bracing himself on the dashboard as Millar took a corner a bit too fast. 'Good thing these seatbelts work.'

'Sorry 'bout that,' Millar said with a smile. 'You'll learn to hold on. So, you're thinking the Chief may be involved?'

'At this point, I don't know what to think. Knowing both Travis and Chief Ravenclaw, I have a hard time believing either of them could be involved. I know I should keep an open mind, but neither of them seems like a murderous type—no one on the reserve really does. But now, with the Chief doing these press conferences, I have no idea what to think. He's definitely strong enough. His arms are about the size of my legs,' Grant said. 'Plus, there are his comments about the note.'

'Well, maybe his wife did mention it to him,' Millar said, taking another turn at top speed. This time Grant was ready. 'We can ask Penner if Sooleawa saw the note, or not. That might be her now,' he said, taking his ringing cell phone out of his pocket, handing it to Grant.

'Millar's phone,' Grant answered. 'Hey, Penner. We're on our way—should be there in about five minutes, or so.'

'Millar got you answering his phone now? I thought he was supposed to be reporting to you?'

'I think it's for the best if he keeps both hands on the wheel. Safer for everyone involved.'

'I hear ya there. He drives like a maniac.'

'I'm starting to learn that. What's up?'

'Just got a call from McGee. He's had a look at the two notes. Not quite as conclusive as we'd hoped.'

'Really? How so?'

'Well, apparently there are a lot of similarities between the two handwriting samples, which would lead him to think they were both written by the same person. But, there are a few differences, too.'

'Enough differences to say he didn't write one of the two?'

'Not quite. McGee said that the differences could be from stress or just from his age. Kids Sammy's age don't have a consistent style of writing—things vary. Happens until they're in their late teens, early twenties.'

'So, the note could have been written by Sammy, or by someone else then?'

'That about sums it up. If it was written by someone else, they did a good job at copying Sammy's style.'

'Well, hopefully Sammy can tell us either way. Is he talking?'

'I think so. His mom and Sarah are in with him right now. I figured we'd give them some time, then we'll go talk to him once

you guys are here.'

'We're just pulling into the parking lot now, so should be there in a minute—if we can find parking.'

'Ask about Sooleawa,' Millar said to Grant.

'Right. Do you know if Sooleawa saw the note?'

'Not that I know of, but she may have seen it before I got here. Why?'

'Just something the Chief said, is all. You won't believe it, but when we got to the reserve, he was giving a press conference again. He actually said Sammy died.'

'What? That doesn't seem very responsible for a community leader.'

'Not at all. Okay, we're parked. We're on our way in. See you in a few,' Grant said as he hung up the phone. 'She didn't see Sooleawa look at the note, but it could have happened before she got there. Sooleawa did drive Sarah to the hospital, so maybe Mrs. Greycrow showed her the note earlier.'

'Make a note to ask her,' Millar said, as they walked up to the hospital entrance. Behind them, an ambulance pulled into the loading bay, lights flashing.

***

'Hey, guys.' Penner greeted Millar and Grant, as they entered the crowded waiting room.

'Sarah and her mom still in with Sammy?' Grant asked, looking around. 'Sooleawa in there, too?'

'No, she left about five minutes ago. The Chief called her and she said she had to go help him with something,' said Penner. 'Mrs. Greycrow said we could go in and talk to Sammy whenever we wanted.'

'Grant, why don't you do the talking,' Millar said. 'You know him the best.'

'Um, okay,' Grant said, a bit taken aback. He had assumed that one of the detectives would have done the interview, but he guessed it made sense. Asking a kid some questions was different than interrogating a suspect. Besides, sometimes kids wouldn't open up to people they didn't know.

Penner led them down the hall, through a set of doors to Sammy's room. She knocked on the door frame before walking through the open door. Sammy was still attached to a variety of machines and had an oxygen tube leading up to his nostrils. He was sitting up, looking a little groggy, but better than he had the last time they'd seen him.

'How's he doing?' Grant asked Sarah, who was sitting on the edge of the bed.

'He's good. Tired and sore, but not too bad,' Sarah said, looking at Sammy. 'Should be able to go home in a day or two.'

'That's great news,' said Grant. 'Is he able to talk?'

'Yeah, which is kind of a shame,' Sarah said, grinning. 'It'd be nice if he'd just keep quiet for a while.' Sammy punched her in the arm.

'Does he remember what happened?' Grant asked, looking between Sarah and Sammy.

'You do know I'm sitting right here, right?' Sammy said, his voice a little hoarse. 'I can answer questions myself, you know.'

'You're right,' Grant said, a little embarrassed. 'Sorry about that. How are you feeling?'

'Like Sarah said. Tired and sore. My neck really hurts. So does my back and the back of my head,' Sammy said, reaching up and gingerly touching the dressing on the back of his head. 'Ended up getting fifteen stiches in the back of my head. May end up with a scar where the hair won't grow any more. Might have to have a little comb over, or something,' he said, laughing.

'Pretty lucky that's all that happened, really,' Grant said. 'So, can I ask you some questions?'

'You already are,' Sammy said with a smile.

'Don't be smart,' Mrs. Greycrow said, slapping his leg.

'Do you remember what happened yesterday?' Grant asked, his notebook at the ready.

'Well, I remember being at the feast,' Sammy said. 'And I remember going outside to shoot some hoops.'

'Anyone else around?' Grant asked, writing as he spoke.

'Yeah. I remember seeing Travis,' Sammy said. 'He followed me out of the hall.'

'Did you talk to him at all?' Penner interrupted. 'So much for leading the questioning,' Grant thought.

'Not at first. He just stood to the side, smoking his pipe.'

'When did you end up talking to him?' Grant asked.

'Well, after a bit, I found it weird he was just standing there, watching me. So, I decided to leave,' Sammy said, reaching up and scratching the back of his head.

'Leave the stitches alone,' Mrs. Greycrow said, giving him another slap. 'The doctor told you not to touch them.'

'They're so itchy!'

'I don't care how itchy they are. Leave them alone.'

'Fine. You can't watch me all the time,' Sammy said, under his breath.

'So, where did you end up going?' Penner asked, trying to get everyone back on track.

'I rode home and grabbed my fishing stuff. Figured it was a nice night and the fish might be biting,' Sammy said. 'I biked down to the pond to try my luck.'

'Did you catch anything?' Grant asked.

'Nah. I had a couple of nibbles, but didn't land anything.'

'So, you said that you didn't talk to Travis at the basketball court, but at some point you did end up talking to him,' Grant said. 'Did you go back to the drop-in centre and see him there?'

'No,' Sammy said. 'It was really weird. After fishing for half an hour or so, I saw him on the other side of the pond. He just came out of the woods and stood there, watching me again. Gave me the creeps.'

'So you talked to him then?' Grant asked, looking at Millar and Penner.

'Not right away,' Sammy said. 'He watched me for a couple of casts, then went back into the woods. I just kept fishing. I was glad he was finally gone. After another half an hour or so, I decided to head home. Fish weren't biting and I was getting tired. It'd been a long day with Jonny and the powwow and the feast and everything. I packed up my stuff and went to get my bike and Travis was suddenly there again.'

'Across the pond?' Grant asked.

'No, standing right behind me at my bike,' Sammy said. 'Don't know how I didn't hear him come up on me—I guess the guy's got a pretty soft foot. I asked him what he wanted, and he just stared at me, smoking his pipe. Super creepy.'

'Did you see him light his pipe?' Penner asked.

'Maybe,' Sammy said. 'I don't really remember. I was getting a bit freaked out and I just wanted to get my bike and go. But he was just staring at me. It was so weird.'

'Then what happened? Did you talk to him then?' Grant asked, writing in his book.

'Yeah, I asked him what he wanted. I just wanted to get out of there. When he finally spoke, he said Chief Ravenclaw wanted to see me.'

'The Chief?' Grant said. 'About what?'

'Said he wanted to ask me some questions about Jonny. I thought that was pretty strange. Why would the Chief want to talk to me at that time of night, when the feast was still going on? Why couldn't it wait until the next day?'

'Did you ask him that?' Penner asked.

'Yeah. He said the Chief had to file a report with the coroner and he needed it done right away,' Sammy said. 'I figured the Chief likes things done a certain way, so maybe it made sense.'

'Did you see the Chief at all?' If Millar's ears could have perked up, they would have at the mention of the Chief.

'No, not after I left the feast,' Sammy said. 'At least, I don't think I did—some things are still a bit fuzzy.'

'That's understandable,' Grant said. 'Just take your time. You're doing great. So, after he said the Chief wanted to see you, what happened?'

'Well, I grabbed my fishing gear and my bike, and went to head back to the reserve,' Sammy said, trying to scratch his head without his mom noticing. But she did. She gave him another slap.

'Did you head back with Travis?' Grant asked.

'Well, yeah. Kinda…' Sammy paused.

'What do you mean, kinda?'

'Well, I started walking my bike back the way I would usually take, but Travis said we should go the other way,' Sammy explained. 'Made no sense to me—the way he wanted to go was longer. But he said that's the way we should go because he wanted to give Chewie more time to run around.'

'So you went with him?' Grant asked, writing again in his notebook.

'Yeah, I did,' Sammy said. 'I probably should have just gone my normal way, but, well, I like playing with Chewie, so I decided to go along with him. I got to play fetch with him while we walked.'

'So you don't remember seeing the Chief, or anyone else, out in the woods?' Grant asked.

'Nope, just Travis and Chewie.'

'Then what happened?' asked Grant.

'Well, that's where it gets kind of fuzzy,' Sammy hesitated as he tried to recall what had happened. 'I remember throwing a stick for Chewie. He ran off, grabbed it and ran back to me, dropping it at my feet. I bent over to pick it up and that's the last thing I remember. Until I woke up here, whenever that was.'

'So, Sammy,' Penner said in a calm, steady voice. 'I have to ask you this. Did you try to hurt yourself last night?'

'Hurt myself?' Sammy asked, looking at his mom and then back to Penner. 'Why would I try to hurt myself?'

'I don't know. Maybe you were sad about Jonny. Or upset about the conditions on the reserve?' Penner asked.

'Well, sure, I'm sad Jonny's gone. Duh. But he's with his ancestors, so that's all good,' Sammy said. 'I know I'll see him again. Plus, if I need to, I can always just talk to him. He may not answer, but he'll hear me.'

'What about the stuff going on at the reserve? Like the dirty drinking water?'

'Well, that definitely sucks. I really don't understand why it's so bad,' Sammy said, his brow furrowing and his face darkening. 'I mean, do you think the Prime Minister has to drink bottled water because he doesn't know if his tap water's safe to drink? Of course not.'

CHAPTER TWENTY-ONE

'And that upsets you?' Penner asked.

'Of course it does, wouldn't you be upset?' Sammy said. 'How would you feel if you'd never had clean water? If your mom had never had clean water? If you were so thirsty and you couldn't just have a drink? If you felt like you were living in a third world country?'

'I'd be pretty mad,' Penner agreed.

'You'd be pissed off,' Sammy said.

'Hey, language!' Mrs. Greycrow said. 'Sorry about that—he knows better.'

'Sorry, mom,' Sammy said. 'But it's true, right?'

'Yeah, I'd be more than mad,' Penner said. 'So, were you so upset that you decided to hurt yourself?'

'What would that do?' Sammy gave Penner a strange look. 'No one's gonna care if I hurt myself. Except my mom and Sarah. Is that going to get the government to give us clean water? No.'

'So, you didn't try to kill yourself like Jonny did?' Penner asked.

'Heck, no,' Sammy said, glancing at his mom to see if he could get away with saying that. 'I like my life. I'm just a kid—there's way too much I have to experience. Besides, I have to be here to help Sarah run for Chief when she turns eighteen. Then things will change.'

Grant looked at Sarah and smiled. He knew she had plans and dreams, but he didn't realize being Chief was one of them. 'Mrs. Greycrow, do you have the note they found in Sammy's pocket?'

Mrs. Greycrow opened her purse and pulled out the folded piece of paper, handing it to Grant. 'Did you write this, Sammy?' Grant asked, passing the paper to Sammy to read.

'Nope,' Sammy said within a second of looking at the note.

'Are you sure? Perhaps you don't remember writing it,' Grant said.

'Definitely didn't write it,' Sammy said, shaking his head. 'Not my handwriting. Plus, I know how to spell Jonny. I made the mistake once of putting an H in his name and never did it again. Took two weeks for my black eye to fade away.'

'Okay, everyone. I think Sammy needs to get some rest.' A doctor briskly walked into the room and stood at the foot of Sammy's bed, looking expectantly at the visitors before asking Sammy, 'Did you want anything to eat first?'

'My throat's still pretty sore,' Sammy said. 'Maybe some ice cream?' he asked, eyes widening with his brilliant idea.

'I'll see what I can do,' the doctor said, checking Sammy's chart hanging at the foot of his bed.

'Do you know when he'll be able to go home?' Penner asked the doctor.

'Probably tomorrow afternoon—if he stops playing with those stitches,' the doctor said, seeing Sammy sneak a hand up to scratch the back of his head.

'But they're so itchy!' Sammy said.

'The more you scratch them, the longer you're going to have to stay here,' the doctor said, putting the chart back.

'Well, if you're getting me ice cream then that's not too bad a trade off, is it?' Sammy said. His mom slapped him on the leg again. 'I'm going to be all bruised by the time I get out of here.'

'Then stop being such a little devil,' said Mrs. Greycrow.

'I think we'll see ourselves out,' Grant said. 'Glad you're doing okay, Sammy. Can we give you a drive home, Mrs. Greycrow?'

'No, I'm going to stay here for a while, make sure he behaves himself and doesn't eat too much junk,' Mrs. Greycrow said. Her voice softened and her eyes started to well up as she added, 'Thank you again for helping my boy.'

'I'm just glad we got there in time,' said Grant. 'What about you, Sarah? Need a lift?'

'No, I've gotta work tonight, so I'm just going to crash here for a bit then walk over. Closer than going home,' Sarah said, giving Grant a hug. 'Thanks for everything.'

'No problem,' Grant said as they left the room. 'Oh, I almost forgot,' he added, poking his head back into the room. 'Mrs. Greycrow, did you happen to show the note to Sooleawa this morning?'

'No, she never saw it,' Mrs. Greycrow said. 'I kept it in my purse the entire time. Until Detective Penner asked to see it.'

'Okay, thanks. Rest up, Sammy. And stop scratching,' Grant said, watching Sammy quickly lower his hand back to his side.

CHAPTER TWENTY-TWO

'So, what's the plan now?' Grant asked as they exited the hospital and walked across the parking lot.

'Well,' Penner said, checking her watch, 'It's getting late and I'm starved…and seriously lacking caffeine. I think we need to talk to Travis again, so it looks like we'll have to crash at the reserve one more night.'

'Yeah,' Millar agreed, standing next to his car. 'If Sammy's getting released tomorrow, I want to make sure it's safe for him to go home.'

'But, if we're staying one more night, I need to pick up a couple of things,' said Penner. 'Probably wouldn't kill you to buy a new t-shirt and some deodorant…just saying.' She wrinkled her nose at Millar.

'What are you talking about? Fresh as a daisy.' Millar feigned offense. 'Reminds me of the old days and twenty-four hour stakeouts.'

'I think there's a bargain department store downtown, next to a pizza joint,' offered Grant. 'Why don't we swing by there, you guys can pick up whatever you need and then we'll grab some dinner and discuss the next steps.'

'Sounds good. Shotgun!' Penner called out, as she quickly stepped around Grant to claim the front passenger seat of the car.

***

'I still can't believe you didn't buy that t-shirt,' Millar said, holding the restaurant door open for Grant and Penner.

'From the back, I thought it looked alright—but then the front had that sequin tiger on it!' Penner shuddered.

'That was the best part! Who doesn't want to wear a bedazzled tiger?' Millar argued as they sat themselves down in a booth.

'So, guys,' Grant waited until the waitress placed the menus down before continuing, 'Do you think we have enough to get a warrant for Travis? Seems like he was the last one to see Sammy before he—what—got attacked, I guess?'

'I really don't know. It's all so circumstantial,' Penner said, reading one side of the menu and then flipping it over. 'Sammy remembers being out in the woods with Travis and that's it. He doesn't know what happened. I'd be really surprised if we got a judge to sign off on a warrant with what we have.'

'You think?' Grant said, sounding disappointed.

'Think about it. The kid's in the woods, playing with a guy's dog. Next thing he knows, he's in a hospital. Easy enough for Travis to say they were playing with the dog and then Sammy left on his own. No one can tell exactly when he got hit on the head, or who tied the rope around his neck. Without more evidence, no judge is going to say we've got enough to make a charge stick.'

'Maybe not,' Millar said. 'But Travis doesn't need to know that.'

'I recognize that look,' Penner said. 'You thinking we play a

177

bit dirty?'

'Just a little,' Millar said, pausing as the waitress brought a pitcher of water and three glasses over. She took their orders before Millar continued. 'We'll call it a night for tonight. Travis knows we've been talking to Sammy, so let's let him stew on that while Sammy is safe in the hospital. Tomorrow morning, we'll tell him we had a talk with Sammy and we have enough to arrest him, see what he says. We know whoever killed Jonny didn't work alone, and I'm thinking Travis was one of the two involved. Let's see if he's willing to let us know who his partner in crime was. I want to see what the Chief has to say about the note, too. If Sooleawa didn't mention anything about it to him, then how did he know what it said?'

'Sounds like a plan to me,' Penner said. 'You can play bad cop, if you want. If you're up for it, that is. I know you aren't really back on full-time duty, yet.'

'This could be just what I need to get back into the swing of things,' Millar said. 'Besides, it could be fun.'

***

Early the next morning, Millar and Penner were sharing a pot of coffee in Grant's apartment while Grant kept watch on the band office from his living room window.

'The Chief and Sooleawa just showed up,' Grant said, letting the blinds fall back into place. 'Should we go see if Travis is there? I didn't see him come through the front door, but, at this time of the morning, he should already be there,' Grant said, looking at his watch.

'Good a place as any to start,' Millar said finishing his coffee and setting his mug down on the kitchen counter. 'Let's roll.'

As they crossed the road and approached the front door, Penner asked, 'So, how do you want to play this?'

'Not too sure, really,' Millar said, hand on the door knob. 'I think we'll just start talking about Sammy's conversation and see if he squirms or talks. If need be, we'll turn up the heat a bit.' He opened the door and they went in.

In the back room, Chief Ravenclaw and Sooleawa were in the middle of a heated discussion. The Chief seemed startled when the door opened. 'Detectives,' he said. 'How's young Sammy doing? I hope he's starting to make a recovery.' He walked towards them out of the back room, Sooleawa by his side. 'We've been so worried that we were going to lose another one of our youth.'

'Fortunately, it seems like he's going to make a full recovery,' Millar said. 'May end up with a scar on his head, but it'll give him a good story to tell later on.'

'That's good to hear,' the Chief said. 'Was he able to talk while you were there?'

'He was,' Millar said warily. 'He talked quite a bit, actually.'

'Oh, really,' the Chief said. 'And what did he have to say?' His voice was calm, but his hands were fidgeting at his sides. Sooleawa seemed to notice, and reached over to hold his hand, interlacing her fingers with his.

'Just told us what he remembers from the other night,' Millar said. 'Rather interesting conversation.' The Chief stared at Millar, as though he was trying to read his thoughts. Neither man was giving up anything. 'Do you know where Travis is?'

'Travis? Why?' the Chief asked.

'Just have a couple of questions for him is all,' Millar said. 'Do you know where we can find him?'

'I haven't seen him yet today,' the Chief said. 'Have you?' he asked, turning to Sooleawa.

'No, I haven't seen him since yesterday,' Sooleawa said. She dropped the Chief's hand and strode over to the window. 'But he should be around. Maybe he's out having a smoke or walking his dog.' She made a show of looking out the window and down the street.

'Right,' said Millar. 'Chief Ravenclaw, I have a question for you.'

'Go ahead,' the Chief said, crossing his arms in front of his body and leaning against Travis's desk.

'The note that was found on Sammy. How did you know what it said?' Millar asked. Grant watched the Chief's expression closely. It never wavered.

'Like I said before, Sooleawa mentioned it when she called me from the hospital,' the Chief replied. 'Why?'

'Well, thing is,' Millar started. 'Mrs. Greycrow said she never showed anyone the note. So, how is it possible you knew what was in it?' he asked Sooleawa.

'She's obviously mistaken,' Sooleawa said, wheeling around. 'Poor woman had just seen her son, her youngest child, brought into a hospital, clinging to life. I've been there. I know how she was feeling. She obviously wasn't in the right frame of mind and just forgot showing me the note.'

'She seemed pretty sure, though,' Millar said.

'Well, I don't know what to tell you,' said Sooleawa firmly. 'I know what I saw and I definitely told Mac about it on the phone.'

'There you have it,' the Chief said, still stone faced. 'Sooleawa saw the note and let me know what it said. Unless you have any other questions, I have things I need to take care of. The community still has to plan the funeral for Jonny.'

Millar looked at Penner who shrugged. 'No, I think that's all for now,' Millar said. 'If you see Travis, let him know we want to talk to him.'

'Will do, Detective,' the Chief said. He seemed to visibly relax. 'Again, thanks to the three of you for helping with Sammy. Our community is forever grateful. We were very lucky that you were here. I feel like you were sent by one of the ancestors.'

'It's been our pleasure.' Millar turned to head towards the door, following behind Grant and Penner. As Grant reached out for the knob, the door flew open, almost hitting him in the face.

'You guys have to come quick!' Barry cried, bursting into the room. 'It's Travis. He's dead!'

'What are you talking about?' Grant asked, putting his hand on Barry's shoulder. 'Where is he?'

'In the woods,' Barry said, catching his breath. 'Looks like he shot himself!'

Millar turned to look at the Chief, who was looking at Sooleawa. 'Not another suicide,' the Chief said. 'You better go and investigate.'

'Why do I feel like you already knew about this?' Millar asked, taking a step towards the Chief.

'I'd be careful what you say, Detective. Slander is very serious,' the Chief said, drawing out the words. 'Remember, you're a guest here and have no jurisdiction whatsoever. Keep it up and I'll have you removed from our community. Now go, tend to Travis. Barry can use your help, I'm sure.'

'I'll be back for you,' Millar said. 'Mark my words.'

'Mark my words?' Chief Ravenclaw repeated in a mocking tone. 'Detective, do you know what I did before I returned to the reserve to become Chief? I was a lawyer. A defence lawyer.

And a good one, too. I know my rights and how the system works. Just keep that in mind. You don't want to go around making unfounded accusations about me or any of my people.'

'Millar, let's go,' Penner said, grabbing Millar's shoulder and pulling him towards the door. 'We'll figure this all out.'

Millar glared at the Chief, who returned the look, a shadow of a smirk playing on his lips. Millar turned and followed Penner out the door, hustling to catch up with Grant and Barry. 'That bastard. He's got something to do with this, I'm sure. And either his wife's covering for him or she's in on it, too.'

'We don't know that for sure,' Penner said.

'Pretty obvious though, isn't it?' Millar said. 'He has to be involved.'

'Maybe so, but don't go pushing him too far,' Penner said. 'If he kicks us out of here now, we'll never be able to solve this. He's right—we're guests and have no power here. We can't go accusing him of anything without more proof. And right now, we really have nothing.'

'Fine,' Millar said. 'But I'm going to make him pay for this before we're done.'

'In due time,' Penner said. 'Come on. Where is he, Barry?'

'Follow me,' Barry said, leading them off towards the woods. If he was surprised by their conversation about the Chief's potential involvement, he didn't let it show.

'Were you the one that found him?' Grant asked as they ran along.

'Yup,' Barry said, panting slightly. 'I was walking to town to get my daughter a gift when I came across him.'

'Sure he's dead?' Penner asked.

'Very,' Barry said. 'Gunshot wound to the side of his head. I checked for vitals, but it was pretty obvious that he was gone. I'd say he's been there for a few hours—probably happened overnight. Oh, and there was a small handgun laying beside him.'

'Did you just leave the gun there?' Millar asked.

'I did,' Barry said, shaking his head. 'Crap, I probably shouldn't have left it there. I wasn't thinking clearly—we don't get a whole lot of gun deaths out here. I tried to call you guys from the scene, but I didn't have any service.'

'Should be okay—I doubt anyone will touch it if they come across it,' Millar said. 'But we should hurry up, just in case.'

CHAPTER TWENTY-THREE

'Do you know the coroner's number?' Grant asked, holding an arm up to ward off branches as he jogged through the woods behind Barry. 'We should probably get him out here right away.'

'It's back in the office,' Barry said, stopping suddenly. 'Do you want to go call, or should I?'

'If you know where it is, probably be easier for you to go back and call,' Grant said. 'Is Travis easy enough to find?'

'Yeah, just keep going down this path,' Barry said pointed ahead of them. 'He'll be a couple hundred yards ahead, just on your right. I'll go back to the station and make the call, then I'll meet you at the scene,' he said, turning around and running back for the second time that morning

'Perfect. See you soon,' Grant called after him, continuing down the path at a quick pace.

'Man, it's been a while since I ran, I guess,' Millar said, panting loudly. 'Crazy how fast you lose it when you don't keep it up.'

'Come on, old man. You can do it,' Penner said, running past Millar, leaping over the occasional root sticking up from the path. 'There he is,' she said, slowing to a stop. Travis's lifeless body was slumped over at the base of a large oak tree.

'Definitely looks dead.' She approached the body and reached down to feel for a pulse on his wrist. 'Cold, just like Barry said.' She looked at his face. His lips were an eerie shade of grey and a river of blood had dried down the side of his cheek. It almost looked like he was made up for Hallowe'en.

'Definitely a gunshot wound to his left temple,' Millar said, leaning over to have a better look. 'Blood's congealed, so I agree with Barry. He's probably been here a couple hours.' Laying on the ground, next to Travis's leg, was a small hand gun. 'Looks like a 22.'

'Is that normal?' Grant asked, pointing at the gun. 'I thought his muscles would have contracted when he died and the gun would still be in his hand.'

'Sometimes, but not always,' Millar explained. 'It really depends on what part of the brain was hit. Hit the right spot and every muscle instantly tightens up. You'd have a hard time getting the gun out if that had happened. But, other times, the muscles just go limp and the gun comes out from the force of the recoil.'

'Any blood splatter on his hand?' Penner asked, trying to have a look.

'Hard to tell,' Millar said, leaning down further to see Travis's hand. 'The way he's fallen over, I can't really see it properly. We'll have to wait for the coroner.'

'Don't suppose either of you have gloves, do you?' Penner asked. 'I don't want to handle the gun and contaminate any prints.'

'I don't,' Millar said, feeling around his pockets.

'Me neither, but I do have a handkerchief,' Grant said, pulling a white square of cloth out of his back pocket. 'Don't worry,' he said to Penner, seeing her expression as he passed it to her.

'I haven't used it,' he added.

'What are you, seventy?' Penner said, taking the handker-chief and holding it gingerly by the corner. 'Who your age carries one of these? And are you sure you haven't used it?'

'I'm sure. When I first joined the force, one of the old-timers told me to always carry one,' Grant said. 'You never know when you're going to need to pick something up. If you always have one with you, it doesn't matter if you don't have gloves,' he said with a smile.

Penner laid the cloth across her hand, reached down and picked up the gun. She tilted her head, looking at the gunshot wound and then down at the ground where she had retrieved the gun. 'Do you know if he was left handed?'

'You know, I'm not sure,' Grant said, trying to remember if he had ever seen Travis writing. 'Maybe. To be honest, I never noticed either way. I think that if I had seen him writing with his left hand, I would have noticed. Lefties kind of jump out at you where you don't see it all the time.'

'Well, he was shot in the left temple—if he was right handed, I very much doubt that he shot himself,' Millar observed. 'No one would use their wrong hand to shoot. And you wouldn't reach around your head, either. We'll have to ask Barry. He might know.'

'So, you're saying he didn't shoot himself?' Penner asked Millar, looking back down at the body.

'I'm just saying it's a possibility,' Millar said. 'We don't know anything for sure at this point. We'll have to wait for the coroner to have a look at the wound, see if it's the right angle to be self-inflicted. And we need to find out if he was left handed or not, but...to be honest,' Millar sighed. 'I don't think I'd be surprised if he said it wasn't suicide. I honestly think the Chief is involved in all of this somehow.'

'Okay,' Penner said, motioning at Millar while still holding the gun at her side, 'Let's just say that the Chief is involved. And that's a big if right now. But let's say he is. Why kill Travis?'

'What do you mean?' Millar asked.

'Well, we decided Travis couldn't have killed Jonny and made it look like a suicide by himself,' Penner said. 'We figured two people had to be involved, right?'

'Right, so Travis and the Chief.'

'But, if they were in on it together, why would Chief Ravenclaw kill his partner in crime?' Penner asked.

'Maybe the Chief was worried Travis would crack and talk to us or to Barry once the pressure was on,' Millar suggested.

'Or, maybe he was pissed that Travis left Sammy alive,' Grant spoke up.

'You know, that's one thing that I don't get with this,' Penner said thoughtfully. 'Assuming we're correct, then Travis knew he was going to have to carry out the attack on Sammy by himself—the Chief was too busy with the feast. He knew he couldn't pick Sammy up by himself to hang him from the tree, so he pre-cut the branch. Or, maybe he cut it after Sammy was unconscious. Either way, he thought ahead and planned it so that it would look like the branch broke and that's why Sammy was on the ground,' Penner continued. 'But, why didn't he make sure he was dead? Seems pretty stupid, really. Go to all that trouble and then leave him alive.'

'Maybe he got spooked before he could finish the job?' Millar said. 'Remember the bear track we found at the scene? Who knows? What if the bear came around to investigate—scared Travis and he took off?'

'Makes sense to me,' Penner nodded. 'If I was out here at night, probably already nervous about being caught, and then heard a bear—I'd be gone like a shot, no matter what I was doing.'

'Maybe it was Jonny,' a voice said from behind them, causing Millar to jump.

'Barry, you scared the crap out of me,' Millar said. 'Did you say maybe it was Jonny?'

'Yeah, I heard what you were saying about the bear,' Barry said. 'Jonny's last name was Two Bears, right? Maybe he sent one of his relatives to help out his best friend.'

Millar scoffed, but then realized Barry wasn't making a joke. 'You really believe that?'

'Sure,' Barry said. 'He was a member of the Bear Clan, so he had a connection with the bears in the woods. If he wanted to help his friend, what better way than to send a bear.'

'Really?' Millar said, unconvinced.

'Detective, you have to realize we have a greater connection with the animal and spirit world than…well, than you. No offence,' Barry added. 'All living beings are connected. We believe that even if you're gone from this world, you can still interact with the living beings. Why else would a bear just happen by? Have you seen or heard a bear since you got here?'

'No, but…' Millar said.

'Neither have I,' Barry said. 'In fact, I've lived here all my life, and I have never seen a bear in these woods. But when one was needed, it just happened to show up. I wouldn't call that a coincidence.'

Penner had been listening intently to Barry and turned to smile at Millar. She liked to keep any open mind, but she knew he would struggle with this explanation. Millar didn't know what to say, so he moved on. 'So, that might explain what happened to Sammy. And if it looked like Sammy might recover, that would explain why the Chief seemed more concerned than relieved that we found him. Or, maybe I'm reading too much into his behaviour. We're pretty sure Travis was responsible, but who was helping him?'

'Did you just look at me?' Barry said to Millar.

'What? No. Well, yes I looked at you, but not because I think you had anything to do with this,' Millar said. 'I was hoping you might have some ideas, that's all.'

'Yeah, right,' Barry said, shaking his head.

'I'm serious. Grant, help me out here.'

'I don't know,' said Grant. 'The way that you swung around and said 'who was helping him'—kind of looked like you were accusing him.'

'You're a jerk, you know that?' Millar said.

'I'm learning from Penner,' Grant said.

'Don't involve me. I'm just minding my own business here,' said Penner. 'So, Barry, got any thoughts?'

'You know, I feel like it could be anyone and no one,' Barry said. 'The Chief's pretty well liked on the reserve. If someone thought this would help him get the funding he needs to change things for the better...'

'They'd be willing to kill for him?' Penner asked. 'That seems pretty far-fetched.'

'Yeah, maybe not kill,' Barry said. 'When you say it out loud, it does sound ridiculous. Let me think. You might kill for your family. And he and his nephew are really close.'

'The carver who did the masks in the great hall?' Penner asked.

'That's the one,' Barry said. 'But, he drove to Ottawa after the feast last night. He had a meeting sometime today with a client about doing a custom carving. As far as I know, he still isn't back yet.'

'So we can rule him out then,' Penner said. 'Anyone else?'

'You know, I can't really see anyone here killing for anyone, not even the Chief,' Barry said. 'Heck, I'm having trouble seeing the Chief killing someone. Are you guys sure he's involved?'

'Sure? No,' Grant said. 'Almost sure? Unfortunately, yes. What about Sooleawa?'

'What? Are you kidding?' Barry asked in disbelief.

'Well, she lied about the note to cover for him,' Grant said. 'They were having a pretty intense talk in the band office this morning. I don't know, maybe she could be involved.'

'Problem is, we have absolutely no evidence implicating either of them,' Millar said. 'Or anyone, for that matter. We should get this gun dusted for prints. I guess we never got the note found on Sammy dusted, eh?'

'No, unfortunately not,' Penner said. 'By the time I got to the hospital, Mrs. Greycrow had been given the note by the paramedics. She had handled it so much, there was no way we would have found any prints other than hers.'

'So, anything else we can look at?' Millar asked.

'Barry, do you know if Travis was left handed?' Grant asked.

'Left handed? I don't think so,' Barry said, trying to picture Travis doing things. 'Pretty sure he always struck his matches with his right hand. Not sure about when he wrote, though. I know I've seen him sign stuff. No, I think he used his right hand.'

'We're going to have to find out for sure. Any thoughts?' Penner asked.

'There are probably a couple of videos of him at some of the ceremonial signings,' Barry offered. 'Any time the band has to enact anything new, both the Chief and the band manager have to sign the official documents. I know the last several signings have been filmed for social media, so there should be video on the computer back at the band office.'

'So, what are we going to do? Just go log onto the computer and start looking at the files?' Millar said. 'That would end up being inadmissible in court—could be considered an illegal search.'

'True—if it was one of us that did it,' Grant said. 'But what if someone who had a legitimate reason to log onto the computer just happened on the file.' He looked over at Barry.

'Me?' Barry said. 'I guess I could find an excuse to use the computer in there instead of in the police station. I could unplug a couple of things so the computer at the station doesn't work.'

'Perfect. So, I think we should start there. I have to head back to Ottawa today, so I can bring the gun and get it checked for prints,' Penner said. 'Speaking of the gun, do you know for sure if this is Travis's?' she asked, showing it to Barry.

'Not for sure,' Barry said, looking at the gun in the handkerchief. 'I think I remember him talking about owning a gun, but I never saw it.'

'Well, I'll get the serial number run while I'm at it,' Penner said. 'Should be in the system registered to whoever bought it.'

'Do you know when the coroner's supposed to show up?' Grant asked Barry.

'They said it would be a couple of hours. Apparently they found the bodies of an elderly couple in town yesterday. They didn't give me any details, but Dr. Dickinson was doing the autopsy when I called it in. Once he's done, he's going to head out here.'

'Well, no point in all of us hanging out here,' Grant said. 'But someone has to keep watch over the body. Do you want to stay, or should I?' he asked Millar.

'Well, I do kind of outrank you—so, technically, shouldn't you stay?' Millar said to Grant.

'True, but didn't the Captain say you were reporting to me out here?' Grant said with a grin.

'Well, yeah. But...' sputtered Millar, unable to come up with a rebuttal.

'Tell you what. How about Rock, Paper, Scissors to decide,' Grant said, glancing over at Penner.

'Alright, seems fair. On three,' Millar said. 'One, two, three!' Millar laid his hand out flat like a sheet of paper. Grant held two fingers splayed apart like a pair of scissors.

'Scissors beat paper. Guess you're staying with the body,' Grant said, winking at Penner. She had once mentioned to him that Millar always chose paper.

'Crap,' Millar said. 'Fine. Just try to hurry back. And bring a coffee. And something to eat, would ya? Have a safe drive home,' he said to Penner, giving her a hug.

'Will do,' Penner said. 'I'll let you guys know as soon as I find out anything.'

Millar watched as they walked back down the trail towards the reserve. He looked around for somewhere to sit. 'It's going to be a long couple of hours.'

CHAPTER TWENTY-FOUR

'So, do you think I should stop into the band office and say good-bye to the Chief and Sooleawa?' Penner asked as they emerged from the woods. 'Or would that be weird? Do you extend pleasantries to someone you suspect may be involved in murder?'

'Good question,' Barry said.

'It's up to you, I guess,' said Grant. 'It might be a good idea. Make him think we don't suspect him of anything. Huh, guess we have cell service here,' he said, pulling his ringing phone from his pocket. 'Hello?'

'Constable Grant?'

'Oh, hi, Captain,' Grant said, looking at Penner. 'Sorry, sir. There's a lot of static on the line—service isn't that good here.'

'I'll keep this short. I just received the results of your sergeant's exam.'

'Really? Already? I didn't expect that to come in for another week. So, do I want to know?'

'Well, I thi...' the call suddenly cut out.

'Are you kidding me?' Grant said, looking at his phone.

'What's wrong?' asked Penner. 'Why's the Captain calling?'

'He was just about to tell me how I did on the sergeant's exam and I lost the signal. And, of course, now I've got no service again. I'll head over to my room and give him a call back.'

'I didn't know you were writing the exam,' Penner said. 'That's great! You should have told me—I could have helped you study.'

'I didn't want to make it too public—in case I tanked horribly,' Grant said, checking his phone again to see if he had cell service.

'How'd you think you did?' Penner asked as they walked up to the band office.

'Don't really know, to be honest,' Grant said. 'I felt good during it, but started second guessing everything as soon as I was done. Hopefully I can get back in touch with the Captain and I'll let you know soon. Make sure you don't leave before I get a chance to say good-bye.'

'No worries. I still have to grab my stuff out of the room,' Penner said, opening the door to the office and letting Barry walk in ahead of her. 'I'll stop by your place on the way.'

'Sounds good,' Grant said, hurrying off to make his phone call.

'Barry. Detective Penner,' Chief Ravenclaw greeted them from behind his desk. 'I didn't expect you back so soon.'

'Millar's staying with Travis's body until the coroner arrives. But I have to head back to Ottawa today, so I just wanted to stop in and say my good-byes,' Penner said.

'Well, I'm glad you were able to come out and be our guest for a couple of days.' The Chief rose from his chair, and walked over to shake Penner's hand. 'I'm just so sorry you had to be here during these troubling times.'

'Troubling times?' Penner couldn't help herself. 'That's what you're going to call them?'

'Well, what else would you call them, Detective?' the Chief asked. 'Two people are dead because of Travis's actions—I'd say that's pretty troubling, wouldn't you? I can't believe your government would send a person like that to work here. Someone so uncaring that he would take the life of a child because he was unable to do his job properly. And then take his own life before he could be tried for his crimes.'

'Whoah. Hold up,' Penner said, looking at the Chief in confusion. 'What makes you say Travis was involved?'

'That's what you're thinking, isn't it, Detective? That's why you and Detective Millar wanted to talk to him,' the Chief replied evenly. 'Besides, I found Travis's suicide note saved on the computer. Seems to me like he confessed to killing Jonny and trying to kill Sammy.'

'Suicide note?' Penner said. 'What did it say? Can I see it?'

'Here,' the Chief said, handing Penner a sheet of paper. 'I printed off a copy. I assumed you would want to see it.'

Penner stared at the Chief in disbelief and took the note. She read it once, silently, and then again out loud.

'To my family and friends, I am terribly sorry for what I have done. I was only trying to do the best for this wonderful community, but, once again, I failed. I was never able to get the government funding required to fix the water issues here on the reserve. If this didn't get the government's attention, then I truly believe nothing I could do ever would. I can't live with the feeling of failure. Every thing I did, I did alone. Travis.'

'Sounds like a confession to me,' the Chief said. 'Glad I was on the computer this morning and came across it. Lucky, really.'

'Yeah, real lucky.' Penner couldn't keep the sarcasm from her voice.

'Speaking of the computer,' Barry said. 'Mind if I use it for a minute? The one in the station is acting up.' He suddenly noticed an empty space on the desk where the computer usually sat.

'Of course—if it was here, but, unfortunately, it isn't,' the Chief said, still looking at Penner.

'Not here? Where is it?' Barry asked.

'When I was working this morning, I came across a virus or something,' the Chief said, his facial expression unchanging. 'A rather disturbing file. Sooleawa brought it in to get the hard drive replaced. Due to the sensitive material on the drive, they're going to make sure to have it destroyed.'

'So, the original file containing Travis's confession is going to be destroyed. That's pretty convenient,' Penner said, looking over at Barry.

'I'd say it's more of an inconvenience, really,' the Chief said, shrugging. 'I really needed the computer to organize my next press conference. Guess I'm going to have to do it the old-fashioned way.'

'You're really a piece of work, aren't you?' Penner said, putting her hands on her hips.

'I don't know what you mean, Detective,' the Chief said. 'As I've said before, I'm just doing what I need to do to make sure my people have everything they need and deserve. And, as a matter of fact, it's working. This morning, after you left, I got a call from the Deputy Minister of Indigenous and Northern Affairs. Apparently one of her assistants saw the press conference on the news last night. She couldn't believe that the conditions here were so bad that our youth were killing themselves. She called it a mental health emergency and a crisis of human rights. She's sending out a team of engineers next week to see what needs to be done. She was very apologetic for letting the situation go on for so long. So in the end, it all worked out for the best.'

'Really. For the best?' Penner said, getting furious. 'Two people are dead, and you say it's for the best! And, no, they didn't kill themselves!'

'Semantics,' Chief Ravenclaw replied. 'All that matters is we're going to be getting the fresh, clean water we deserve. We've been treated as second class citizens for far too long.'

'Unbelievable!' raged Penner. 'We know Travis didn't work alone in killing Jonny. Nor did he kill himself. And we have a very good idea who else was involved.'

'Oh really, Detective?' The Chief's voice lowered and it felt like the temperature in the office dropped several degrees. He took a step closer to Penner, looking down at her. Barry took a step backwards, but Penner stood her ground. 'I'd advise you to tread carefully, Detective Penner. Didn't you say Travis shot himself, Barry? Sounds to me like he killed himself.'

'You're not going to get away with this,' Penner warned him.

'Detective, you and I both know you have absolutely no evidence to prove that anyone other than Travis was involved,' the Chief said. 'And, you can't even prove that he was. Without the note he wrote—that I found and helpfully gave to you—you have nothing. So, I'm very sure these cases are closed and done with.'

'Once they do an autopsy, I'm sure they'll find something,'

'Oh, I almost forgot to tell you,' the Chief said, walking over to Travis's desk under the window. 'I called and told the coroner not to bother coming out. When I was going through the computer, I found this,' he said, handing Penner some papers stapled together. 'It's a copy of Travis's will.

Seems like he didn't want an autopsy—against his religion or something—and he wanted to be buried on our land in a traditional manner, as quickly as possible after his death.'

'I'll get a warrant to stop you.'

'You can try,' the Chief challenged. 'But, just remember, you have zero evidence and zero jurisdiction here. Technically you are just a common citizen, with no greater power than anyone else walking the streets. Your badge means nothing here. And since Travis died on tribal land, we can handle this as he wanted. We strongly believe in respecting an individual's wishes. If he wanted to be buried in a traditional manner, without an autopsy, then that's what will be done.'

'How do you know he died on tribal land?' Penner asked, grasping at straws, hoping that he would say something, anything, incriminating.

'Barry said he found him in the woods,' the Chief answered, walking back over to Penner. 'That's our land. Barry, I think it's time for our guests to leave and head back to the city where they belong. Do me a favour and go get Detective Millar. No point in him waiting in the woods any longer. I'll make some calls to have Travis's body brought back for burying.' He paused before continuing, 'Oh, and you can let Constable Grant know that we won't be needing his services out here anymore. We'll find someone else to help out at the drop-in centre.'

Barry looked back and forth between Chief Ravenclaw and Penner. His head dropped. 'Sorry,' he said under his breath to Penner as he stepped outside to retrieve Millar from the woods.

'I don't know how you can live with what you've done here,' Penner said softly, looking the Chief in the eyes. 'Don't you have any morals?'

'You're going to talk to me about morals?' the Chief asked, returning her look with venom. 'After what your people have done to us for hundreds of years? How can you live with yourself, knowing you're living on stolen land, forcing us, the original residents, to live in slum-like conditions? You take what you want, destroying the land, with no thoughts of the consequences.' The Chief snorted with contempt. 'Get off your high horse, Detective, you're just as bad as I am. But at least I'm trying to make a difference. Now, if you don't mind…get off of our land,' he said, walking past Penner and holding the door open.

For once, Penner was at a loss for words. After a few seconds, she walked out through the door, barely clearing the step before the Chief slammed it behind her.

CHAPTER TWENTY-FIVE

Penner stood outside, trembling with fury and helplessness. She tried to think if there was anything they were missing. She still had the gun to be tested—maybe they could get a print off of it. Or maybe off of the note found in Sammy's pocket. She knew it was a long shot, but that was all they had. One of them would have to stop by the hospital to get it from Mrs. Greycrow. 'I should have taken the note as soon as I saw it,' she thought to herself. 'Tried to keep it from being handled too much.' She knew there was no point in regretting what couldn't be changed, but still—she hated to think that she may have let a piece of evidence get away. She started walking back to Grant's place. She had to let him know that they had to leave. Let him know that she had kind of just got him fired from his side hustle. Sure, it was all volunteer time, but still—it was something he enjoyed. She walked past the coffee shop and was assaulted by the smell of roasting coffee beans. 'Oh, I'm going to miss this place,' she thought. Walking up the wooden stairs, she opened Grant's door without knocking.

'Hey, Detective.' Grant looked up from where he sat on the lumpy sofa. 'All packed and ready to go?'

'Um, no, not yet,' said Penner..

'Is something wrong?'

'Well…I kind of had it out with the Chief.'

'Really?' Grant said, surprised. 'I thought you were just going to say good-bye. Was Barry able to get onto the computer?'

'No,' Penner said, sitting down. 'Sooleawa took the computer into town to have the hard drive destroyed and replaced. Said they found a virus. Oh, and the Chief said he found this on the computer.' She took the printed copy of Travis's confession out of her pocket and passed it to Grant. 'Take a read. Nice little work of fiction. But again, I can't prove who wrote it. Or what it really means. Argh.' Penner put her head in her hands. 'This whole computer virus thing. I guarantee he was trying to get rid of evidence.'

Grant looked up from reading the note. 'Think we can get to town before it's worked on?' he asked.

'Wouldn't do any good. We don't have a warrant, so we can't seize the computer,' Penner said, her head still in her hands. 'And, with the little we have to go on, we wouldn't get a warrant.'

'There's gotta be something we can do?' Grant said, more as a question than a statement.

'If there is, I don't know what,' said Penner, slumping down in her chair in defeat. The door opened again and Millar walked in, followed closely by Barry.

'So, you got us kicked out of town, eh?' Millar said. Grant looked at him, then to Penner.

'Yeah,' said Penner. 'Sorry, Grant. Looks like your services here are no longer required. Chief Ravenclaw wants the three of us to leave the reserve. Doubt we'll be allowed back any time soon.'

'Really?' Grant said with disbelief. 'I didn't expect that. So, that's it then?'

Penner sighed. 'I think so. Unless we find a print on the gun or Sammy's note, I don't know what else we can do. The Chief is too smart to say anything to incriminate himself, and you can bet he told Sooleawa not to talk to anyone.'

'I can ask around the reserve—keep it on the down low. Just see if anyone has any info,' Barry offered. 'What about getting a warrant for searching the band office? Maybe the Chief left something there?'

'I don't think we would get one,' Penner said. 'We don't have enough evidence against the Chief.'

'No, but we have a note supposedly written by Travis, right? If a judge sees that, it's a confession that he killed Jonny. And Travis wasn't a member of the band—he was a Federal employee. We may be able to get a warrant, just to verify that it was him.'

Penner's face lit up. 'And if we can get that, then it could include the computer, right? We might even be able to check the timestamp on when the supposed suicide note was written. Maybe we could prove that it would have been impossible for Travis to have written it. Barry, you're a genius! How quickly can we get a warrant out here, do you think? I have no idea when Sooleawa took the computer to town, so it may already be too late.'

'I'll go right now, see what I can do,' Barry said. 'With any luck, I'll get it signed off on within the hour.'

'You have Grant's number?' Millar asked, as Barry was heading out the door.

'I do. I'll give you a call as soon as I can,' Barry said. 'Stay out of the woods, so you have a signal.'

CHAPTER TWENTY-FIVE

'Do you know where she took the computer?' Grant asked.

'All I know is she took it to town,' Penner replied. 'I'm guessing to an electronics repair shop, but I didn't get a name.'

'I'll go see if Barry knows where she may have taken it. I should be able to catch him before he drives away,' Grant said, sprinting out the door.

'I don't think we have a snowball's chance in hell of nailing him,' Millar said, stretching out his legs and crossing his ankles.

'Me, neither. But, we've gotta try, right?' Penner said. 'If he gets away with this, what's to stop him from killing someone else the next time he wants to get attention for a cause?'

'Well, let's hope Barry can convince the judge we have a good reason to search the band office,' Millar said, turning his head as the door opened again.

'So, there's a particular shop in town where the band has an account,' Grant said, panting slightly. 'Tang's Electronics. Maybe we should go straight there. See if we can stall them from working on the computer—if it's not already too late.'

'Sounds like the best plan we have,' said Penner.

'Well, it's the only plan we have, so that makes it the best,' Millar said, standing up. 'The quicker we get there, the better. I'll drive.'

'If anyone's going to get us there quick, it's you,' Penner said, as they headed out the door. 'Afterwards, we should stop by the hospital and get the note from Mrs. Greycrow. I want to dust that to an inch of its life, and hope we find something.'

***

'Alright, so I think it should be just up here,' Grant said, studying a map on his phone from the back of Millar's car.

'Turn right on the next street.'

Millar turned the corner, checking the addresses on the facades of the buildings. 'Should be on your side,' he said to Penner.

'There it is,' Penner said. 'Pull up just there.'

Millar pulled up alongside the curb, just past Tang's Electronics. 'Is that Sooleawa?' he asked, looking in his rearview mirror as he backed into the parking spot.

Grant turned to look out the back window. 'Shit, it is,' he said. 'And she's carrying the computer. We're too late!' Sooleawa walked to her car, carrying the computer tower. She put it on the ground while she fumbled with her keys and opened the back door. After putting the computer on the back seat, she closed the door and walked around to the driver's side. Without a second glance, she got in and drove off.

'Maybe not,' Penner said. 'The Chief said she was coming in to get the hard drive replaced and to have the old one destroyed. She may have had the new hard drive installed, but the old one may still be there, waiting to be destroyed.'

'I guess we're due to catch a break on this case soon,' Grant said. 'Let's go see what they have to say,' he said, unbuckling his seatbelt and stepping out of the car.

Grant held the door to the electronics store open for Penner and Millar. Computers and other types of electronic material were piled along the perimeter walls. Some of the equipment stacks looked like they could topple over with the slightest bump.

'Hello? Can I help you?' an elderly Asian man asked, shuffling out of a back room.

'Um, yes, hopefully,' Penner said, pulling her badge out of her pocket. 'Are you Mr. Tang?' He nodded, and Penner continued, 'Mr. Tang, one of your customers just left—we believe you replaced the hard drive in her computer. Have you started working on the old hard drive, yet?'

Mr. Tang reached down for a pair of glasses that hung around his neck from a gold chain. He put them on and moved closer to examine Penner's badge. 'Ottawa Police? What is Ottawa Police doing here?'

'We're investigating a case,' Penner said. 'Can you tell us if you've started working on the hard drive?'

'This is not Ottawa,' Mr. Tang said, shaking his head. 'I can't help you.'

'We are in the process of getting a warrant,' said Millar.

Mr. Tang slowly turned to look at Millar. 'Do you have it now?'

'No, I said we're getting it,' Millar said.

'Then I can't help you. Now, if you will excuse me, I have work to do,' Mr. Tang said, turning to go back into the back room.

'If you start working on the hard drive before we're back, you can be charged with tampering with evidence,' Penner called out in desperation.

'No, I can't,' Mr. Tang called back. 'Without a warrant, it's not evidence yet. I have work to do.'

Penner thought for a second. 'When we get the warrant, it will just be for a hard drive,' she said, looking around the store interior. 'Seems like you have a lot of hard drives here. Probably have to take them all with us to make sure we have the right one.'

Mr. Tang slowly turned around. 'That's not how warrants work. You can only take what is outlined in the paperwork,' he said, not sounding as confident as he had before.

'Maybe. Maybe not,' Penner said. 'But it's up to you if you want to take that chance. If we have to take every computer out of here, if could take us months and months to analyze them before we could return them. How do you think your customers will like that?'

'Are all Ottawa Police dirty like you?' Mr. Tang asked, looking at Penner with barely concealed disgust.

'I prefer resourceful.'

'I think you're bluffing.'

'It's up to you,' said Penner, motioning to Millar and Grant to walk out of the store. 'Take your chances, if you want. We'll be back, either to take one, untouched hard drive, or everything in your shop. Your choice.'

They walked out of the store, leaving the man to contemplate his next move.

'Didn't see that coming,' Grant said. 'You always seem so nice.'

'I thought I was pretty nice,' Penner said. 'There's a difference between being not-so-nice and being intimidating.'

'And a fine line between the two,' Millar said. 'Right, might as well head to the hospital—see if we can get the note back.' He checked his watch. 'Doubt Barry will have the warrant any time too soon.'

***

On the drive over to the hospital, Grant's phone rang. 'Hello? Barry, so what's the word? He will? That's awesome! How long? Okay, good. Give me a call when you have it in hand. We're on our way to the hospital to pick up the note from Mrs. Greycrow. We'll want to get to the electronics shop before going back to the band office—no guarantee the shop owner's going to hold off on destroying the hard drive. Perfect, talk to you soon.' Grant hung up.

'He got it?' Penner asked, excitedly.

'Not yet, but the judge has agreed. Said it would be good to make sure Travis was actually the one involved,' Grant said. 'Should have everything signed off in the next fifteen minutes, or so.'

'Maybe we have a bit of luck working with us after all,' Millar said, pulling into the hospital parking lot. 'Why don't you run in, grab the note. I'll just circle around until you're back out,' he said to Penner, pulling up by the main door.

'I'll be quick,' Penner said, hopping out of the car. She walked through the main lobby of the hospital and turned down the hallway towards Sammy's room. She came to an abrupt halt. 'What are you doing here?' she asked, seeing Chief Ravenclaw walking towards her.

'I came to see how our young lad was doing,' the Chief said, walking up to Penner. 'I thought you had gone back to where you belong.'

'You're not getting rid of us that easily,' Penner replied. 'Not by a long shot. I'm going to find something on you. You're not that slick. You had to have made a mistake somewhere along the way.'

'A mistake?' the Chief scoffed. 'Not likely. Ravens don't make mistakes. Have you ever watched a raven in the woods? When they have excess food, they'll hide what they don't need until later. If they see they're being watched, they'll pretend to hide the food in one place, then actually hide it somewhere else. They leave no trace, leave no clues.'

'Aren't they also seen as inherently evil, too?' Penner said.

'Sounds about right.'

'Oh, Detective Penner. And I thought we were going to be friends when you first arrived,' the Chief said, walking past her. 'A shame, really. You could have been a good ally to have back in Ottawa.'

'Yeah, dream on,' Penner said, watching the Chief walk towards the exit. She hurried on towards Sammy's room. When she got there, Sammy was standing up beside the bed and his mom was helping him put on his shirt. 'Well, look at you,' she said. 'Good to see you out of bed. Heading home soon?'

'Yup,' Sammy said. 'Doctor just came in—said I could go home today.'

'As long as he promises not to scratch the stiches and to rest,' added Mrs. Greycrow.

'And he agreed?' Penner asked.

'Of course,' Sammy said, and with a sly look added, 'Well, I agreed not to let mom catch me scratching. But, I can't be watched all the time, can I?'

'What am I to do with him, eh?' Mrs. Greycrow said to Penner. 'It was much easier when he was a baby. Just wrap him up in a swaddle so he couldn't move.'

Penner laughed. 'Could try that now, I guess. Would need a big swaddle, though. Glad you're feeling better,' she said to Sammy. 'Mrs. Greycrow, can I get the note that was in Sammy's pocket? We want to run some tests on it.'

'I don't have it anymore,' said Mrs. Greycrow, her eyes growing instantly worried.

'What do you mean? What happened to it?' asked Penner.

'I gave it to Chief Ravenclaw,' Mrs. Greycrow explained. 'He said he was going to give it to Barry. Said he was going to help figure out what really happened.'

'The Chief? The Chief has the note?' Penner asked. 'I've gotta go,' she said, running out of the room and into the hall.

CHAPTER TWENTY-SIX

'That bastard,' Penner thought, running through the front doors of the hospital. She stepped out into the sunlight and frantically searched for the Chief. He had a few minutes' head-start on her, but he couldn't have gotten far. 'Where is he?' she cried. She started running through the parking lot, looking for the Chief's SUV. A car honked its horn behind her and, as she looked over her shoulder, she saw that it was Millar.

'What's going on? You look like a crazy woman,' Millar said as Penner got into the car.

'Did you see the Chief?' Penner asked, still scanning the parking lot.

'The Chief? No, why?' Millar asked. 'Is he here?'

'He was,' Penner said. 'Mrs. Greycrow gave him the note. He told her he was going to get Barry to test it.'

'You've got to be kidding.' Grant pounded his seat in frustration. 'Just when I thought we were catching a break. Now what?'

'I guess we wait for Barry to get the warrant,' Penner said. 'When's he supposed to call?'

'Soon,' Grant said. 'Why don't we head back towards the electronics shop. Grab a coffee in the neighbourhood and wait. That way we'll be ready to roll as soon as we hear from Barry.'

'Sounds good to me,' Penner said. 'I can't believe the Chief got the note!'

'We'll find something on him,' Grant said. 'Well, I hope so, anyways.'

'Me, too, but I have my doubts,' Millar said, taking a right turn onto the main street. 'It's seeming less and less likely. He was one step ahead of us on the computer, on the note. What else is he ahead of us on?'

'I think our best bet is the hard drive,' Penner said. 'Hopefully, we scared the store owner enough into thinking that we're going to take everything out of there that he leaves the drive alone. Time will tell, I guess. There's a coffee shop,' she pointed. 'Let's wait for Barry there.'

Millar pulled over and parked. The smell of fresh coffee wafted out the door of the coffee shop as Penner opened it. Walking in, they failed to notice the Chief's SUV drive down the street behind them.

***

'Hi. We'll get three coffees, please. Black,' Grant said to the girl behind the counter.

'For here or to go?'

'Make them to go, just in case,' Penner said from behind Grant.

'Six fifty, please,' the cashier said as another girl started pouring their coffees.

'Here's seven, thanks,' Grant said, passing the girl a five dollar bill and a toonie.

211

'There you go. Enjoy,' the cashier said, giving Grant back two quarters.

'Thanks,' Grant said, dropping the change in a tip cup. The other girl put the coffees on the counter. Grant passed a cup to Penner, a cup to Millar and then grabbed his own. They sat down at a table by the window and drank their coffees in tense silence.

'Finally,' Grant said, as his phone rang. 'Barry? Hey how's it going? You got it? Perfect! We'll meet you outside of Tang's. Later.' He hung up his phone. 'Alright, we're good to go. He should be here in five minutes.'

'I hope we're not too late,' Penner said.

'We'll find out soon enough. Let's go see,' Millar said, popping the lid on what was left in his to-go cup and standing up. Leaving the coffee shop, they turned left and walked down the block to the electronics shops. And then they waited.

'There he is,' Grant said, pointing down the street. Barry was walking along, paper in hand.

'Sorry, guys. Ended up taking a wrong turn,' Barry said, passing the search warrant to Millar. 'So, we're allowed to take any computer equipment dropped off that belongs to the band. Let's see what we can get.'

Penner opened the door of the shop and walked in. A little bell above her tinkled and the elderly man from earlier looked up from behind the counter. 'Ah, the dirty cops are back. And you brought a friend.'

'We have a warrant for any computer equipment that belongs to the band. That includes whatever was dropped off by Sooleawa Ravenclaw earlier, and anything dropped off by anyone else recently,' Penner said, handing the sheet of paper to Mr. Tang. He put on his glasses and read over the form, nodding his head.

'Okay. Here you go,' he said, pulling a computer hard drive out from under the counter. 'Figured you would be back,' he said, handing the drive to Penner. 'Do you want a bag? See, that's how you be nice.'

'Thank you,' Penner said, biting her tongue and taking the drive. 'No bag, thanks. Do you have anything else from the reserve?'

'No, nothing. This is the only thing they have dropped off in the last six months,' Mr. Tang said.

'Well, that's all we need then,' Penner said. 'Thanks for your co-operation. Let's go.'

The old man watched them leave and then went back to what he was working on. 'Alright, that was easy,' Grant said. 'So now we can go search the band office.'

'Well, not exactly,' Barry said, stopping on the sidewalk.

'What? Don't tell me the judge wouldn't give you a warrant for the office,' said Millar. 'I thought he was going to.'

'He did,' Barry said. 'But, while I was there, the Chief called. He filed a complaint against Penner and got a restraining order against the three of you. You're not actually allowed on the reserve.'

'That bastard!' Penner said. 'He really is one step ahead, isn't he?'

'What about our stuff?' Grant asked. 'I never cleaned out my room—I wasn't expecting to have to leave.'

'I did ask the judge about that,' Barry said. 'He's going to allow you back on the property next Wednesday. With a police escort, of course. If there's anything you need before then, I can go get it. So, either you come back next week or I can box up your stuff and meet you somewhere—it's your call.'

'With any luck, we'll be back before then with a warrant for his arrest,' Penner said.

'Oh, what about our cars,' Grant said. 'We took Millar's car today, but Penner's car and my car are still there.'

'You can follow me back and wait outside the reserve's property line,' Barry said. 'I'll bring your cars out to you.'

'What a pain,' said Penner. 'I'm disliking the Chief more and more.'

'So, are you still allowed to do a search of the band office?' Millar asked Barry.

'Yup. Got it right here in writing,' Barry said, holding up a second warrant.

'Well, that's good at least,' Penner said. 'Is there anyone that can help? I don't feel good about you executing the search on your own.'

'I contacted a guy from the city police. He's going to come out and back me up,' Barry said. 'He used to live on the reserve but moved off a couple years ago.'

'Perfect,' Penner said. 'As soon as we pick up our cars, we'll head back to Ottawa, get the hard drive processed and dust the gun for prints. If you find anything in your search, get in touch right away. We'll let you know if we turn up anything on our end.'

'Will do, Detective,' Barry said. 'If there's anything to be found, we'll find it.'

'Right, we'll follow you back to the reserve, then,' Millar said, as they walked back to his car.

'I can't believe he filed a restraining order against us,' Grant said. He looked at Penner. 'What did you say to him?'

'Nothing too bad, I don't think,' Penner said with a shrug. 'I may have implied that we thought he helped Travis kill Jonny.

And that he was probably responsible for killing Travis, too.'

'So, normal stuff, then,' Grant said, getting into Millar's car.

'I couldn't help it. He was so smug. I got mad, and it just came out,' Penner said. 'I was kind of hoping he would say something that would help the case. But, unfortunately, he didn't.'

'He really doesn't seem like the type that's just going to let something slip,' said Millar. 'Unless we turn up something concrete, I think he may get away with this.'

'Any chance Sooleawa may say something to someone?' Penner asked, turning back to Grant.

'Doubt it,' Grant said. 'I think she's even stronger willed and more determined than the Chief is. I can't see her incriminating the Chief.'

'Guess this is as far as we can go,' Millar said, seeing Barry pull over to the side of the road. Barry got out of his car and walked back to Millar's.

'Right, so you both have cars here, right?' Barry asked.

'Yeah,' Penner said, grabbing her keys and passing them over to Barry through Millar's open window.

'Thanks, Barry. I appreciate this,' Grant said, passing his keys.

'No problem,' Barry said. 'Give me a couple of minutes. I'll drive in and grab someone to help drive out the other car. Be back in a bit,' he said, walking back to his car.

Ten minutes later, a convoy of three cars pulled up across from Millar's car. Penner and Grant got out and walked to their cars.

'Thanks, guys,' Penner said. 'Really appreciate the help.'

Barry got out of his own car. 'Well, hope you guys have a safe drive back to Ottawa. We'll let you know if we find anything.'

'Sounds good, Barry. Do me a favour and keep an eye on Sammy,' Grant said, 'And you be safe, too. I don't trust the Chief.'

'Don't worry about me—I'll be fine,' Barry said, walking back towards his car, followed by the two other drivers. 'Later!'

Penner leaned against Millar's door and checked her watch. 'It's three o'clock now. Takes an hour to drive back—I'm going to bring the gun and hard drive straight to the precinct. I'll see if I can call in some favours and get these processed right away. Feel like grabbing a bite to eat after?'

'Sounds good to me,' Grant said. 'I have to stop in and talk to the Captain.'

'Oh, I totally forgot,' Penner cried. 'So, how'd you end up doing?'

'I passed!' Grant said, trying to contain his excitement. 'It was killing me, waiting for you to ask.'

'That's fantastic news!' Penner said, shaking Grant's hand. She wasn't much of a hugger.

'Passed what?' Millar asked from his car window. 'What am I missing?'

'Our little Constable is going to be a Sergeant,' Penner said.

'Really?' Millar said, getting out of his car. 'I didn't know you wrote your exam. Congratulations,' he said, shaking Grant's hand.

'Thanks, guys. I'm pretty chuffed,' said Grant. 'I'd been worrying about it ever since I wrote the stupid thing. It'd be nice if you could just get a promotion without having to jump through hoops.'

'Now, what fun would that be?' Penner asked. 'Alright, we definitely have to go out and celebrate tonight. You in, Millar?'

'Sounds better than eating by myself,' Millar said. 'I'll meet you guys at the precinct,' he said, getting back into his car. 'Last one back buys the first round.' With that, Millar pulled away in cloud of dust, leaving Penner and Grant standing by their cars.

CHAPTER TWENTY-SEVEN

'So, that cop that stopped you, how fast did he peg you?' Penner asked Millar, squeezing beside him in the precinct elevator. 'Did he give you a ticket?'

'No, he let me off,' Millar said with a smile. 'Told him I had a meeting to get to with the Captain and that I was late. Guess he felt bad for a fellow man in uniform.'

'I'll have to borrow your horseshoe sometime,' said Penner. 'I still don't know how you beat me here. When I saw you on the side of the road I figured I had you beat for sure.'

'I took some of the back roads. Can't legally go as fast as on the highway, but there's not as much traffic, so it's all good,' Millar said as the doors opened.

'Legally being the key word, I presume?' Penner said, pulling a hair off of Millar's shoulder. She held up the paper bags containing the gun and the hard drive. 'I'm going to run these down to FIS—see if I can sweet-talk them into getting started on the processing right away. Where are you going to be?'

'I think I'll head to my office and see if there's any emails or voicemails I should delete,' Millar said. 'It's been a while since I've checked.'

'So, think you're going to start back full time soon?' Penner asked.

'Going to have to talk with the Captain,' Millar said. 'When he recommended I work out at the reserve with Grant, I don't think he expected it to only last a couple of days. I'd like to come back. Working this weekend didn't bring up any bad memories about Tina. At least none worse than what's usually there, so I think I'm ready. We'll see what he says.'

'Well, it'd be good to have you back,' Penner said. 'I'll come find you in a bit.'

'Sounds good,' Millar said, walking off to his office.

***

'What in the…how the heck did they both beat me here?' Grant said to himself, seeing Millar's and Penner's cars in the parking lot. 'I was sure I was going to win,' he thought, getting out of his car. He looked at his watch. 'Captain should still be here, I think.' He swiped his ID card at the garage entrance and headed for the elevator. Just as the elevator doors opened, his phone rang. 'Crap,' he said, choosing to answer his phone and letting the door close without getting in. 'Grant,' he answered.

'Hey, Grant. It's Barry.'

'Hey Barry. How's it going? Wasn't expecting to hear from you—we just left an hour ago. What's up?'

'Just wanted to let you know that we'll be executing the search warrant in the next ten minutes, or so. The local cop just got here.'

'Really? That's great. I'll make sure my phone's on. Give me a call when you're done. Or, if you find anything partway through. Thanks, Barry.'

'No worries. Talk soon.'

Grant pressed the button for the elevator again. 'Millar and Penner are going to like this.'

219

When the elevator doors opened on the main floor, Grant exited and walked down the hall to the Captain's office. He peered in and saw the Captain sitting at his desk, reading some papers. His usual pose. Grant knocked on the door frame.

'Come,' the Captain called out without even looking up.

'Evening, Captain,' Grant said, walking into the office.

'Constable Grant,' the Captain greeted him, taking off his glasses. 'Or should I say, soon-to-be Sergeant Grant.'

'That sounds kind of strange, sir,' Grant said. 'Nice, but strange.'

'I'm sure you'll get used to it soon enough,' the Captain said. 'Glad you're here, actually. Got a phone call about you and Detectives Penner and Millar earlier.' His tone shifted toward serious.

'You did?' Grant said, surprised. 'From who?'

'From a judge, actually,' said the Captain. 'He told me that he had to issue a restraining order against the three of you. Millar and Penner were out there with you for what, two, three days and you get a restraining order placed against you? Care to explain?'

'Crap,' Grant thought. 'Well, sir, we were investigating the deaths out at the reserve, and, well, we may have told the Chief we thought he was involved.' He felt a bead of sweat suddenly appear on his forehead and quickly wiped it off. Technically, it was Penner who accused the Chief, but Grant wasn't going to throw her under the bus—they were all in it together.

'I assume you must have a lot of evidence, then?' the Captain said. 'I know you wouldn't have made an accusation like that if you couldn't prove it, right?'

Grant's mouth was going dryer by the second. He could hear his heart beating in his ears. 'Well, sir, we have a lot of, um, circumstantial evidence,' Grant said, his legs shaking. 'Nothing really, um, concrete.' He wiped his brow again. 'May I sit, sir?'

'Please,' the Captain said, motioning to a chair.

Grant sat down heavily in the chair. All he could think was how his promotion was going to be withdrawn. Having a restraining order filed against you had to be an infraction of some sort of police code. Could he lose his job over this?

'You do realize,' the Captain said, slowly. 'That this doesn't only look bad for the three of you, but it looks bad for the entire precinct, right?'

Grant swallowed hard. 'I do, sir.'

'Well. Luckily, the judge also told me that he issued a search warrant for the band office and some computer equipment. He explained the reasoning behind issuing the warrants—seems like your police friend from the reserve did a good job of explaining the possible involvement of the Chief.'

Grant sighed. He could feel his shoulders drop as he relaxed slightly. 'We have a lot of reason to believe he's involved, sir. Just not a lot of solid evidence, unfortunately. The guy's pretty slick.'

'Do you know when they're executing the search of the office?' the Captain asked.

'Right now, actually,' Grant said, checking his watch. 'Barry, the cop from the reserve, is going to call me when they're done.'

'Good. Keep me informed,' the Captain said. 'I know it's not our case, but I am curious.'

'Will do, sir,' Grant said, more at ease now.

'Were you able to find the computer equipment you were looking for?' the Captain asked, taking a sip of a coffee. He made a face—the coffee had gone cold.

'We did, sir. A hard drive,' said Grant. 'Detective Penner was running it down to get it looked at by forensics. We also have a gun we want processed for prints.'

'Well, hopefully you find something,' the Captain said, switching gears. 'So, for your promotion ceremony. I was originally planning on doing it next week, because I thought you were going to be out of town for a couple more days. But, seeing as you're back, what if we did it tomorrow?'

'Tomorrow, sir?' Grant said with surprise.

'If you want. If not, it will have to wait until late next week. I have to go to my daughter's wedding. Bit of a surprise, really. She called last night—seems her fiancé is in town for three days. He's in the Navy and their ship is in Halifax for repairs so he's flying in. They've decided to go to City Hall to get married.'

'Congratulations, sir,' Grant said.

'Thanks. Would have preferred a bit more notice, but I like the fact they're not spending a fortune on it. The wedding's just one day—the marriage is for the rest of their lives. Well, hopefully, anyways. I don't understand people who spend tens of thousands of dollars on a wedding. Why start life off together going into debt?' the Captain said. 'Anyway, if you want, we can have a small ceremony tomorrow morning. Of course, if you need more time to invite some family or friends, I understand.'

'No, tomorrow would work for me, sir,' Grant said. 'Thank you, sir. I'm just planning on inviting my mom and dad. I'm sure mom can get the time off work and dad's retired, so shouldn't be a problem.'

'Excellent. Then we'll set it up for ten tomorrow morning,'

the Captain said, making a note on a scrap of paper. 'Have you thought about where you want to work, once you get your new stripe?'

'Honestly, I haven't, sir,' Grant said. 'With everything that's been going on, I haven't had time to really let it sink in that I'm getting promoted. Wherever I'm needed, I guess.'

'Good answer. I was thinking one of two places would be good for you. You could move over to the guns and gangs unit. There's an opening for a sergeant there. You would be running a team of five. Pretty hectic these days, unfortunately. A lot more gang activity moving into the city.'

'That sounds like it could be a great opportunity,' Grant said, thinking how that could help advance his career. Running a team of five people would look great on his resume. 'Thank you, sir.'

'Did you want to hear the second option?' asked the Captain.

'Oh, of course. Sorry, sir,' Grant said.

'Now, this one's a bit different, and maybe not the best fit,' the Captain began.

***

'Hey, Millar,' Penner said, walking into his office. 'Almost ready to grab some food?'

'I am. I'm starved,' Millar said, standing up and grabbing his keys. 'I haven't seen Grant yet, though.'

'Assuming he didn't drive like my grandma on the way here, he's probably still with the Captain,' Penner said. 'Wonder how he's going to take the fact you got us banned from the reserve,' she added off-handedly.

'Me?!' Millar said. 'No, no, no. I was in the woods when all the shit went down. You're not pinning this on me.' He shook his finger at Penner.

'Come on. Let's go find Grant,' Penner said, laughing.

'What did FIS say about the drive and the gun? Are they going to get to them soon?' Millar asked, closing his office door.

'Hopefully this evening,' Penner said. 'Apparently they aren't swamped for a change. They're going to call my cell when they're done.'

'We'll see if they actually get to it that quickly.' Millar was skeptical. 'They talk a good game down there.'

'Maybe you only get the runaround from them because you're a jerk. Ever think treating them nicer would help your cause?'

'I'm nice to everyone. When they deserve it.'

'Okay. Keep telling yourself that,' Penner said as they turned the corner and headed towards the Captain's office.

'Thank you, sir,' Grant said, walking out of the Captain's office into the hall. 'I'll see you in the morning. I'll have a decision for you then.' He turned and saw Penner and Millar. 'Ready to go?'

'We are,' Millar said. 'So, I guess you're buying the first round—you got here last.'

'Only because I abide by the law,' Grant said. 'I just have to call my mom real quick.'

'What, to ask permission to go out?' Millar chuckled.

'No, to invite her to my promotion ceremony tomorrow. I was going to invite you, too, but…now I'm not so sure,' Grant said. 'You can still come, Detective,' he said to Penner.

Penner smiled at Millar. 'See, being nice to people pays off. Being a jerk, not so much.'

'Whatever,' Millar said. 'How about you meet us in the garage. If you guys want, I'll drive.'

'Sure, it should only take a minute,' Grant said. 'Well, if my mom answers. She's not much of a talker on the phone. May be a bit longer if my dad answers.'

'We're pulling out in five,' Millar said. Penner gave him a slap on the back of his head. Grant chuckled, watching them walk away.

CHAPTER TWENTY-EIGHT

'Alright, let's go,' Grant said, sliding into the back seat of Millar's car.

'That was quick,' said Penner. 'Were they not home?'

'Oh, yeah. I talked to my mom,' Grant said as Millar started up the car. 'Told you she wasn't much of a talker on the phone. In person, she'll talk your ear off—but, she's definitely not a phone person.'

'So, your promotion ceremony's tomorrow? That's pretty quick,' Penner said, buckling her seatbelt.

'Captain's got some personal stuff going on so it was either tomorrow or next week,' Grant said. 'Figured I might as well get it done sooner than later.'

'So, what time's it going to be?' asked Millar, pulling onto Metcalfe Street.

'Ten,' said Grant. 'Hope you guys can make it. If you want, of course.'

'Yeah, we'll be there,' Penner said. 'Well, I will be anyways.'

'Me, too,' Millar said. 'If the Captain's going to be off for a bit, I should probably talk to him—find out if I can come back to work yet, or not.'

'So, Constable-soon-to-be-Sergeant, any idea what your

next assignment's going to be?' Penner asked. 'Did you not see that stop sign?' she said, turning to Millar.

'I saw it,' Millar said. 'I totally slowed down—no one was coming.'

'I don't know how you still have your license,' said Penner. 'So, did the Captain give you your assignment yet?'

'Sort of,' Grant said. 'He gave me two options.'

'Options are good,' Millar observed. 'I don't think I got any choices when I got my promotions. I was just told where I was going to work. And who I was going to work with, unfortunately.'

'I'm just going to ignore you for a while,' said Penner.

'So, like I was saying,' Grant continued, 'I can lead a team with the guns and gangs unit, which I think could be a good career move.'

'I'd say,' Penner said. 'Leading a team is a great way to get noticed and move up in your career. That could be a pretty high profile assignment.'

'That's what I was thinking, too,' Grant said as Millar pulled into the parking lot of The Fat Cat Bistro. 'I've never eaten here before. Is it good?'

'Yeah, it is,' Millar said. 'I ate here last week with my publicist. I had a T-bone, cooked to perfection.'

'Sounds good to me,' Grant said as they got out of the car and walked towards the restaurant.

'Give me a minute,' Penner said, taking her vibrating phone out of her pocket. 'It's forensics. I'll meet you inside.'

'Wine?' Millar asked.

'Please. House white,' Penner said. 'Penner.'

'Hi, Detective. It's Sergeant Wilson.'

'Hey Sergeant. So, have you got good news for me?'

'*Well, not really. We dusted the gun, but we didn't find any prints. As you suspected—no prints means it's not a suicide. But, unfortunately, it means there's no evidence to incriminate anyone else, either.*'

'Huh. Well, that's kind of what I was expecting. What about the hard drive?'

'*We should be getting to it in the next half hour or so. We're a bit short-handed tonight.*'

'Alright, give me a shout when you're done. Cheers.'

Penner hung up her phone and walked into the restaurant. Looking around the crowded space, she saw Millar and Grant sitting in a booth by the kitchen. 'Surprised you were able to get a table—the place is packed.'

'Yeah, kind of surprising,' Millar said. 'Wasn't nearly as busy the other night. So, FIS find anything?' he asked, as the waitress came by with a glass of wine for Penner, and two pints of beer for Millar and Grant.

'Do you need a couple of minutes with the menu?' the waitress asked.

'Please,' Penner said.

'Take your time.'

'Well, cheers, Grant,' Millar said, raising his beer. 'Congrats on the promotion. Not sure you deserve it, but I'm not the boss.'

'Thank goodness for that,' Grant said, clinking his glass with Millar's and Penner's. 'Thanks, guys.'

'So, forensics checked the gun but didn't find any fingerprints. Not even Travis's,' Penner said, with an arched eyebrow.

'That sucks,' Grant said. 'What about the drive?'

'They're just getting to it,' Penner said, taking a sip of her wine. 'With any luck, we should get a call before we're done eating.'

'Let's hope it's better news,' Millar said, opening his menu. 'So, what's the other option the Captain gave you?'

'Oh, right,' Grant said. 'He said I could join major crimes and actually report to the two of you.'

'Really?' Penner said with surprise. 'Don't know the last time we had a sergeant working on the team. Must be four or five years now.'

'Probably five,' Millar said. 'I think Merasty was the last sergeant we had, and he's been in Toronto for a few years now. Quite the different choices,' Millar looked at Grant over the top of his menu. 'Be a team lead, or be the bottom rung on the ladder.'

'Any idea which way you're going to go?' Penner asked. 'Oh, this looks good, the blackened salmon on rice pilaf. Think I'll go for that.'

'I'm torn,' Grant said. 'Being the boss is really appealing. Plus, guns and gangs would be a good place to work. Get to help clean up the city and get some weapons off the streets. That's really why I became a cop—to try and make a difference.'

'Are you ready to order, or do you need more time?' The waitress appeared at the table, notepad poised.

'I'm ready,' Penner said. 'Millar?'

'I know what I want,' Millar said.

'Okay, you guys order, I'll decide quick,' said Grant, scanning the front and back of the menu.

'I'll get the salmon, please,' said Penner.

'I'll try the bison burger with bacon and cheese. No lettuce, no tomatoes. No condiments. Just meat, bun, bacon and cheese,' Millar said. Penner looked at him, giving him a strange look. 'What?! I don't like to hide the taste of what I'm eating.'

'And for you?' the waitress asked Grant.

'Um, I'll go for…for…the steak frites, please,' Grant said.

'How would you like the steak?'

'Medium rare, please,' Grant said, passing over the menu.

'Hopefully you have an easier time choosing a career path than choosing your entrée,' Penner said to Grant, watching the waitress walk away. 'Major crimes could be a good fit for you. You have a pretty good knack for interviewing suspects and a keen eye when it comes to looking at crime scenes. If you eventually want to become a detective, I think it could be the best choice. Not many detectives working guns and gangs, so I think you would learn more about what's involved. Tough call.'

'Well, I don't need to decide today, which is good,' Grant said, finishing his beer. 'I told the Captain I would let him know tomorrow, so I can at least sleep on it.' His phone vibrated on the table. 'Excuse me,' he said, answering it. 'Grant. Hey, Barry. I was starting to think you forgot about us. So, how'd it go? Right. Right. That's it? Right. So, you still have a job? Well, that's good at least. Okay, thanks for letting me know. We'll get in touch about picking up our stuff. Later.'

'So?' Millar asked.

'Apparently, the band office had been cleaned up,' Grant said. 'Almost all the paperwork was gone. The only thing they ended up taking was a saw.'

'A saw? That's it?' Penner said.

'That's all there was,' Grant said. 'Barry brought it back to the station and dusted it for prints. He was able to identify two. One was Travis's and the other was Sooleawa's.'

'Really?' Millar said.

'Yeah, but Sooleawa had an explanation ready for that. She said she had knocked it over and picked it up,' Grant said. 'No way to prove if that's true or not.'

'So the gun and the search were a bust,' Penner said. 'Now our last hope is the hard drive.'

'Keep your phone out,' Millar advised. 'Don't want to miss the call when it comes in. Food's here,' he said, as the waitress set their plates down.

'Do you need anything else?'

'I think we're good for now, thanks,' Penner said.

'Enjoy,' the waitress said.

'This smells good,' Penner said, watching Millar lift the top bun off of his burger. He put it back, flipped the burger over and took off the bottom bun. 'What are you doing?'

'What?' Millar said. 'Oh, just making sure they didn't add any stuff to my burger. Way too often you ask for a burger to be plain and it still comes with ketchup and mustard. Or worse, a pickle.'

'You're a strange man,' Penner said. 'Well, enjoy, guys,' she said, cutting into her salmon.

***

'How was everything?' The waitress reached across the table to gather their plates.

'Delicious,' said Penner. 'That salmon was so nice and moist.'

'Good, glad you liked it. Can I get you all anything else?'

Penner looked at the time on her phone. 'I could go for a coffee. Are you guys having any dessert?'

'I'll grab a slice of chocolate cake, if you have any. And a coffee, please,' Grant said.

'Yeah, that sounds good, I'll have the same,' Millar said.

'So, three coffees and two slices of chocolate cake.'

'Can I get ice cream on my cake?' Grant asked. 'Sounds like a good celebratory dessert.'

'No problem,' the waitress said. 'And you?' she asked Millar.

'I never say no to ice cream. Thanks.'

The display on Penner's phone lit up and she quickly picked it up. 'This could be it,' she said. 'Penner. Hey, Sergeant. So, what'd you find. Really? Oh, okay. We can be there in twenty minutes, if you're still going to be there. Alright, see you then.' She hung up, looking perplexed.

'Why do we have to go in?' Millar asked. 'What did she find?'

'I'm not really sure, to be honest,' Penner said. 'All she said was there was only one file on the drive and we should come and see it for ourselves.'

'That's pretty weird,' Grant said. 'What do you think it could be?'

'No idea,' Penner said. 'But I guess we'll find out soon enough.'

The waitress placed their coffees and desserts on the table. 'Do you need anything else?'

'Just the bill please,' Millar said. 'I'll get it.'

'Wow, that's a shocker,' Penner said.

'Just my way of celebrating Grant's promotion,' Millar said.

'Thanks, Millar. I appreciate it.' Grant saluted Millar with a forkful of cake before shovelling it into his mouth. 'Oh, this is delicious,' he said, crumbs falling down his chin.

***

Millar paid the bill and drove them back to the precinct. He pulled into a parking spot next to Penner's car—the garage was nearly empty. From the garage, they went through a side door and straight down to the FIS lab. Penner scanned her ID card to unlock the door.

The lab was empty, with the exception of two technicians—one in a white lab coat and the other already in her street clothes. 'Hey, Sergeant,' Penner greeted the officer in the bomber jacket and denim. 'Sorry to keep you so late.'

'Ah, Detective Penner. No problem.'

'Sergeant Wilson, this is Detective Millar and Constable—sorry, *Sergeant* Grant,' Penner said, winking at Grant.

'Nice to meet you,' Sergeant Wilson said. 'So, we hooked up the hard drive and did a complete scan.'

'And you said you only found one file?' Penner said.

'Yes, ma'am. And it's a strange one,' Wilson said.

'Strange? How so?' Millar asked.

'Well, probably easiest if I show you,' said Wilson, walking over to a table with a computer monitor set up. 'So, when we scanned the disk, we found this file called the_raven.mpg.'

'A video file?' Grant said.

'Yeah,' the sergeant said. 'Ready?' She clicked on the file, opening a video player. On the screen, an Ottawa Police badge appeared. An animated Raven flew onto the screen, landing on top of the badge. The Raven squawked, digging its claws into the badge. It raised its wings and flew off the screen, carrying the badge away with it. In its place, a skull wearing a feather headdress appeared. The video ended.

Penner stood, staring at the screen with her mouth open. 'What the hell was that? That son of a bitch!'

'How did he do that?' Grant asked. 'How did he have the time?'

'Unbelievable,' Millar said, shaking his head. 'Any way of knowing who created this?'

'Unfortunately not, sir,' said Wilson. 'I can tell you it was uploaded to the hard drive this morning at around ten. That's about it.'

'At ten this morning? So it would have to have been made before then,' Penner said. 'I don't know how long something like that would take, but I assume it's not quick. Definitely pretty custom graphics.' She ran one hand through her hair in frustration. 'So, again, he was ahead of us. He knew we were going to confiscate the drive and had this made up. Either it was in the computer Sooleawa dropped off, or he switched it out after.'

'The Chief didn't strike me as super tech savvy. How did he find someone to do this?' Millar asked, leaning against the desk.

'Didn't Sooleawa say she used to be a computer animator? She could have done this,' said Penner. 'So, she probably is involved.'

'But how are we going to prove that?' asked Millar. 'There was no other computer out there. And you can be sure that if he had another computer anywhere on the reserve, it's long gone by now.'

'There has to be something else we can do,' Grant said. 'Right? Guys?'

Penner stood, staring at the screen. 'I hate to say it, but I think Millar's right. Ravenclaw's won.'

'So that's it?' Grant said. 'There's nothing else we can do?'

'Unfortunately, not,' said Penner. 'Sometimes, no matter how hard we try, we just can't get the evidence we need. Sergeant Wilson, thanks for your help.'

'You're welcome. I'm just sorry we couldn't be of more help. Did you want a copy of the file?'

'No, thanks,' Penner said, walking towards the door. 'I'll come pick up the drive tomorrow—bring it to evidence lock-up until we return it.'

'I'll put it aside for you.'

Grant followed Penner and Millar into the hallway. 'I guess I'll call Barry, let him know. I can't believe Ravenclaw's going to get away with this. It just doesn't seem right.'

'Don't take it personally,' Millar said, patting him on the shoulder. 'The best thing you can do is put it behind you and move on. But don't ever forget about it. Use what you've learned for your future cases.'

'Thanks,' Grant said. 'I just don't like the idea that he got the better of us.'

'No one likes it, but it happens,' said Millar. 'Not often, thankfully. But it does.'

'Well, I'm going to head out. I'll call Barry when I get home,' Grant said. 'Not sure I can handle working in major crimes if people like the Chief can end up walking away free.'

'Just remember, more often than not, we get the arrest—we close the case,' Penner said, trying as much to make herself feel better as Grant. 'And it doesn't matter what department you're in, you won't always make the arrest. Petty crime, major crime or guns and gangs—sometimes, the bad guy wins.'

'I guess,' said Grant. 'This is just a first for me.'

'I'd say it gets easier, but that would be a lie,' Penner said. 'It sucks each and every time, but it makes you work harder for the next one. Go home, have a glass of scotch and a good night's sleep. We'll see you tomorrow at your ceremony. And if you need more time to decide where you want to take the next steps in your career, I'm sure the Captain will understand.'

'Thanks. See you guys tomorrow,' Grant said, shoulders still slumped as he walked to the elevator .

CHAPTER TWENTY-NINE

By the next morning, the heatwave had broken and Millar had enjoyed a full night's sleep back in his own bed. He dressed carefully, thinking that Grant's promotion ceremony might require something a little more formal than jeans and a t-shirt. Back at the station, he decided he would stop in and see the Captain before the ceremony. It was still only eight-thirty. He had plenty of time. He walked up to the Captain's office and looked through the open door. The office was empty. 'Guess I could have slept in after all,' Millar said to himself. He walked down the hall to the kitchen to grab a coffee—he was still pretty tired. After being off of work for so long, the last three days had worn him out. But, truth be told, it was a good type of tired. The kind of physical and mental exhaustion that he'd been missing. Sitting around the house all day was tiring, too, but that was different. Being tired from boredom was very different than being tired from adrenaline. The last year had taught him that he needed to work, and the thrill of the last couple of days really drove it home. Oh, he was looking forward to retiring alright, but not just yet. For now, he wanted to work. He walked into the kitchen and saw that someone had made a fresh pot of coffee. He grabbed a mug from the cupboard and poured himself a cup.

'Don't take it all—I just made that,' the Captain said from behind Millar, making him jump and spill his coffee.

'Morning, Captain. Still lots left.' Millar recovered quickly, grabbing another mug and pouring a cup for the Captain.

'Thanks,' the Captain said, taking the mug. 'You're here early.'

'Wanted to talk to you before things got too hectic today,' said Millar. 'Do you have a minute?'

'Sure,' the Captain said. He sat down at one of the tables in the lounge and motioned for Millar to do the same. 'What's on your mind?'

'Well, sir, I think I'd like to come back to work,' Millar said, sitting across from the Captain. 'I know we were going to re-evaluate my situation after a couple weeks of working with Grant, but, well, obviously things kind of changed.'

'You could say that,' the Captain said. 'Back for just three days and you've got a restraining order against you and Grant's been fired from his job.'

'When you say it like that, sir, it really doesn't sound too good,' Millar said with a grimace. 'But, whether I was there or not, I think Grant still would have lost his job. Chief Ravenclaw wasn't going to let anyone snoop around, so he would have gotten rid of him either way.'

'It's possible. Maybe probable,' the Captain said, sipping his coffee. 'But still doesn't look too good, does it?'

'No, sir,' said Millar, looking down at the tabletop. This wasn't going quite how he had envisioned.

'When are you supposed to go back out to the reserve to collect your stuff?' the Captain asked. Millar was surprised that he knew about that.

'Next Wednesday, I think,' Millar said. 'I'll have to check with Grant—see when Barry's going to meet us there.'

'Right. Okay, if you think you're ready to come back, then why don't you start back next Thursday. Take a couple more days—make sure your head's in it. If things are feeling good, come back. If not, you still have the six months like I mentioned before.'

'Thank you, sir,' Millar said, relieved. 'I appreciate it.'

'Just make sure you're ready, alright?' the Captain said. 'There's no need to rush.'

'Sounds good.'

'Did you talk to Grant last night? Do you know what team he's leaning towards?'

'Couldn't say, sir,' said Millar, remembering the events of the previous evening. 'He seemed pretty unsure when he left last night. The fact the Chief is going to get away with murder really hit him hard. I'm not sure if he'll want major crimes after that or not.'

'Do you think he'd be good in major crimes?' the Captain asked, finishing his coffee.

'I think he'd be good wherever he decides to go, sir.'

'Good to hear.' The Captain stood up. 'If there's nothing else, I have to get ready for the ceremony. I assume you'll be there?'

'Yes sir. And thanks. I'm looking forward to getting back in the saddle.'

'Good. It'll be good to have you back,' the Captain said, putting his mug in the sink and walking out of the kitchen.

Millar checked his watch. 'Still time for another coffee,' he said, pouring himself a second cup. He sat back down at the table and pulled out his phone. He saw he had a text message from Penner.

'Hey! Just got to the station. Saw your car in the garage. Where are you? Coffee?'

He started typing a message back, but only got halfway through before Penner walked into the kitchen. 'I was just sending you a message,' he said. 'Coffee's on.'

'Let me guess—had the volume down on your phone again?' Penner asked, grabbing a mug out of the cupboard. 'I don't know why you bother having a phone if you've never got the volume loud enough to hear messages or calls.'

'I always end up getting them,' Millar said. 'Just, sometimes, not right away. But I get them eventually—that's what matters.'

'Yeah, that's what matters,' Penner said, sitting down. 'How was your night?'

'Not bad. Took a while to fall asleep,' Millar said. 'Just kept thinking of that stupid video.'

'Me, too,' said Penner. 'I can't believe he would taunt us so blatantly like that. Friggin' sociopath. And you know what the worst part is?'

'What's that?' Millar asked, sipping his coffee.

'I forgot my coffee beans back on the reserve!' Penner said. 'All those lovely, lovely beans and I totally forgot to grab them from my room before we left.'

'You think that's the worst part about all this?' asked Millar. 'Who's the sociopath, now?'

'Shut up. You know what I mean,' Penner said, taking a drink from her mug and then looking at it sadly. 'Hopefully it's still there when we go back next week to grab our stuff.'

'You and your coffee. Did you hear from Grant at all this morning? Wonder how he's doing.'

'I don't know. He sure seemed to take it hard last night.'

'Yeah, he did,' Millar said. 'I remember the first time I knew someone was guilty but we couldn't prove it. Owner of a construction company here in town ended up dead one day. Shot in the head, buried in concrete at one of the job sites.'

'If he was buried in concrete, how'd you find him?' Penner asked.

'We got an anonymous tip that he was there, so we got a company out that uses ground penetrating radar. Ran this machine over the concrete and they saw an anomaly in the pad. Got a backhoe and dug it up. Sure enough, there he was.'

'Lucky you got the tip,' Penner said, finishing her coffee.

'No kidding,' Millar said. 'Without that, I don't think we ever would have found him. Not like we could just start digging up every construction site in hopes of finding him. So, based on all the information we had about the company, we were sure his business partner was responsible. But, no matter how hard we tried, we just couldn't find that one all important clue. He had never owned a gun, but his brother did.'

'Did you get that tested?'

'Couldn't,' Millar said. 'It was actually reported stolen the week before the murder. His house was broken into when he and his wife were out for dinner. Only thing stolen was the gun, so whoever took it must have known it was there.'

'Let me guess, no fingerprints?'

'No prints, no nothing,' Millar said. 'Person gained access through an open window, so they didn't even have to really break in.'

'Did the cops think it was an inside job?' Penner asked.

'What, the theft?' Millar asked. 'At the time, they had no reason to think it might be. The murder didn't happen until a week later.'

'Makes sense. What else did you have?'

'Well, the company was in trouble, financially. They had lost a lot of money. They had worked on a bridge and the concrete that they used wasn't up to par. City engineers wouldn't sign off on the work and they had to tear it down and start again. Ended up losing almost a million and a half. Lots of money for a small company.'

'So, why did that point to the partner?'

'They each had a large life insurance policy on each other, so if one of them died, the other would get two million, which would help the company stay afloat.' Millar narrowed his eyes as he looked at Penner. 'Don't think I would ever enter a deal like that with my partner. I could just see it now—you'd have me poisoned so fast, no one would see it coming.'

'Trust me—I've already thought about how I'd do it, too.'

'I'd like to think you're joking, but…' Millar said. 'Anyway, there were a lot of rumours of infighting between the two. Lots of stuff was telling us that this guy did it, but we couldn't convince the Crown Attorney's office to give us the arrest warrant. They didn't think they could make the charges stick. That case is still technically open, but there hasn't been any movement on it in years.'

'I know we all end up with cases like this, but man they sting,' Penner said. 'I try not to keep track of the cases I couldn't close, but there's been a few. Each one hurts.'

'Hopefully Grant realizes that there's no point in dwelling on this one,' Millar said. 'And hopefully, with all the attention we've put on the Chief, he'll think real hard before he commits another crime in the future.'

'We'll have to make sure Barry keeps an eye on him,' Penner said. She looked at her watch. 'I guess we should start thinking about heading to the ceremony—make sure we get a seat.'

'So, what team do you think Grant's going to choose?' Millar stood and carried both mugs to the sink. 'If you were him, which way would you go?'

'If I was him?' Penner thought for a minute. 'New in my career, I might lean towards the guns and gangs. The idea of actually leading my own team—that would be pretty appealing.'

'Yeah, I'm sure it would be,' Millar said.

'But, I know he wants to end up as a detective, eventually,' Penner said, standing and stretching her lower back. 'So, I would think working major crimes might be a better path to take. You're not going to get to supervise anyone, and you'd probably end up doing a lot of grunt work. But, having the opportunity to work with a group of detectives every day? I think that would be a quicker way to get to the end goal.'

'Definitely curious to see what he decides,' Millar said. 'Either way, I think he'll do alright. Grant's got a good head on his shoulders.'

'You're going to make me blush,' said Grant, walking into the kitchen.

'Well, well, well. Look at our little Constable, all dressed up in his dress uniform,' Penner said, straightening his tie. 'Looks like you may have pulled a Millar.'

'Pulled a Millar?' Grant said, looking at Millar. Millar shrugged.

'Put on a bit of weight since you got your uniform,' Penner said, tapping Grant's stomach. 'Looks like that button's holding on for dear life.'

'Geez, thanks for that,' Grant said, trying, unsuccessfully, to suck in his stomach. 'Now all I'm going to be able to think about when the Captain's giving me my stripe is bursting the button and taking someone's eye out.'

'Now that would be funny,' Millar said. 'Well, not if someone actually lost their eye, of course, but if the button went flying across the room.'

'Glad I invited you two,' Grant said.

'So, how're you doing?' asked Penner. 'Come to terms with the fact we're not going to get Ravenclaw?'

'Not really, but I know we did everything we could,' Grant said as they walked out in the hall to head to the ceremony. 'I just really hope he doesn't try anything like this again. I don't know if I could live with myself if he ended up killing someone else.'

'You can't take it personally,' Millar said. 'But you never know—he may slip up at some point and say something to the wrong person.'

'Or he and Sooleawa may break up,' Penner said.

Grant looked at her, a bit confused. 'I don't see how that would help.'

'When couples break up, they tend to talk. Especially if one of them has dirt on the other—they'll tell anyone who will listen,' Penner said. 'I've had a few cases where I was able to make an arrest years after a crime was committed because a husband cheated on his wife. The wife is pissed and wants to get back at him. She feels the best way to do that is to tell the cops about her husband's dirty little secret and she gives you the little piece of evidence that you were missing. Doesn't happen often, but it does happen.'

'Well, let's hope they break up then,' Grant said as they walked up to the conference room where the ceremony was going to be held. 'Here we are. Last day as a Constable.'

'Congrats again,' said Penner, patting him on the shoulder. 'You deserve it.'

'Thanks, ma-am,' Grant said. 'It's been fun working with you. The two of you. Right,' he straightened his shoulders and took a deep breath, 'I'll see you after the ceremony,' he added, walking into the room and sitting down in the front row.

'Did that sound like he wasn't going to be working with us anymore to you?' Penner asked Millar.

'Kind of did, didn't it?' Millar said, looking into the room. 'I gotta say, I was kind of thinking he was going to choose major crimes.'

'Me, too,' Penner said. 'Huh. Well, guns and gangs is a good unit, too. He'll be an asset for them. Should we grab a seat?'

'After you,' Millar said, letting Penner enter the room first. They chose two seats towards the back of the room and sat down.

After only a few minutes, the Captain walked into the conference room, buttoning his jacket with one hand and smoothing his hair with the other. He greeted a few people and shook a few hands as he made his way up to the podium. A respectful silence settled over the room as everyone sat down and stopped talking.

'Thanks, everyone,' the Captain said. 'Constable Grant? Would you join me up here?' Grant got up and walked to the front of the room, standing beside the Captain.

'Is he still sucking in his gut?' Penner whispered into Millar's ear.

'I think you got into his head,' Millar whispered back, trying not to laugh. He kept an eye on that second brass button doing all the work—secretly hoping it would fly off.

'Constable Grant, it's been my pleasure to watch your

progress over the past couple of years. I would like to be the first to officially congratulate you on your promotion to Sergeant,' the Captain said, handing Grant a new rank stripe for his uniform with his left hand, shaking his right hand. They both turned slightly to face the official department photographer. Penner pulled out her phone and took a picture as well. 'Ladies and gentlemen, please help me congratulate…Sergeant Grant.'

'Woohoo!' Penner yelled out, as everyone started clapping. Grant turned red, but couldn't keep the beaming smile from his face as he thanked the Captain and returned to his seat.

'Right. There will be coffee and cake available shortly, so please stick around,' the Captain announced to the small gathering.

Millar and Penner stood and walked over to where Grant was talking to a few of his beat cop buddies. They overheard one say, 'It's not detective, but it's a step in the right direction.'

'Thanks, Spicy,' Grant said to his friend, Constable Curry. 'Any idea when you're going to try the exam?'

'Probably next month. I kind of missed the ball with the last one. I ended up booking my vacation without realizing it overlapped with the exam date.'

'My advice—study up. Some of the questions were harder than I thought they would be,' Grant said. He looked over Constable Curry's shoulder, smiling. 'Excuse me, guys,' he said, walking over to an older Black couple standing off to the side. 'Mom. Dad. So glad you made it!'

'We wouldn't have missed it,' Grant's dad said, giving Grant a hug. 'Kind of a short ceremony, isn't it? I thought there would have been speeches or something.'

'No, these are usually short and to the point,' Grant said,

giving his mom a hug. 'Pick up the new stripe for the uniform and then head back to work. After some cake and coffee, that is.'

'Well, I thought it was just fine,' said Grant's mom, looking up at him with pride. She was a petite woman, much shorter than Grant and his dad. 'And your Captain is quite the looker. You never told me he was so handsome.'

'Really, mom?' Grant said. 'You let her talk like this?' he said to his dad.

'Oh, he knows he's the only one for me,' his mom said.

'And you know there's no stopping her. If she wants to say something, she's going to say it.'

'Just try not to say anything to the Captain when I introduce you, alright?' Grant said. He spotted Penner and Millar lurking by the cake table. 'Detectives, I want to introduce you to my parents.' Penner and Millar walked over. 'Detective Penner, Detective Millar, these are my parents, Tom and Mary-Ann Grant.'

'It's a pleasure to meet you,' Penner said, shaking their hands. 'I didn't realize you were adopted,' she added in an aside to Grant.

'Adopted?' Grant said. 'What makes you think I'm adopted?'

'Wait. What?' Penner stammered. 'Well, you're white and your parents, are, um…not.'

'I'm not adopted.'

'Really?' Penner said, looking at Grant, then at his parents. 'Really?'

'No, I'm kidding,' Grant laughed. 'But you should have seen your face! I was adopted when I was two.'

'When we saw him at the orphanage, we just knew little Cornelius would make a great addition to our family,' Grant's mom said. 'He was such a cute little thing.'

Penner gave a sharp look at Millar and then looked back at Grant, 'Cornelius?'

'Yeah, Cornelius. You knew that was my name, right?'

'Uhh,' Penner said, looking again at Millar and hoping he was going to bail her out.

'Seriously?' Grant said. 'What did you think my name was?'

Millar's mind was racing. It suddenly occurred to him that he had no idea what Grant's first name was. 'Umm…Constable?' Millar said, sheepishly. Grant's parents watched the proceedings with amusement.

'You didn't know my name?' Grant said. 'After all this time working together? I can understand not knowing I was adopted, but my name? How could you not know what my name was?'

'I guess it never came up,' Penner said. 'You've always just been Grant.'

'I don't know how I should take this,' Grant said. 'You really didn't know my name?'

'Sorry?' Penner said, hoping Grant wasn't too mad.

'You both owe me a drink,' Grant said.

'No problem, Cornelius,' Millar said. 'Never going to forget your name now, that's for sure.'

'It's a family name,' Grant said, defensively. 'It was my granddad's name.'

'I like it,' Millar said. 'You look like a Cornelius.'

'Really?' Grant said. 'Alright, enough of you two. I'm going to introduce my folks to the Captain. As long as mom promises to behave herself.'

'I can't guarantee anything,' said Mary-Ann with a mischievous grin.

'Congrats again, Cornelius,' Millar said as Grant and his parents walked over to the Captain. Mary-Ann gave the Captain a big hug under Grant's watchful eye. 'You didn't know either?' Millar said to Penner.

'I had no idea,' Penner said. 'Trust me, I would have remembered it if I'd heard it. Probably should have gotten to know his name at some point over the last year, I guess.'

'Yeah, might have been a good idea,' Millar said. 'Let's get some cake.'

'It's like, twenty after ten,' Penner said, checking the time on her phone.

'And your point is?' Millar asked, walking back over to the cake table by the window. A large vanilla cake, covered in royal blue icing, was waiting to be cut.

'Don't you think it's a little early for cake?'

Millar looked at Penner with a serious expression on his face. 'Absolutely not. It's never too early for cake. Especially free cake,' he added, picking up the knife and cutting the largest slice he dared. He dumped it on a paper plate and traded the knife for a fork. He took a bite—making sure to get equal parts cake and frosting. 'Mmm,' he said, 'that's some good cake. You should have some.'

'Maybe later,' Penner said.

'Don't know if there will be any left later,' Millar said between bites.

'It's a chance I'll have to take I guess,' Penner said. Then she looked closer at Millar. 'Stick out your tongue.'

'What?' Millar said, taking another mouthful of cake.

'Stick out your tongue,' Penner said again. 'Well, swallow first.' Millar finished chewing the cake in his mouth, swallowed and stuck out his tongue. 'It's so blue!' Penner cried, laughing.

'Really?' Millar looked at some of the other people eating cake, trying to see what their mouths looked like. He noticed a woman beside him had blue teeth. 'I assume it will fade eventually,' he said, taking another mouthful.

'Hey, Captain. Sergeant,' Penner said as the Captain and Grant walked over to grab a slice of cake. 'Just a warning—it'll turn your mouth blue. Look at Millar.' Millar smiled and stuck out his tongue.

'Is it good, at least?' the Captain asked.

'It's delicious,' Millar said, finishing his piece and grabbing another one. 'Penner didn't want hers,' he explained.

'Well, if it's good, it's worth a blue mouth,' the Captain said, helping himself to a moderate slice.

'So, Grant, have you decided which assignment you're going to take?' Penner asked.

'I think so,' Grant said. 'I thought about it a lot last night and this morning. I think I've changed my mind about a dozen times so far—it's a big decision.'

'But you've decided now?' Penner asked again, her curiosity getting the best of her.

'I have,' said Grant. 'Both positions would be challenging. They'd each give me different opportunities. Being a supervisor would be amazing. And guns and gangs sounds like a great place to work. But, working in major crimes would give me the chance to learn from detectives like you two. Plus, I could hopefully learn more about profiling if I got the chance to work with Millar.'

'You're killing me,' Penner said. 'What did you decide?'

'I think the best choice for me, at this point in my career and considering where I want to end up, would be with major crimes.'

'That's fantastic,' Penner exclaimed. 'I thought for sure you were going to go with guns and gangs. I figured the way the case with the Chief went would have turned you off major crimes.'

'Actually,' Grant said, 'that was one of the deciding factors for me. I want to learn as much as I can so people like him don't get away with their crimes.'

'Well, welcome aboard,' Penner said, shaking Grant's hand. 'So, when will you start with us?'

'You know, that's a good question,' Grant said. 'Captain?'

'Well,' the Captain said, his teeth blue from icing. 'I spoke with your current Sergeant—he wants you to finish off the week with him. They'd be a bit short-handed if you transferred right away. Finish off the week. Then you can start when Millar comes back. When was that? Next Thursday?'

Millar struggled to finish the cake filling his mouth. 'That's correct, sir.'

'Does that work for you?' the Captain asked Grant.

'Absolutely,' Grant said. 'It will be good to spend a couple of days with the old team before moving on.'

'Perfect,' the Captain said, taking another bite of cake. 'This really is good cake.'

CHAPTER THIRTY

Grant pulled open the door of Joe's diner and looked around. It was early in the morning, but Penner and Millar were already there, drinking coffee at one of the tables by the window. 'Hey, guys. How's it going?' he greeted them, pulling out a chair and sitting next to Penner.

'Doing well. And you?' Penner asked. 'How was your last week with your old team?'

'It was good, but it seemed to go by really slow.' Grant noticed Joe, the owner, walk by. 'Hey, Joe. Can I get a coffee when you get a chance?'

'No problem, Neil,' Joe said.

'See, even he knows my name.'

'We're never going to live that one down, are we?' Penner said.

'Probably not,' Grant said, grinning. 'But you never know. How was your last week off?' he asked Millar.

'It was good,' Millar answered. 'Stopped in and saw Tina, which was nice.'

'How's she doing?' Grant asked, as Joe stopped by with a mug in one hand and a coffee pot in the other. 'Thanks, Joe. I'll have the usual, please.'

'No problem,' Joe said. 'Sue?'

'I'll go for the crepes today. Extra whip cream,' Penner said. 'Sounds good. Terry?'

'I'll get two eggs, sunny side up. Bacon, sausage and hash browns, please. Oh, and white toast.'

'I'll get the order in right away,' Joe said. 'More coffee while you wait?'

'You know me,' Penner said. 'Thanks.' She held out her mug and Joe topped it up.

'So, Tina? Doing well?' Grant asked again.

'Yeah, she is,' Millar said. 'She's doing well with her classes and the psychologist seems to be helping her come to terms with everything.'

'That's great,' Grant said. 'Is her leg finally healed up?'

'She's still doing physio,' Millar said. 'She has some pain from time to time and a bit of a limp. Gunshot wounds are no joke. Seems like it's getting better, though.'

'Hopefully it keeps improving,' Penner said.

Millar spotted Joe carrying three plates of food towards their table. 'What time's Barry planning on meeting us to escort us onto the reserve so we can grab our stuff?' he asked Grant.

'Quarter to ten, so we're going to have to head out as soon as we're done eating,' Grant said. 'Thanks, Joe,' he said as a stack of pancakes was dropped off in front of him.

'Well, eat up,' Penner said. 'This looks delicious. And we might need our strength.'

***

Millar rode with Penner out to the reserve and Grant followed behind in his own car. It was 9:40 when they arrived at the entrance, but there was no sign of Barry. They parked, one in front of the other along the side of the road, and shut off their engines. Grant walked up to Penner's car and motioned for her to roll down her window.

'I guess we're a little early,' he said, leaning down.

'I really hope we don't end up seeing the Chief while we're here,' Penner said. 'I can't be held responsible for what I might say. Or, worse, do.'

'Technically, if he has a restraining order against us, he shouldn't be around during the time we're allowed on the property,' Millar said, leaning across the centre console towards the driver's window.

'Well, technically you aren't supposed to kill people but that didn't stop him, now did it,' Penner said.

'If he's smart, he won't be around. But if he is, we'll just try and ignore him, right?' Millar said. 'Right?' he emphasized again to Penner. He had his doubts that Penner would be able to do that.

Ten minutes passed and Barry still hadn't shown up. 'Do you think he forgot?' Penner asked, checking the time on the dash.

'I called him the other night to confirm the time,' Grant said. 'Maybe he's just running late. I'll give him a call and see where he is.' He took out his phone and dialled Barry's number. 'Went straight to voice mail,' Grant said. He tried again. 'Must be in one of the dead zones.'

'Hopefully he shows up soon, I don't feel like sitting on the side of the road all day,' Penner said.

'You can always stand.'

'Not a bad idea,' Millar said, opening his door. 'I could use a stretch.' Penner and Millar joined Grant in leaning against the hood of her car.

A cloud of dust appear on the dirt road ahead of them. 'That's probably him,' Grant said, watching a car appear out of the dusty haze. He could make out a driver and someone in the passenger seat. 'Is that the Chief?'

'What the hell's he doing here?' Millar asked as the car pulled up beside them. Barry opened the driver's side door and stepped out, but the Chief stayed in his seat, staring straight ahead.

'Why did you bring him?' Grant asked, walking over to Barry.

'I can't stay—I have to go back to work,' Barry explained. 'So, the Chief agreed to bring you in to get your stuff.'

'Can't stay? What do you mean you can't stay?' Grant asked, looking at Millar and Penner. 'Couldn't you have had someone else bring us in?'

'Look,' Barry said, rubbing the back of his neck. 'There's been some developments since the last time we talked.' He glanced over at the Chief, who still hadn't moved.

'What type of developments?' asked Millar.

'Well, yesterday the Chief came to see me,' Barry said. 'He wanted me to dust the note from Sammy for prints.'

'Really?' Penner said in disbelief. 'Why would he do that? Did you find anything?'

'I did,' Barry said. 'Obviously, it was plastered with Mrs. Greycrow's prints. But, we found another print as well.'

'Travis's?' Millar asked, confident of the answer.

'Actually, no. It was Sooleawa's,' Barry said.

'You're kidding,' said Millar, the shock evident on his face. 'Well, I didn't see that coming.'

CHAPTER THIRTY-ONE

'You're not the only one,' the Chief said. No one had even noticed him get out of the car. He hardly seemed like the same man. Gone was the bravado—he seemed broken. Like he was carrying the weight of a great sadness on his shoulders.

'So, maybe she did see the note at the hospital, then?' Grant suggested.

'I don't think so,' the Chief said. 'I spoke with Mrs. Greycrow, Sammy and Sarah about it, and all of them were adamant that she never saw the note.'

'So,' Penner started slowly, 'maybe I'm missing something, but how did her print get on it?'

'Well, that's what I asked her,' the Chief said. He paused and crossed his arms before continuing. 'At first she told me that they were all mistaken. Or they were lying. I wanted to believe her, but there was something that just didn't make sense to me. Why would Travis have wanted to commit these crimes? It made no sense at all. He had nothing to gain. He was getting paid whether the funding came in or not—and all he had to do was stick it out for a couple of years and he would have retired with a sweet pension. I pressed Sooleawa, asking her what she knew about the crimes and she finally caved.'

'Caved? What do you mean?' Penner asked.

'She told me everything,' the Chief said, shaking his head. 'Several months ago, Travis had taken a couple of days off to visit his sister. While he was gone, Sooleawa opened up some mail that had come for the band. Travis usually took care of all the mail. It was a letter from the Government—a receipt for a payment they had made to the band for $9500.'

'Is it normal to get payments like that from the Government?' Penner asked.

'It is. They send periodic payments in hopes of making up for the conditions here. Never quite enough, but it's something. Anyways, Sooleawa looked at the accounting ledgers and there was no mention of the payment ever coming in. So, she started to do some digging. After a couple of days, apparently she figured out that Travis had been stealing from us for almost as long as he worked here. Writing himself cheques from the band accounts, signing over cheques from the Government to a fake account. Probably $100,000 or more over the years.'

'And you didn't know?' Grant couldn't keep the skepticism out of his voice—he wasn't sure he believed the story.

'I had no clue,' the Chief said, looking him in the eye. 'I had nothing to do with the books or the accounting—that was Travis's job. I had no reason to believe he was stealing from us. When he told me funding hadn't come in, I just figured we were getting screwed over again. Nothing new.'

'And Sooleawa didn't tell you?' asked Penner.

'No, she kept it to herself. Well—not entirely to herself. She confronted Travis when he came back to work and he admitted it right away. He begged her not to report him to the police or to his bosses—to give him a chance to pay the band back. But there was no way to pay us back. The money was gone and, even though he had a good salary, he couldn't come up with that type of money. So, the two of them hatched a plan to guilt the Government into giving us enough money to fix the water supply and, they hoped, anything else that needed improving here.'

A stunned silence followed the Chief's speech, as they each slowly came to realize the implication of his words. Finally, Millar broke the silence. 'So…they decided to kill Jonny and Sammy?'

Chief Ravenclaw flinched as the words were spoken out loud. 'That's right,' he said. 'Sooleawa figured that kids killing themselves would get us the sympathy we needed and things would improve. There had been suicides here before, so she didn't think it would be too far fetched.'

'Like Amanda,' Grant said.

'Yes, like Amanda,' the Chief said, looking over at Grant. 'When Amanda killed herself, it broke a part of Sooleawa. It was like part of her spirit died with her that day. She changed.' He took a deep breath before continuing. 'I blamed myself for Amanda's death. When Sooleawa and I got married, we decided to move back to the reserve so I could try to become Chief. I didn't think about the effect it would have on Amanda. She had grown up in the city—she had no idea what it would be like to live on the reserve. It's not easy, Detectives.' The Chief looked up at Millar and Penner and quickly wiped a tear from his eye. 'I blamed myself. I blamed the Government for treating us like second-class citizens. But, Sooleawa—she blamed Jonny. And when she and Travis came up with this outlandish plan, she decided Jonny would be their first victim. She had always claimed that Amanda's suicide was his fault. She figured something must have happened while they were dating. But I never thought that—they always seemed so happy together. I thought Jonny was one of the best things to happen to her.'

Penner was trying to make sense of it all. 'Why did they choose Sammy?' she asked.

'Easy target who was at the right place at the right time, apparently,' the Chief said, shaking his head. 'Sooleawa was mad at Travis after they killed Jonny because he screwed up the note—he hadn't made it look like Jonny's hand writing. The night of the feast, he saw Sammy and remembered that he had a paper Sammy had written. So, he went back to his house, forged the note, then went and found him in the woods. I don't know all the details—all I know is that Sooleawa was furious that he hadn't actually killed Sammy and she was terrified that Sammy might eventually remember what had happened that night and tell someone. She told Travis that he was going to have to try again when Sammy was back home, but Travis refused. He said he was done helping her out and that he would pay back the money he could out of his salary. Apparently that wasn't good enough. Or, maybe she thought she couldn't trust Travis any more. But, the night before you left, she followed him out to the woods when he was walking Chewie and shot him.'

The Chief's shoulders sagged as he finished speaking. Barry looked at the ground, kicking the dirt with his toe. Finally, Millar cleared his throat and said, 'No offence, but it sounds pretty crazy to me. How could all of this been going on under your nose? How do we know you're not involved.'

'Detective, I am not a murderer,' the Chief said. 'I admit, I thought that Travis may have been involved in some way, and I was willing to let you think that. I was even willing to let you think that I had something to do with it, just to protect the tribe. And to keep you guessing. But, as soon as I found out the truth, I gave the note to Barry to test and told him everything. I loved Sooleawa, but I wouldn't cover up this type of crime, no matter who had done it.'

'It's true,' Barry confirmed. 'Since he came to see me, he's been giving me total access to anything I need. We hired a forensic auditor to check the accounts and it seems like Travis was definitely stealing. And he was the only one accessing the accounts, other than Sooleawa.'

'And, if I had anything to do with this, do you really think I would be here telling you all this?' the Chief asked. 'As I told you before, I used to be a lawyer. No lawyer would explain a crime to the police if they were involved. I don't care how good a lawyer someone was, that would be stupid.' For the first time, Chief Ravenclaw showed some of the same aggression as before.

'So, where's Sooleawa now?' Penner asked. 'Did you arrest her?'

'Well,' said Barry slowly, 'That's why I need to get back to work.' He glanced over at the Chief. 'After Chief Ravenclaw came to see me about all of this, I got an arrest warrant signed by the judge. But, by the time I got back to the reserve, she was gone.'

'So you don't know where she is?' Millar asked, his voice raising. 'Great. So you finally had a chance to arrest her and she's disappeared?'

'Not exactly disappeared,' Barry hesitated.

'What?' Millar said, looking between Barry and the Chief.

'She was found dead this morning,' Barry said. 'Just at the edge of the woods. There was a group out turkey hunting early this morning and it seems like it was an accident—probably a stray shot—but, we'll see what the coroner says to be certain.' He looked at his watch. 'Chief, do you mind bringing them in to get their stuff? I have to meet the coroner—I'm already late.'

'No problem,' the Chief replied. 'I'll come and see you when we're done.'

Without another word, Barry got back into his car and pulled away. 'Right, if I can get a ride with one of you, we can get your things,' the Chief said.

Grant looked at Millar and Penner, neither of whom would make eye contact with him. 'I'll take you,' he finally said, turning and walking back to his car. He opened the passenger door for the Chief and waited for him to get in before walking around the front to the driver's side. He shook his head at Penner and Millar. 'We could have at least rock, paper, scissored for it,' he said. 'I'll see you guys there.'

'We'll follow you,' Millar said, slapping the roof of Penner's car and getting in.

Penner put on her sunglasses and started the engine, but left it in park. Turning to Millar, she said, 'So...what are you thinking?'

'I'm thinking that I'm still not sure I'm buying what the Chief is selling.'

'I hear ya. I can't believe Sooleawa was the mastermind behind everything,' said Penner. 'But grief and bitterness are powerful emotions—they can make you do crazy things. And the Chief does seem pretty broken up. He made a good point—he could have just let us think that Travis was behind it all.'

'I still have a lot of questions. But I don't think we'll ever get all the answers.' Millar watched Grant's car disappear into the dust ahead of them.

'So, we're considering this case closed?' Penner asked as she shifted to drive and started to follow Grant onto the reserve.

'It's not airtight—but it's closed. Now let's go get your coffee.'

***

'So, you really didn't have anything to do with all of this?' Grant asked the Chief.

'I swear to you,' Ravenclaw said. 'I'm willing to do a lot for my people, but something like this is beyond me. But, some good has come out of all of this madness. The government engineers have already been out and investigated the water issues. Looks like it should be fixed within the year. So, as much as I condemn what she did, Sooleawa actually did some good for our community. I will miss her, but I think she finally got what she wanted—she's together with Amanda now. And maybe she got what she deserved.' They drove the rest of the way in silence until they reached the band office. 'Drop me off here. I'll get the keys and let you guys into the rooms.'

Grant pulled over and let the Chief get out. He rolled down his window. 'Chief? Are hunting accidents very common?'

'Pardon?' the Chief asked, turning back around.

'I know hunting accidents happen, but they're pretty rare, no?' Grant said. 'Seems like a pretty big coincidence that a murder suspect would end up getting killed by a hunter's stray shot, I would think.'

The Chief leaned down until his head was level with Grant's in the window of the car. 'You know, my mom used to have an expression she used all the time. Don't ask questions you don't want the answer to. See you in a bit, City Boy.'

About the Author

Kevin Hopkins grew up in the suburbs of Ottawa after his family moved to Canada from England. The middle child of three boys, he has always enjoyed the creative side of life, from playing music, painting and sculpting to writing.

Kevin now lives in an old farmhouse East of Ottawa with his wife Juanita and their two cats, Lenny and Carl.

'Reserved For Murder' is Kevin's second novel.

A note from the author

Although the Black Beaver Coffee Company is purely fictional, it was inspired by Birch Bark Coffee Co., an Indigenous-owned and operated Ontario company. Birch Bark Coffee Co. offers organic and fair trade coffee that is grown and produced by South American farmers who are Indigenous descendants and is one of only three Canadian companies with SPP certification, helping true organic farmers. On top of this, they also hire people through Flower Cart to put the labels on their bags.

Despite government efforts and pledges, thousands of Indigenous families in Canada continue to go without clean drinking water. Some communities have been under boil water advisories for more than 25 years. Set proceeds of Birch Bark Coffee Co. sales are used to purchase water purification systems that are installed, for free, in Indigenous community homes across Canada. For every 100 bags of coffee sold in retail locations, and every 50 bags of coffee sold online, Birch Bark Coffee Co. is able to equip one home with a certified water purification unit, at no cost to the family.

You can learn more about their mission and how to purchase their excellent products at www.birchbarkcoffeecompany.com. Detective Penner recommends the Summer Solstice Dark Roast.

You can connect with me on:
- http://www.kevinhopkinsauthor.com
- https://twitter.com/@author_kevin
- https://www.facebook.com/authorkevinhopkins

Subscribe to my newsletter:
- http://www.kevinhopkinsauthor.com

Also by Kevin Hopkins

The Ottawa Detective Series is the first series of novels by Kevin Hopkins

A Striking Similarity
The first murder was a tragedy.
The second was a mystery.
The third was an epiphany.

Detective Terry Millar doesn't believe in coincidences. As a criminal profiler, he's built his reputation on identifying patterns and perpetrators.
But he's never encountered a killer like this.

Millar and his team are being led on a macabre treasure hunt around the city of Ottawa, and they're desperate to find a connection between the crimes before the killer strikes again.

The murders bear a striking similarity to one another, which should make it easier for the renowned profiler, but the evidence seems to point in an impossible direction.
With every secret that's revealed, Millar is a step closer to realizing that nothing will ever be the same again.

The Art of Murder

The Ottawa Detectives are called in to investigate when a well-known local politician goes missing on the night his family is dedicating a new art exhibit of pieces from their private collection in the Canadian Museum of History.

During the investigation, their efforts are side-lined as the RCMP, Canada's national police force, gets involved.

There seems to be more afoot than just a missing Member of Parliament, and the Detectives are determined to get to the bottom of things, whether the RCMP are receptive to their ideas or not.

Look for The Art of Murder, the third book in the Ottawa Detective Series in the Fall of 2020.